THE END OF IT

THE END OF IT

by **Mitchell Goodman**

a novel

1980

Second Chance Press

Sagaponack, NY

First published in 1961 by Horizon Press

Manufactured in the United States of America

SECOND CHANCE PRESS, INC.
Sagaponack, NY 11962

Where do we come from? What are we? Where are we going?

—title of a painting by Paul Gauguin

The End of It

Mitchell Goodman

The war is fact. All the rest is the truth of imagination. Any resemblance that may seem to exist to real persons is purely coincidental.

THE END OF IT

1

Mid-Atlantic. Mid-winter. A big ship in cold darkness, alone, in a hurry. Waves eighteen feet high. A lonely world of water. The world was full of death. Where were they going? They did not know. Inside the tight steel container the young soldiers tried to sleep, against the creaking and the groaning of the steel. They were afraid. Ten thousand men lying side by side. Strangers to one another. Replacements. It was easy for them to believe that the ship might break up under them.

On this night in February the troopship worked through the wilderness of sea alone. Worked hard, heaving and rolling. Inside they waited, silent, hanging on, in fear. God what a sea. Where was the land? Had the world all turned to water?

A big fast liner with no escort, no convoy, hurrying with no lights into darkness. To them inside it was as if the sea had tilted high up to touch the sky, as if the world would turn over. A sea?—it was more like a flood. The Flood. Alone now, no one else on the earth.

These young soldiers—no one had told them. It was new to them, and terrible. The violence of the sea hurled them helpless against one another, sickened them, rolled them in their own vomit. It ripped them from what they knew and hurled them toward what they did not know. As long as they had stood on their own ground the war had been unreal. Now the sea rocked them and made it real. It came at them, howling. The sea. The war. The shuddering drive of the ship's engines against the swinging, tilting sea was like no machine they had ever known.

Morning. Nothing but the cold steel of the sea. The crew was telling them scare stories about submarines. The poor damned fed-up crew.

Sure they were scared, but not by the crew. They had been scared from the moment they passed Sandy Hook in the early morning and watched the frozen rose facade of New York drop into the sea behind them.

Now Europe. What in Christ's name was Europe? What's it got to do with me? And the war—what the hell is a war, what happens?

Look around, on the decks, below: the lean figures of men in battle dress, the half-familiar faces, all wondering (while they make talk), Who's going to die there in Europe, which one of us?

Maybe it was the sea that made them wonder. The sea was a warning. There were more boys than men among them.

Not frightened? Call it what you like—loneliness, uncertainty. There had never been much enthusiasm. They had belonged to the outfits with which they had trained—it had been their known world, their safety. Now they belonged to nothing. Casual labor, to fill the holes in the line.

They move over a heartless sea toward what they do not know. Whatever it is they do not want it. Someone had said to them, Let's play soldiers—and they had played. Now that was over.

On deck or below there is hardly room to move. Eating, sleeping, they are pressed up against one another, and they do not know one another. They do their complaining into the air, like people in a tenement who don't know who their landlord is. At home, far behind them now, are their people, who do not know what they want from the war. It is like a celebration back there—after a lousy ten years of stagnation they need this excitement. They are a people with a need to believe in the purity and heroism of soldiers. The soldiers knew of this need. But at this moment neither the soldiers nor the people knew what war was, and only a relative handful were going to find out. It was a shot in the arm, anyway. That much they knew.

On the ship there was an officer in charge of morale. But he did not try to tell them why they would fight. They did not want to be told any more. They had heard it many times. And against the sound of the sea those big words would not ring for them. A job—let it go at that.

Instead, when the sea allowed, they tried to break their tension with boxing, wrestling, amateur shows on the canvas-covered hatchways. (From the sun-deck the officers and nurses and Red Cross girls looked down—the educated ones who knew what the war was all about.) At other times they were kept busy with cleaning and repairing their equipment. But they found their own surest relief in card games and crap games. Money held its own. The strong taste for money. The next card, the next roll gave them some kind of a future.

They were called replacements and most of them were very young. They had been taken out of infantry divisions and replacement training centers to fill the holes in the line. So they had lost their outfits, their buddies—all the familiar landscape of their army lives—and they did not like it. It had happened in this way to the young field artillery lieutenant, the one called Gil Freeman, who lay stretched out on his bunk in what had been the first-class lounge. He did not like it either, this being broken off from the men he knew and had counted on. But there was a difference: for him the war was right and necessary. And he thought he would find in it something he was looking for. Experience? Excitement? A way into manhood? Who knows. He had no name for it.

The world was burning, armies were on the move, his own country was coming to life. He was young, his body was hard and strong, he was a lieutenant of field artillery who had made the guns roar and seen the targets disappear in fire and blast. In fact, he was a knight and his lady had thrown him a rose, and he would prove himself. But of course he did not think of it in this way. He dropped the book he had been reading and with his eyes open day-dreamed of Anne—the sudden unexpected way she had given herself, the newness and eagerness of her body, its uncertainty and instinctive grace. He felt her eyes on him; he felt himself swept forward with the ship, felt the power of it as it struggled against the sea; he let himself go with it to the point of elation.

His eye was caught again by the gilt of the ceiling and the dark polished wood of the panelling, the remains of a world of luxury and privilege that would never be quite the same again. Never. This was the end of it. He was sure of it, as Anne was sure. Something was happening: he had seen it, in railway stations, on trains, on the streets of Oklahoma City and New York. It was in the air, a common understanding: If there is going to be dying, let it be worth something.

A sense of expectation, arising out of promises. Promises. Things will be different, we promise you that. Something for everybody, no more hogging. Something was wrong—we'll fix it. A new time. New era. After the war . . . The President of Harvard says we need American radicals . . . that there should be no more inheritance of wealth . . .

the end of privilege . . . equality . . . The President of the
United States says that no man should be allowed to earn
more than $25,000 a year. The Vice-President says it will be
a new world, he says that—. If you come back. What is it to
be killed, now, in two or three months? What happens? To
die. To be killed not as by lightning but by the deliberate
working hands of another man. What was it the small muscular man had said, the man with the broken face of an old
boxer? *Whaddya got thumbs for boy? Use 'em! Stick 'em
in the Jerry's face and gouge his eyeballs out. Like this! See?*

At night, as the sea rolled the helpless bodies against
the steel walls of the ship, the fact of a man killing a man was
almost believable. The knee in the groin, the knife in the
back, the rifle butt in the face. Promises. When the ship
strained against the dark sea who could believe the promises
that might be believed in the day, under the sun and in sight
of the horizon? At night each man is alone on the cold sea,
and the war is only a continuation of the angry waters.

But as the ship moved closer to Europe the anticipation of fighting—and of the return to routine—threw them
clear of doubt, neither believing nor unbelieving, swept forward into sunlight, the smell of the land—into the oncoming
facts of war. First came the destroyer escort to lead them past
Gibraltar, then the friendly planes hunting submarines. They
saw the dim black hills of Africa as they went in to the
Mediterranean, and from there it was all sun and quiet sea,
the ship rolling playfully toward Naples. It was a hot sun, a
real sun, that shone on the hills and turned fear into exhilaration. Europe, a human landscape, trees on the hills, women.
Let it come.

Here was the rush of confidence again. The young
lieutenant standing eagerly at the ship's rail with other men
of his country watched it come, watched the land rise to
present villages on the hills in the freshness of morning. At this

moment the picture of what he was was clear. An officer, Lt. Gilbert Freeman, Army of the United States—boots, pistol belt, helmet, insignia, the close-fitting combat uniform over the tall lean body. Ready, reaching out for what might be in it—the experience. The shared experience, of men in the open, together, depending on each other, moving forward, unlocking prisons.

Along the rail they stand and watch.

Hey look—what the hell are those? Look at 'em come out of the water. Look at 'em go. The streaming blue-shining leap of the porpoises made them forget the dark Atlantic. The sun striking the big fish on their arched backs, the ship plowing easily now—things weren't so bad. The clenched bodies opened up under this sun, the blood ran free, believing again in its own immortality. Around the Mediterranean there has always been more living than dying. The old center of life. Here the sun makes itself known.

At moments like this they let themselves believe they knew what war was. With the heat of this sun in them they could be cocky. But the ship moves closer to the land, and the land is strange. The mood changes. Underneath they knew, they didn't kid themselves. They knew who they were: they were infantrymen, most of them—riflemen, automatic weapons men, machine gunners. Ditch-diggers. Lousy dangerous work. The army was made of bosses, technicians, clerks and common labor. They were the common labor. And right now they were casual labor, being shipped to strange organizations. Very far from home, among strangers, each a number on an IBM card, destination unknown, alone. *I don't know any of these men. Who are they? Do they know who I am? Do any of them care what happens to me? Where are we? Where are we going? What will they do with us?*

Suppressed voices of fear. On the edge of the un-known.

But then again, simple. It was a job. A lousy job. They didn't like the bosses. But it wasn't a job you could quit. They had to go through with it. They had their reasons, and these reasons had nothing to do with War Aims. But right now they didn't have to think. There it was. There was the land, dark green, terraced, with the sun soaking into it, as solid as a good meal. And now into the warm shelter of the Bay of Naples (after the dirty trains and the nameless depots and the transient camps that had led to the windy sheds and the gangplanks of the embarkation center).

Here—look—a luscious fruit of a city hung on hills. One of the oldest, singing and stinking with life. *Hey look at that you guys. Sunny Idaly. Hey Luigi, where do they keep the women? What's that? A volcano?*

Yeah man, this is one hot town. (All along the rail they leaned in their laughing excitement, watching it come at them pink and brown with blurs of green leaf here and there.) *Lotsa stuff here, huh? Might be worth the ride over. They're supposed to know a thing or two. A guy in the crew told me. Yeah. Hey doc, what's Italian for tail?* (And then there were the quiet ones who stood and stared.)

Flat against the hills the color-washed travel poster moved toward them, changing, and they began to see the de-tail of the corpse—the city—paint peeling, ripped open and beginning to rot. It was not yet completely plundered. It was wide open. They saw it as a woman, to be taken. To be raped.

Some guy in the crew says you can buy anything here, and he means anything.

You men better not be forgetting these guinea bas-tards is the enemy.

Or they was. Now they ain't nothin' at all. Man, this is shit creek itself we're sailing up.

What the hell—they asked for it, didn't they?
So this is Italy—of all the goddamn stinking—
(There was garbage on the oil slick on the blue bay. British and American garbage—the Italians were eating theirs.)
Boy it sure makes you appreciate what we've got in the good old U.S.—
What the hell you want boy, there's a war on. You're seein' the world aintchya?

The sun poured its heat into the dirty corpse of the city. They came in closer; they saw it move. Life. The corpse would not lie still. Flies, rats, men, women, children. It stank, it festered, but it lived.

They came crowding to the rail to see the land, Vesuvius, its ashes, and the whole great pastel-colored junk pile of history under it. *Hey, look at the goddamned castle, willya? Palm trees, get a load o' that.   Boy what a pastin' these guinzos did get.*   A loaded harbor; live ships bobbing and swaying, in and out; dead ships, belly up, nose down, leaning twisted superstructure quiet in the gay water.   *What a shithole. Ain't these wops got any idea how to live?*   The loudmouths spilled their fear; the others stared in awe at the revealed guts, the private parts of the city. The smell of drains, and death. Brown and gray ruin; buildings sliced, gouged and crushed to rubble. Plumbing. Wallpaper. The tumbled tilted gutted harbor, its shells and skeletons, came close as they came up the bay to dock at one of the concrete causeways built over the hulls of sunken ships. Luxuriant naked death. Along the curve of the promenade the cracked shells of the pink and white and blue hotels, the elegant apartment houses. Dead balconies, hanging. On the walls: VIVA! VIVA IL DUCE! VIVA STALIN! VIVA! VIVA! Long live anything and everything.

When he got down on the dock a public relations

officer wrote in his notebook: "The squalor depressed the men and at the same time by contrast reminded them of the kind of life they were on their way to fight for." That's the kind of thing that would go good when they got ready to write the history of the Fifth Army in the Mediterranean theater. Pretty soon they would have a radio station set up. Morale booster. The voice of the salesman. You had to keep selling it to them, at home and abroad.

Naples. With nothing to live for—as we measure it— they live. The dirty inextinguishable wops. Singing, crying, grinning in the teeth of death, they lived as the Germans and the Englishmen and the Americans had never lived. And these hated them for it. Before they were off the boat they were busy hating the wops. A few came to love them; but for most of them it did not change. Contempt, hate—it was hard to conceive of such hate. *Sigarette! Caramelle! Amore! Hey Joe, mia sorella— My sister is a virgin, clean. Capito? Mille cinque cento lire. Cheap.*

The Italians had taken so much shit from so many armies—to live. The simple fact of being alive. They gripped it and hung on. They hung on with their teeth. The persistence—over and over, everywhere: *Sigarette Sigarette Cambio. Hey Joe. I gotta cousin in Bridgeport. Wanna sell something. Hey Joe.* They'd been waiting for a miracle, America was miracles, and now they were getting their miracle. *Lucky Strike, Baby Ruth, Milky Way, Hershey.— Mia sorella* . . . In Naples a miracle is a miracle. Immaculate con- Conception. Consumption. Contraception. Contempt.

If the guinzos get in your way, knock 'em the hell off the sidewalk. They asked for it.

Their city a corpse—but they go on loving it, pumping their life into it with the big open gestures of love. No matter what happened. Bellissima Napoli. Their city. They cared. The warmest damn people on earth, some of them stealing, some pimping, some scavenging—taking what they could get to live, only to live, any way they could get it. If there is work, they work hard, with love of the work.

Watch 'em Eddie, they're tricky as hell.
Tricky my ass—we've got 'em where we want 'em, ain't we?
Screw the ass off 'em. Watch 'em crawl. Outsmart 'em every-
time. Buncha wop bastards—

The life of the city rising like some wild growth from the rubble. Coming from deep down—under every house Roman stones, and under those, Greek. But America, they want to know about America, what it's like there, how much money you can make. Crazy to get to America. For the good life. On all the big streets, in the Galleria, they come to stare at the Americans. Fascinated. They come from the narrow streets where they have lived for a thousand years to see the new men, the men who carry no past on their backs, who eat well off a new world. The father, *Duce*, was gone, and they were waiting for a miracle.

And here down the crawling street come the long-legged men, the Americans. Heads up. Embarrassed, defiant, tough, cocky and bewildered. Conquerors, who can't help it. Operators of an almost automatic war machine. Serving the machine and waiting for the chance to go home. Immaculate contraption.

2

During his first days in Naples the Lieutenant was uneasy. All around him were these people who had been the fascists, the enemy. Now they pretended to be something else. They shifted with the wind. Or did they? He watched them as he walked their streets. From old dark doorways of crumbling houses they watched him pass by. He was the conqueror;

they watched him to see what he would do with his power. The children out of their great starved hollow black eyes looked up at him. He was not like them. He was tall, his body was loose and rambling as it moved; his long high-boned face and the deep-set eyes were alive with energy and good blood. They were small, and shrunken with hunger. Serious dark faces, gentle eyes. The enemy.

In a small cobblestoned square he stopped by a fountain, awkwardly, to look around him. The children approached in a ragged half-circle. When he smiled they met his eyes and smiled. A warmth and a directness of a kind he had never seen before. Farther back, in the doorways, the women watched and smiled. Not sadly. Not to prove anything. Only glad of any sign of life. From one of the windows a song, a woman singing. He looked up. Fullness of arms and breasts stretching to push back the shutters. She stopped singing. Frankly she looked at him, as a woman who knows herself as a woman will look at a man, a man of another kind than she has known. Her eyes told him, You are a man, you are a man worth looking at. And I am a woman. The soft impact of her womanliness was altogether new to him; he lowered his eyes. She turned away, satisfied, and was singing again. The children came closer, closer—to touch him and examine the ornaments of his uniform. Where do you come from, they asked. Where are you going? What is your name?

This, the enemy?

From day to day he walked the steep narrow streets of this ancient maze, looking down into deep wells of humanity, deeper than anything he had imagined to exist. They were defeated, they accepted it. But they would not give up their lives. Life was to be lived. Bread, wine, the sun, a song. The deep heat of the women. The joy of a man whose house has burned down, who feels his need deep in his soul and waits to build anew.

On his fourth day among them they were not the enemy. On the sixth day he began to try to talk with them. Because he tried to speak their language, they gave him their warmth. Soon he loved them, opened himself to them in a rush of naked feeling, glad of the heat of their lives that entered him and lifted him to a new kind of joy in life. They gave him their wine. They sang to him. They withheld nothing. With wide open gestures they welcomed him and embraced him, showed him the secret places of their much loved city. And asked for nothing.

Death hovered in this city. But the shout, the gesturing hands, the sudden song were thrown in its face. The kids rolled and scattered and grinned and clustered, springing like weeds out of the old stone of their city. Lives had fallen on lives to make of this stone a kind of soil, as trees and leaves fall to make the earth new. The Lieutenant watched, listened, and went with them. Vitality, a willingness to live, like nothing he had ever known.

Death had its hand in. There were many funerals that moved through this fight for life. The plumed horses, the plumed and gilded black hearses of ornamental wood. The procession, led by the priest. The smell of death, the sour smell of drains, as if all the sewers had been broken open by the explosions. Typhoid fever. The plague. And still the life kept rising out of the death and the rubbled ground; it spurted up in fountains and geysers everywhere, and fell to make a warm mist.

Sightseeing: The rusting corrugated iron of the public urinal. Men selling a handful of oranges. Women waiting for bread. The elaborate carved stone of palaces pocked by gunfire. A girl thrown from a hotel window by Americans having a party. Small boys looting the bodies of drunken soldiers. A city broken open.

Some of the sightseers knew what they wanted: the guys on leave from the front going straight to the sources of warmth and nourishment. Making love against any wall, standing up, lying in hallways, amid the rubble of a deserted inner court, the sour stench of wet broken plaster, brickdust, pipes broken open. Empty windows. The smell of cheap perfume and urine and dead flesh, mixed. Sneer at them, buy the warmth of their bodies (and get more than you paid for); but look: how they grip their lives, how the warmth flows from them. A few miles to the north the old barbarians and the young primitives are slaughtering each other in a cold muddy dream. And here is life, piled up like fruit: the soft worn faces of women, their slow sure bodies waiting to be filled—all glowing in the face of death.

Once they had come back to this city from the slaughter—those who had fought and lived (on leave, in a hospital)—how could they make themselves go back to it again? After a taste of this?—And some did not go back. They had gotten the taste of death in their mouths and spat it out and turned their backs on the cold mountains, to go deep into this city, to eat, to drink, to be lost in the living flesh of it. So warm, after the cold storms of death in the mountains. How is it they did not all do this, given the chance? There were many who did not go back.

Everywhere in the city another kind of fruit: the round green globes of the prophylactic stations. And on the near hills, oranges. (If the man who is about to die picks an orange from the tree and eats it, if he can still taste the life in it, will he then allow himself to be led quietly away?)

The Neapolitans have always lived for miracles. They waited for the miracle from America, and piece by piece they got it. The miracle of the armed corporation. They came in the ships, the new men, young and well-fleshed; they unloaded their new civilization. And they moved it into the large and small palaces of the city. And there it flourished, calling itself 5th Army HQ, Peninsula Base Section, Mediterranean theater. It was a miracle of re-creation: an American transplant, whole. Out of the old stones and the smells it grew. And it grew. An ant hill of offices, corridors, offices, corridors, offices. Brass and steel and paper. On the fertile rot and dust of Naples there grew up a fat corporation, fat and breeding in on itself, fed from the liberty ships that kept coming; or feeding off the land, fattening. They never had it so good. Un miracolo.

The Neapolitans reached out for America, that golden legend that had stuck deep in their heads. They were ready to love the new men from the new world. America had come to them and brought some of its miracles, managed by a nonprofit, tax-supported corporation in the shape of an army. But more than an army. A government, a father, a way of life. A coke machine. A vacuum cleaner. A chocolate bar. One of the biggest corporations the world had ever seen—spilling itself on to the docks, carting itself away, throwing its weight, running wild, soberly keeping accounts. It handled everything from safety pins to magic cures for syphilis and the plague. It bought and sold, it gave itself away. It ran a newspaper, it dumped cans of spaghetti into the surprised mouths of the spaghetti eaters. There was nothing it could not do. It was the Universal Corporation. It was Cadillacs, refrigerators and good cold beer. It was the secretary on every knee and the bottle of whiskey in the bottom drawer. It laughed and scolded, hired and fired, could make or break, and gave away dimes. It printed money and inspected the whore houses. It ran tours to Pompeii. It washed socks and pressed pants. It kept itself busy. A miracle. The Italians were goggle-eyed.

It was not lovable. Yet it was America, and America was a dream, and they tried to love it.

It gave them jobs, and paid them badly, and rapped their knuckles; it kicked them in the ass, and put them in their place, and spat on them, and instructed them in the benefits of democracy. Yet they were willing to love it.

3

When the ship had docked and the men had moved off in trucks, an officer who was later to serve as a unit historian wrote in his notebook: "The close proximity of war fired the men's imaginations."

No. Not war, but the close proximity of life, Naples. A woman for a cake of soap. It was the new world of free love and oranges that fired the imagination. Promiscuity in chaos. If you don't like this woman, throw her away and buy another. Or step on her, she'll lie there and take it—for a pack of cigarettes. Screw them and screw them and screw them. Show them how much of a man you are. Live a little. They came off the ships, out of the cold Atlantic, and they smelled death. They saw the tired men back from the frontiers of death. This—right here, now—was a place to live, to live before you are asked to die. And you know it. But you are green and raw in the midst of ripeness.

The Corporation began to process Lieutenant Freeman, the Field Artillery replacement. Freeman, Gilbert Morse, 2nd Lt. F.A., 0527946, Blood type O, Religion Protestant, Battery Officer. Filed on the IBM card. Another unit of the corporate machine.

But far from the palace of the filing cabinets the Lieutenant walked in the depths of the city, talked, sat in quiet cafes, came to know the Italians, to love them, to drink their wine. By the men he was taught the sad history of their country; by the women he was taught the secret uses of his body and of theirs. Little by little he began to understand, and the hot blood of life welled up from the hidden places of his being. It came from deep down, from mysterious springs, and drove him headlong in a rising spiral of expectation and fulfillment. He knew—he began to know—how much life there was in him to be lived.

Outside of the city was the Replacement Depot—labor pool of the A.U.S., Inc. (as distinguished from the mother organization, the United States Army, Inc., with an interlocking directorate). Nissen huts, tar-paper shacks, storehouses, latrines, PX, a coke machine. Wholesale, retail —you name it, we've got it: Pants, gloves, guns, contraceptives, chewing gum. Cooks, truckdrivers, riflemen, typists, tankmen, bakers—the works.

The replacements kept coming, off the ships and out of the hospitals. They hung around, killing time as they could. Crap games, movies, card games, waiting for orders, waiting for work, waiting to go somewhere else, indefinite waiting. They were tight and edgy with the waiting, imaginations fired by the close proximity of the unknown, and of the starving, willing women. Money moved fast in the card games; money was the link with home.

Some got orders and moved out. The others watched them go—wondering, waiting. What was a war? What happened? They sat on their duffle bags and waited. The sun shone bright. The oranges fattened on the trees. They were neither here nor there. Waiting, wondering. How many would die? Who? Was death a person? Was he watching them? They sat in the sun on the edge of safety. Beyond those mountains was the war, the unknown. They listened for sounds, for rumors, from the unknown. They heard wild stories from men who had been there, or who said they had been there. They remembered training films they had seen, lonely men and tanks stumbling through the smoke and mud holes of a moon-landscape, a scabby crust of land attached to nothing, leading nowhere. In all the pictures and the stories there was something alien, something untouchable, almost unnatural about the enemy. Look, they seemed to say, look closely: here is the place, and here is the man who will try to kill you. Imagine it: two men, you and him, face to face. You come around a corner and there he is. Now kill! Kill or be killed. Kill and be killed. Watch him, he is trying to rip your bowels with a piece of steel. The point! Kill him. Quick!

And they were old enough to remember the anti-war journalism of the thirties: the Hearst papers every Sunday (better than Buck Rogers or any other *jokes*): broken corpses, faces becoming skulls under tilted helmets, dead meat hanging on barbed wire. The First World War. Wholesale anonymous death. Promiscuous.

Here on the frontier between the known and the unknown quick, heated friendships were made and sharply broken by the receipt of orders. (The memories, the fears, the private pictures of death and mutilation were not shown around. Unmentionable.)

Quietly, each alone, they read a pamphlet they had been given called Combat Tips For Fifth Army Replacements. It read like the reassuring advice from a big corporation to new traveling salesmen who were going into a strange territory. But there was one line that reached them, came up and touched the living flesh: *When you go up to your battalion, be dressed in the clothes you are going to fight in.* Fight in. Die in? They were processed feverishly, then they waited.

The orders they waited for came from the main

office in Naples. In Naples they had everything by now, a Big Business installed in old and new Palazzi, equipped by the International Business Machines Corporation. You need a rifleman? Punch a button, a card falls out, orders are cut, he is put in a shipment, and shipped. From the training center to the grave: punch a card. Nothing is left out in this universal corporation, the vertical and horizontal corporation. All phases: Marketing, Transport, Supply, Legal, Archives. Insurance. Information. Public Relations. Entertainment. Medical, Surgical, Dental. Psychiatric. Graves Registration. Religion. Finance. Justice. Police. All strung on the chain of command: office boys, clerk-typists, bookkeepers, junior executives, vice-presidents, The Boss. The Boss's secretary who doubles as his mistress, with the rank of captain. Typewriters, filing cabinets, desks—rows of rows. Corridors leading out of corridors into offices that lead to other offices. Inner offices, outer offices, warehouses, clubs, prisons.

Palazzo after palazzo full of the Corporation, grinding out way-bills, due-bills, requisitions, contracts, memos, orders, procedures. It grew, as all the best corporations grow, until it was beyond the comprehension of any one man, and existed for its own sake. After twenty-five lean years business was booming. Big cars, big executives. Heavily capitalized. Unlimited resources. Limited liability.

This corporation was in the shape of a wedge, shoved into the raw flesh of Italy. This—in Naples—was the fat end. Somewhere up around Cassino it tapered to a small point, a spearhead of armed men. For every fighting man there were five or six middlemen. For twenty-five years the directors of The Corporation had been small businessmen who played soldier and bridge and golf in out-of-the-way places. Now suddenly they were big, and they wrangled for supremacy among themselves. They hired public relations men, they had their pictures taken, they made speeches. They hoped to expand, to set up offices in Rome, Florence, Bologna, Milan, as business picked up. The biggest corporation the world had ever known, a miracle of—

Name, rank, serial number, organization. The clerk-typist completed the processing of Lieutenant Freeman. "That's all sir. Thank you and good luck to you sir." He was a neat little man who knew his typewriter and was thankful for his niche in the corporation. He took Naples as he had taken North Africa, as a competent tourist. The war was far away, yet near enough to charge the atmosphere. A job was a job (he remembered his days of unemployment). And it was nice to work abroad. "You'll probably be around for two or three weeks sir. Things are moving slowly. If you don't mind my saying so, I hope you enjoy your stay in Naples."

In the days of waiting the Lieutenant walked deep into the crevices of the city, into the alleys that rose and turned and fell to hidden flights of steps that rose to still other levels—losing himself in it. It was good to be lost, to be caught in the rising and falling tides of its life. So much weight and vitality in its voice, its gestures, its comings and goings. The stone was so old, rubbed smooth by the passage of life—almost a living substance. Even the paving, the cobbles of the streets were worn to a kind of softness, as of soil, where human beings had grown and died for 3000 years, layer on layer. As leaves fall on a forest floor to form new layers of earth. Where the bombs had fallen it smelled: the explosions had disturbed the deep complex of man-made ground to release its gases, out of its wet half-decayed enriching layers—as the fallen leaves will smell if they are disturbed before the process of their transformation is complete. The city had suffered death. But in the decay there was a seed. And this was the end of winter.

2

When his time was running out the Lieutenant met a woman who was truly of this city. So completely did she belong to it that finally they were inseparable in his mind. She had lived as it had lived, and died as it had died, and now, together, they struggled back into life. He was a man from what looked like paradise—the new world—and he was on his way to the unknown mountains where Death was holding its Olympic Games. She had, as a girl, gone down into hell. Now, a woman at 22, she climbed back into life. At the moment when they met they knew one another instantly. He saw her beauty behind the mask of grief. She saw his serious regard for her, his glow of newfound manhood, his innocence of death and suffering. Together they made what must be called a marriage. In ten days they had lived a lifetime together.

Among the steep dark lanes of the city, in a small piazza surrounded by old houses that had once been palaces, he had found a café that he liked. It was far from the great palaces of the armies, it belonged still to the people of these streets. It was here that he met her, a small dark cave of a place where old men talked over red wine. She was alone. The Germans, before they left, had killed her husband.

From the window of the room where they had lived, the Germans had made her a witness of her husband's death. They had hung him from a lamppost in the street, and had left him there. No one was to touch him, they said; he was to be left as a warning. He had been in the Resistance, as she had.

The Lieutenant listened to her story in silence, watching her eyes where the dark waves of sorrow and anger welled up. In the night, she said, with the help of friends I cut him down. Two nights later she invited a German officer to her room and killed him with a knife as he slept. Then she had come to live here, on the other side of the city, and had given way to despair.

Her face was hard; the candle burning in the bottle on the table could not soften it. Only her eyes showed the passionate life that now flared up in her again, and the hope that would not die in her. A kind of hope so ferocious in its intensity that it seemed like a mystical challenge to the future. As if a new race of men was to be born out of the war. My country will be made clean, she said. It will be a renaissance. It will erupt like a volcano and make new ground to live on. You will see.

Until very late at night she spoke with an intensity that was like madness. The Lieutenant did not know what to think. But finally her passion moved him to belief. Still there was nothing he could say. In the face of her agony and her belief he remained silent, fascinated, in awe. She told him stories of the Resistance—of life in the mountains, of sabotage, and the terrible inhumanity of the Germans. She prayed that Germany would disappear from the earth. He was forced to turn away from the glittering hate in her eyes.

Toward morning, softened by the wine, she was calm, and they sat together in an unstrained silence, watching the cats prowl the wet cobblestones of the quiet piazza. He was thinking of all that she had lived through, and of the trivialities of his own life. What could he say to her? Yet he knew there was no need to say anything. In her speaking and his listening they had come very close to each other.

She turned to him and faintly smiled. He took her hands and held them. In that moment he was aware of some new dimension of love. It was not, I love you—Do you love me? It was as if he had just now set foot in this country and knew, all at once, why he had come here. As if he had himself made the decision to come. Why? Why then had he come? He could not find words for it. It was no longer as simple as it had been. What is it for, the war? What? She is Italy, he thought, and she wants to live in a new way, and I love her for it. It sounded foolish, this way, but it was as close as he could get to understanding what had happened to him.

Later she took him to her room, high over the piazza, and fell asleep in his arms. He was content only to hold her. He could not sleep. The good earth smell of her black hair gave him great pleasure. It was the very opposite of the smell of death that permeated the city.

His mind drifted from the cold sea to the city to the mountains that waited for him. The warm curves of her body were under his hands. He thought, She has seen it all. Everything that has happened here. She knows what it is. The Germans. They hung him from a lamppost. They hung him before her eyes and left him hanging in the street where he had lived. From the window she could see him, the feet pointed toward the ground, the head hanging to one side of the stretched and broken neck.

In the days that followed he saw her as often as he could. She took the food that he brought her, simply and directly; she cooked for him; she walked with him and showed him how the city lived. Its children's games, its songs, its peculiar rituals and ceremonies—these she gave him, with her sensitive hands, her fine eyes. Gave willingly, out of her fullness—in the same way that she touched him, freely, with reverence for the life in his body. She turned to him and followed him as a flower turns to the sun.

Alone with the bare white walls of the high sun-filled room she took him as a man, not as a soldier; she laughed softly at the anonymous clothes of the soldier and told him she liked him much better without them. When he had taken them off and was himself, she told him—in whispered words and with the sure delicate touch of her hands—that he was a man, that it was good to lie close to him, beyond the need to think or speak. From the cell of his self-consciousness he was released a man. Something came to life at the very center of his being that he had not known was there; it moved and burst from him like a flood to meet her own onrushing passion.

He looked: he saw the roundness of her shoulder, the subtle rise of her breasts, the tapering fullness of her arms, the calves narrowing to ankles. This was the form of a woman. The detail. Look at it. It is alive. It is the most beautiful thing on earth. And with her, in the same way, he began to see flowers, the faces of children and old men, trees, the shape and proportion of buildings, the reptile scales and shimmer of the sea. With his hands and his eyes he began to take hold of the facts of life, to touch, to relish.

A marriage. All life was one—fused, created in the giving and receiving of two living bodies. She took an orange from a tree and held it out to him. He peeled it, bit into it, tasted it. From the shade of the trees on this hill they looked down and saw the complex irregular cubes of the city, the shining blue of the bay. All in a lifetime. They turned and looked at each other.

He got up from the bed—it was sunset of one of their last days—and went to the window of the room where she lived, to look out over the city that breathed and murmured low under the final glow of light. He looked for a long time; in the intensity of his pleasure he smiled to himself. He heard himself say, I am here, she is here with me, what more could there be? He wanted to wake her and tell her how it all seemed to him: herself as a woman, the city that was a part of her, the war that he had been waiting for and was no longer waiting for. He was here, he existed in this sense of completeness, because she had created him. And there was the city, in its fight for life—a world that had weight and vitality, that he knew by sight, by touch, by heart. In its stone were the colors of life, the clay colors: yellow, pale pink; colors of earth at sunset: umbers, burnt sienas, faded rose of very old brick. A living thing.

He looked around at the woman sleeping. She was the same—unforced, of the earth and the sun. She did not strain for life. She did not pursue happiness. They appeared from within her, as from the sun or the earth.

He looked down at himself; he laid a hand on himself, felt the beat of his heart. Alive. Pumping blood. New blood, freed in him, by her. She had her life, rooted, out of the ground she stood on. She had given him some of it, enough to release him. He felt himself changed, as if he had made the leap from an imagined life into an actual life, so that his whole being was alive in the world and at one with the world that was all good to look at and to touch and to taste. He felt himself to be in effortless motion, like some animal in the woods in the spring that opens itself from sleep into the life opening around it. And the war—the hunt—a long way off, in the mountains, unthinkable.

He went to the bed and lay near her, leaning on an elbow, to touch her. His hand, in its pleasure, moved to caress her. There had been a time when it might have drawn back from her nakedness. Not now.

She stirred, opened her eyes, moved to be closer to him. She did not say, Talk, talk to me, tell me things, do you love me, will you always love me, is it all right, what will we do, what are you thinking? None of that. She stayed close to him, her head on her arms, glad of the warmth of his hand.

Each day might be their last together; there was no future. Yet with her there was no time: there was only now, time for everything. A lifetime. There were the cool white walls of this room, the clean angles of the plaster where the walls met the ceiling, the woven straw of the chairs, the shutters closed at noon throwing ribs of shadow on the ceiling. A man and a woman. A bed. A table. Wine. Throw open the shutters in the afternoon and there was the ripe breathing city that she belonged to. A smell of the sea. And that was all, there was nothing else in the world. Nothing.

Very far from him now was the cold stone and steel of his own city, the rigid upstanding body of it, its endless rows of cells, its mechanical shuttling clatter.

"What is it?" she asked once. "Your city. Is it a great city?"

He could not tell her. He did not know. In my city, he thought, we have the tallest building in the world. It has 102 stories. Tell her that? And at the top there are men who are hired to see that no one throws himself off.

There was a day when he came in very late to find her sitting at the window, the room dark. She had given up on him. It had been two days since he had last been able to come to her. They did not speak. There was a glow on the sky above the port, the rest of the city was dark. Finally, without turning to him, she spoke.

"It is strange that you should be here. Why have you come?"

"Strange? Why?"

"You are not a European. You live in another world."

"There is a war—"

"We have our own way with each other. It is not something that you can understand."

"There is a war, there are the Germans— What else is there to understand?"

"We have had wars before. We know what they are. What do you know of them? You come from a place where there are no wars."

"We have had wars." He watched her. She was avoiding his eyes.

"But you have never seen the destruction of a city. You have never—"

"Why do you ask these things? I am here because I must be here."

Quietly, her face showing nothing, she said, "Have you ever watched a man die? A young man who is a human being, who is gentle and full of life and desire. In five minutes he is nothing. Less than nothing. Broken. Empty."

He said nothing. For a moment, in the darkness of the room, he did not know who she was. He was afraid of what she knew.

"This is a place to die," she said. "It is a slaughter house." She hesitated. "To see him hanging gave them pleasure. If it goes on we will all become like that."

"Then it is necessary. The sooner it is ended . . ."

She shuddered and pressed her hands to her eyes. "In the beginning it is necessary, but in the end it is nothing. It is something else. It changes."

"But we change too. Perhaps there is something we learn."

"Perhaps. I do not know."

She reached out for him with both her hands and gripped his arms. "Be careful. Don't let them kill you."

"If I come back to Naples, will I find you here?"

"I am not sure. The home of my family is in the mountains, to the south, in Apulia. Perhaps I will go there."

"I will write to you."

"Yes, write to me." She stood up. "But we must not talk so much. What have you brought? I will cook supper for you. You must be hungry."

3

On the tenth day since he had known her he climbed the worn stone stairs to her room high above the small piazza. Pinned to the door was a note. She said that she was going to her parents' home in the mountains. She did not want to be there when the time came for him to leave. You are very good, she said. Do not let them take your life. When it is over, she said, there will not be many good ones left. At the bottom she had added, You must live before you die. She had signed herself Francesca. He had never known her last name. There was no address.

For what seemed a long time he stood in the dim corridor without moving. I love her, he thought. I'll come back and find her. She's gone. Now it's time to go.

Down the stairs he went without thinking. Her dark eyes watched him across the table in the candle light as they ate. Her voice. Hands. His body was charged with her love.

When he reached the street and the life-smell of the street he knew that she was gone. But the sense of her courage and hope remained with him. A last look around the piazza—the fountain, the doorways, the kids rolling their hoops. He saw it as she had shown him how to see it. Because of her it belonged to him. And then he thought of Anne, the last days in New York, and tried to remember what she was. It was hard to remember. And yet he loved her. But how do I love her? That was not me, he thought, that was in another life. He stood still, trying to get it clear. This was the beginning of his life; the rest had fallen away. Along the street the shops were opening, women hurried with their baskets for something to eat. The shoemaker looked up from his bench and smiled at him. He raised a hand to wave. The life of the street pulled him into its flow, its will to live. He let it take him.

Then he was alone again, until he met Davis, the infantry lieutenant. The first time Lieutenant Freeman saw him, Davis was sitting at a cafe table talking over his wine to the proprietor and whoever else would listen, in a wild mixture of two languages. "Wanna go to America, huh? What the hell you think's in America, anyway? Paesan, lemme tell you something. You got a great country. Stick with it." He drank a lot of wine and talked a steady stream. A lonely man. "Work? You wanna work. Lemme tell you something. You ever hear of the CCC? That was my work, for the CCC. With a shovel. Not a woman for a hundred miles. Listen—." When he caught sight of his countryman he stopped short. "Lieutenant, tell this man what kind of work we had over there. He's seein' too many movies."

He came over with a glass in one hand and a bottle in the other and sat down. "Lieutenant, did it ever occur to you, if we stayed around here we might learn something? Or maybe you're one of these big-shot types who don't go for Italians. Well lemme tell *you*—."

"These are the best people I've ever known."

"Right. OK. We're friends. Put it there." He shot out a big hand; then he sat down and leaned over the table.

"I tell you, they know something, these people. Something we don't know. They got something." He filled both glasses and went on without waiting for a response. "Where I come from they call 'em wops. Ignorant bastards, that's how much they know. Listen, the first week off the boat I went around hating them. Wops. Yeah. Then they lost my papers, so I got to hang around. I'm still here. A reprieve, you might call it. Well I found out something. I want to stay here. Right here, an' they can keep their lousy war. The women. Man, if a trainload of these women turned up in my home town they'd put the local girls right out of business, married and unmarried. These are women, buddy, women."

He drank some of the wine. "Nobody ever told me there were women like this. What the hell did I know, I took what was going. But these are women. And lemme tell you, it isn't only the women either. It's all of 'em. They're great. I'm telling you they're great people."

He stopped and looked at the man across the table. "You think I'm crazy?"

"No.—How long you been here?"

"Twenty two days. Best days of my life." He looked over his shoulder and was silent for a moment. "I'm due for a shipment. As for me, if they lose the papers and never find 'em, it'll be too soon." He looked down at the table, picked up the glass and put it down again.

"You know what it is," he went on. "I'm scared. I'm full of wine but I'm still scared. When I got off the boat I was OK. Now I don't know. I got a feeling I'm not going to make it. I never should have seen this town . . ."

"What do you mean?"

"You get so you don't care too much. You take a lot of shit and you crawl in the mud an' you think, well maybe the next guy is going to get hit, but not this kid. Maybe, maybe not. Anyway, you go along. Then you see a little life, some real people, and you wonder what it's all about. I guess I'm not making much sense. To hell with it—"

"No. Go on. Finish it."

"What I mean is, I've had it. That's all. I'm done. I found out, and that's the end of it. The condemned man ate a hearty meal . . . That's how it goes, huh?" He broke off a laugh and finished the wine in his glass. "I've had mine. A taste. A teaser. Now I go out an' pick up the check." He picked up the bottle of wine. "You see this stuff. I like it. I like it very much. It makes me want to—. I want a little more time."

He looked at the man across the table. There was no answer. He went on looking at him. The muscular face and the blue eyes were almost blank. What does he want? Freeman thought. What does he want me to say?

To break the silence he said, "Who knows. Maybe if you want to live, you live. Maybe—"

"Who the hell you trying to kid? You know what's going on in those mountains? You know what the percentages are? For a guy who's wearing these, and these?" He poked a finger at the gold bars and the crossed rifles on his uniform. "You're another lousy second lieutenant and you talk like that? Why don't you wake up?" There was anger in his voice as he finished. He went back to the wine, hard. The other lieutenant watched him for a moment. Then he picked up his own glass and drank. And refilled it. He waited. He wanted to hear more. He wanted it and he didn't want it.

Davis said, "You know what I've been thinking?" He stopped for an instant. His voice was perfectly level. "I'll tell you. I've been thinking if I got a dose of the clap they'd keep me here." He looked in the other man's face for a response. There was nothing. "I like it here. But I won't do it. There are guys who do it. You know that? But not me. I'm too thick. I'll go along . . ."

"Take it easy. You've got too much wine in you."

Davis didn't hear him. "No one asked me if I wanted to come over here and stop a bullet. They told me. You're it. And then I see all these office boys sitting on their asses and complaining. This isn't good enough for them. Too many Italians. They see a street full of whores and a few of the black market boys and right away they know all about the Italians. They want to go home. Yeah. They don't like it. It's dirty. It ain't like home. That's all they know. All they want is to be big shots here and then get home to some clean little blonde who doesn't know what the hell she was made for. To hell with 'em. Let's get another bottle. Hey paesan, un altro litro. Vino."

For as long as they were in Naples the two lieutenants stayed together. When he was not alone Davis could forget that he was a replacement, that he would go up alone, among strangers in a strange country. They walked, and drank wine in the small cafes, and took the women where they found them. They laughed, they sang, they played Santa Claus to kids in the streets. For hours on end everything they did would seem hilarious to them. From the warm stone and flesh of Naples they took what they could find to feed the ravenous life that burned in them. Women. Not as prey, as conquests—but as warmth, heat. Women not as ornament, decoration, charm, ideas—but as forms in the natural world, flowers, fruit of the earth. Neck sloping to breasts, back curving to hips, to the tense rounded thrust of thighs. To be loved in the direct way they made love, the body as free as the voice that sings.

Out of their openness, their unconstraint, a friendship grew. They spoke of the time after the war, of when they would meet again. They would come back to this city, these people. A week later Davis got his orders and was gone.

Three weeks later he was dead on the slope of a hill that had no name but a number.

When his own orders came in early March he was not sorry to go. For a week after Davis had gone he had been restless in Naples, the spring coming and nothing to do. It had become a vacation that lasts too long. He had begun to be afraid of what was happening to him here, how the war came to seem more and more remote. The rhythm of his forward motion had been broken; he wondered how it would seem when it came time to move again. He knew that he had come too close to this city, he had taken too much of it into himself. He loved it, he wanted to come back, but now he had had enough.

Then it was time. At the Replacement Depot he packed his equipment and dressed himself in the clothes he was going to fight in.

4

He was glad of the jarring speed of the truck as the convoy went up through the freshening valleys of the early morning. The sun was up; the machine guns on the trucks were pointed into it; but no planes came to break this luminous sky. Over the first hills they moved through dark corridors of green, alight with the gold of oranges. On Bailey Bridges they crossed the swelling rivers and streams that chewed at the ruins of the old bridges. The mountains glistened, the olives were silver wet after rain, pouring their sheen down the steep slopes. There were wild flowers here and there. Blue, yellow, purple. White oxen moved among them and up through the dull blaze of the orange trees. The farmers looked up, waved, watched the long column of trucks move away. They seemed only to be interested in the things growing, in the sun that warmed them, in the fat blue of the grapes. Dust on the road, in clouds. Another convoy. The war had passed through them and was gone out of their lives altogether.

Climbing, winding, the truckloads of replacements went over hills, under trees, into mountain valleys. It was getting colder. Here and there a dry village. No sign of life.

They passed a rough sign on a pole that said, TIMES SQUARE, WHAT'S YOUR HURRY? WAR WON'T BE OVER UNTIL MARCH. They rolled through the bones of a broken village, even the church was down. But the fields around it were plowed, a deep red. The sky was a high brilliance: beneath it the objects stood out in lines and planes as clear as playing cards: black and white, blue, red brown violet. Sand and gold tiled roofs of stone farmhouses. The fire-blackened body of a gutted tank. Umbrella pines in a grove; chestnut, oak on the slopes. A piece of a gun, a truck on its side, a field of charred airplanes. A wooden cross with a German helmet hung on it. A field of whitening bones: someone said cattle. They weren't saying much, the replacements; sitting in rows on benches in the steel bodies of the trucks; anonymous rows of steel helmets, rifles between their knees. Out of the open backs of the trucks they watched the road unwind. Only the drivers could see what lay ahead of them. Houses pried open and hollowed out. Rocky slopes. The trucks fifty yards apart, a long line of force boring into the mountains.

The wide open column swinging on the curves came as close to the fighting as it could get. At the end, in what looked like a mining camp, the Negro drivers got down, stretched, gathered to crack their jokes and smoke. They were not allowed to be "real" soldiers and they no longer cared. The men in the trucks sat still, waiting, uncertain, unaware that they had arrived anywhere. Then they saw the men—the lean unkempt men of the war. Different from themselves, as if they had always been here in the mountains. Years away from houses, cities, women.

Up here on the flat below the next line of mountains it was very cold. The wind bit down hard. In the hubbub of vehicles among the huts and tents of the Division Replacement Center long lines of mules waited quietly. Lieutenant Freeman stood by his equipment and watched the

men who were of this unknown place. He could not tell much about them. But he sensed that they were somehow distinct from him, that they were of a kind of brotherhood, and that he was not yet one of them.

He glanced at the new men, each one alone, committed to nothing, who sat subdued by their packs and rifles, waiting. They did not speak. The air was sharp, good to breathe. It was all spare and clean. No ceremony, no pretension, no buying and selling. He was glad to be here. He was moving. After the confused waiting in the overripe city he felt clear and sure again. Sharply he remembered Francesca, who had led him into this country. But as suddenly as she had come to him she was gone. Behind him. He was here, caught up in the forward motion—everything here moving forward. Clear and sure, aware of the hard force of his body, its readiness for what might come, he waited.

There above them—the snow still on them—were the hostile mountains. The Lieutenant looked up at them. He was not frightened. He was almost calm, and under the calm was something like the eagerness of a mountain climber before the ascent. Here on the edge of the known world he looked hard at the mountains, thinking about nothing, thinking about what might be up ahead, trying not to think. There were the mountains, here around him were men who had been in the mountains, men who seemed more closely involved, easier with each other than men he had known. They seemed not to recognize the existence of the men who had come in the trucks. Now and again he would meet their eyes. There seemed to be something to be read in their eyes, but he could not read it. They did not stop, they went about their business. Were they saying, We're glad to see you? Or were they indifferent? Or was it: It's terrible here, but here we are, and now here you are, and all any of us can do is to keep going. There was no way to ask them. Yet it was simple. They were moving. Others were waiting up ahead. A low current of excitement ran through his body. It was not the end of life but another life.

He was returning to something he knew, the life of the artillery forward observer for which he had been trained. For month after month he had lived with the infantry companies on maneuvers. Now he was on his way to join them in the mountains, they who lived and died in their own way, close to each other, depending on each other. Up on the farthest edge he would be with them, the young infantrymen; he would go with them and support them with the fire of the artillery battalions. He wanted to be with them.

The replacements stood on the threshold, waiting. This was the Division Replacement Center, the entrance to another world. There was a spareness here, the world of men stripped to essentials. The unshaven men in the plain working clothes of soldiers, the sharp clean lines of the trucks and guns, the nameless mountains against the sky, the sun on the mountains. Cloud shadow moving over them. Stone farmhouses scattered on the bare plateau. The remains of the bombed village, the simple church tower. Here there was no rivalry among men. That was behind them. They shared their lot.

They worked from hand to hand, they looked straight at one another. They could not do without one another. Their speech was hard and direct. There was firmness in their bodies, a sure measure in the way they walked. No posturing, no bluff.

They had learned why they were here. They were here for the sake of each other. For no other reason. To support one another in their fight to go home. To go home. Their war aim. Here no one knew what else the war was for. It was a war, they were in it; God only knew how or why. God and the statesmen. All they could see to do was to fight their way through it until they came out at the other end, to the daylight, where the objects of their dreams lay piled up, waiting. There, at the other end of a long tunnel through these mountains (they rarely spoke of it) was what they hoped for, unclear but real: a way of life different from what they had known before. A job, a house, a car. But something more: A life something like what they knew now, but without the killing and the fear; of men together, who were not afraid to love one another—though even here they did not often know how to love one another, or how to speak of it. Here they had found one another. They were face to face. Then it was all love? No. But at moments they came as far toward it as they had ever come. At times they embraced. They talked together, in sorrow and fear. They looked into the blank white face of death (it was good just to be alive). At some moments they were not afraid to weep.

But for the replacements these things did not yet exist. They were on the threshold. They were innocent.

They waited. The wind bit through them, the mountains were suddenly dark under fast-running clouds. The replacements sat on their packs, each one separate, each unknown to the others. Nothing had happened. The young Lieutenant walked back and forth over the frozen ground; up toward the wall of mountains, back toward the quiet waiting men. He tried to read what was in their tight-locked faces and in the glances they threw now and then at what lay around them. They were kids. Lost. When he looked at them he was afraid. They did not speak. Were they afraid? Would someone help them, show them what to do? He wanted to be moving again, to be committed, to have no chance to look back.

Where are we? Somewhere in Italy, above Naples and below Rome. A Division Replacement Pool centered on a nameless village. In it and around it nothing had a name—it was all codes and symbols and numbers. More trucks were coming in. The Lieutenant watched the young soldiers spring from them, look around, settle quietly down to wait. All around them moved the ritual fraternity of men at war, which did not yet include them.

A tall sergeant came in a rambling walk from the nearest farmhouse with papers in his hand. At his command the infantrymen—wary, uncertain—fell into line. He told them to leave their heavy equipment for transport by truck to their battalions. Three other sergeants came up, names were read off, the men were sorted into three groups. The top sergeant spoke patiently in a tired voice: The next stop was the regimental replacement pools. Any questions? No questions.

They settled their packs on their backs, took up the rifles and moved off, alert now, in loose single file on either side of the dirt road that climbed toward the mountains.

Five yards apart they went, in the last light of the cold afternoon, trying to hold the long casual stride, the new combat boots creaking on the hard ground. They went as separate men, alone. From the regimental pools they would go to the battalion "Kitchen areas," where they would be sorted again, to wait for the mule teams carrying rations up to the Company command posts. Then in darkness and silence each, separately, knowing nothing and nobody, would be led by a guide to a platoon leader, and from there to the squad leader. And when daylight came each would look up from his hole to see the new world of the war: the squad, the shattered mountainside, and the unknown enemy who faced him over the naked ground.

The Lieutenant watched them go. They carried extra socks, underwear, an entrenching tool, water-purifying tablets, an insecticide to fight the fleas in the foxhole straw, toilet paper, sometimes a pocket knife, a pencil, a few small snapshots, a letter or two. The winding road rose to the first ridge, and went down. They were gone. He, who had always been a forward observer with an infantry division, expected to be with them soon.

2

But it turned out that he was wrong. The battalion of artillery he was assigned to was not part of an infantry division. It was one of those separate battalions of long range guns that are organized into Corps Artillery Groups for what is called general support. Usually they do not work in close support with the infantry; they reinforce the artillery fire of the battalions attached to each division, or they are concentrated for special missions, as when a barrage is fired in preparation for an infantry assault.

They told him he was lucky, he was going to be with the technicians and not with the common labor. It was a very different life from that of the division artillery, where the guns were brought up close and the artillery observers spent their days in muddy holes with the infantry companies; and where, when the fighting swung wildly back and forth, even the battery positions might be overrun by tanks or infiltrating infantry. No, this corps artillery was a very different kind of life—where the officers could go right on being gentlemen, and every last man expected that he would live to go home. It was the difference between coal miners and engineers who drill for oil.

So it went. The jeep took him up a dirt road into a valley of stones and brush where the battalion was dug in on either side of a broken farmhouse. It was very bare. The harsh encircling mountains pressed in close, except for the gap through which the guns fired. There were no trees, nothing really growing—only the polished steel of the twelve long eager guns under the camouflage nets and the relaxed figures of their servants, the gun crews.

Twelve enormous guns—clean, glistening engines of propulsion, silent now in repose. Like so many huge dogs sitting back on their massive haunches. Feed them and turn them loose and you change the face of the earth.

The Lieutenant, the stranger, went to "A" Battery—four guns, 40 or 50 men, and four officers, one of the three batteries that, with a service battery, made the battalion, the 501st F.A. Battalion, part of the 23rd Artillery Brigade, attached to XII Corps, 5th Army.

There was nothing else to be seen. The battalion seemed to be fighting a private war, attached to nothing. From somewhere it was fed food and ammunition and orders. For the rest, it was alone, hidden in this valley, firing, waiting, firing, waiting. It never saw the targets or the effect of its fire. There were trucks, jeeps, instruments for surveying and aiming, stacks of huge shells, and a telephone whose wire ran into the battalion switchboard which was connected, somewhere back in the valley, to a group of technicians elaborately organized in the cellar of a small farm building—the Fire Direction Center—which was connected to Brigade, and Corps, and finally ran into the main office somewhere in Naples.

Day after day, and sometimes in the cold quiet nights, the commands came down to the Battery switchboard and were relayed by the Executive Officer to the guns. Each series of rounds fired was called a "mission" or "fire mission."

Sometimes there would be peace at night, the men sleeping near the guns, and out of the darkness would come the voice of the Exec: *Battery adjust!* to alert them; and after a pause would come the litany that made the crews push their frozen bodies to the service of the guns. The insatiable guns. "Shell HE. Charge Three. Up one zero. Right one hundred." And the response from the gun sergeants: "Number one is ready"— "Number three is ready"—"Number four gun is ready"—"Number two is ready." And: "Fire!" And again, and again—the fat shells forced into the night, shark-like, speeding to find the ripe belly of a house, a bridge; or only to break open the night, to ruin the sleep of German infantry on a mountain ten miles away.

At times the shells went out as regular as subway trains, harassing, interdicting, ripping guts and nerves. The valley walls would scream and roar with the echoes of the guns. But always, for these men living here in the valley with their guns, the end was remote. When the shell left the gun that was the end of it—they saw nothing, they heard nothing more. That was their war, that and the business of loading up and moving when the infantry got too far ahead; finding a new position and settling down again to housekeeping and the service of the guns.

But now in these days of the late winter they did not often move. The war was frozen, locked, and the two armies held each other in a nervous embrace, from mountain to mountain, tormenting each other with patrols and the intermittent shriek of shells. Wrestlers shifting and gripping, lurching, jockeying for a foothold, for position to lunge and throw. It would come, the lunge, the push; would come as inevitably as the lengthening days of sun that would loosen them from the clench of cold, give back the full use of the hands that could kill.

But not yet. This was a holding operation, locked tight, while the corporation built up its inventory for the coming season. Men died one at a time, or in small bunches.

It rained. It rained for a week without end. Cold winds off the mountains cut through the valley. The cannoneers in their clumsy raincoats and helmets plodded through the mud, digging out the holes that had caved in, keeping the mud from the immaculate cold surfaces of the guns. They looked like garbage men working in a dump on the edge of a city. They grumbled. They fought with one another over trifles. They fell silent.

But the guns were indifferent. In the rain and the wind they went on with their noisy rejoicing. The big barrels reared and plunged in the shiny sliding mechanisms of their well-oiled carriages—howling, spitting flame. Then there would come a lull. There was no work; the great precision machines stood silent in the mud of the valley. The men huddled under their raincoats and in the pup tents. But the wet and the cold would not leave them alone. There were a few houses left in the nearby village, but their roofs were gone.

The new Lieutenant watched the play of the twelve giants, their slow precise movements. Again and again he watched as the almost immovable shells took flight out of the valley toward some unknown destination. Their power gripped him. They were of another dimension than the guns he had known; they were beyond the human scale.

Yet it was all part of a routine, day to day, and soon it began to pall on him. Nothing to be seen, only the broken ground of the valley and the bleak stone of the encircling slopes. Like living at the bottom of a well. Nothing moved. Nothing happened. The rain fell. A heavy gray sky closed down to shut them in.

The trucks that hauled ammunition passed through the shells of three dead villages, and now and then they saw the dazed faces of peasants driven down by hunger from the caves in the mountain where they had hidden themselves. To break the routine the Lieutenant sometimes made the trip back to the supply dumps. Along the main road the dead were being moved back, and the wounded; and the living moved forward to replace them. Beyond that, nothing. Back down the side road in the valley were the workers and their machines—as if they had come here only to build a road through the mountains. A job.

From Naples the Allied Radio spoke apologetically of the slow progress of the armies, spoke of the difficult terrain. (And on the rocky slopes men wondered why the generals had not foreseen the difficulties of the terrain.) The radio voice was confident: preparations were going ahead on schedule, all contingencies would be met, all factors were known. In fact, nothing was known. It was like the eruption of a volcano: no one knows how it will go or where it will end.

From both sides of the line artillery fire kept the war going—chewing roads, eating villages, biting men in half.

In the isolated valley the Lieutenant thought of Naples, of the sun, the body of a woman, the view of the city from her window. The hanged man. And Davis—what had become of him? In his mind he saw an infantry company up on the line, so different from these gun-servants in the way they worked, and stayed close to one another, and died.

Some died. But not here. Here they ate, slept, wrote letters, cleaned and fed the guns, wiped the mud from their boots. Lieutenant Freeman saw to the concealment of the trucks, inspected the guns and the kitchen, controlled the ammunition details, warned the men to dig their holes deeper. Change your socks. Shave. Keep your helmet on. Bury the shells deeper. Keep the powder dry. When these things were done he stood under the dripping camouflage nets and looked for something to do, something to stop the erratic tossing of his mind, that would not be still, would not be satisfied but would haggle, would cry out for action, would ask questions about shells that destroyed empty villages and men who did not go willingly but hesitated and were ordered to their deaths. (How can a war be fought with anything but volunteers; how can you ask a man to die until he has offered?)

To stop the crumbling of his simple certainties he worked harder than he needed to work. He worked with the men of the gun crews and the ammunition parties, blindly, to exhaustion, for relief. And because he wanted to be a good soldier. Whatever else was true, untrue, necessary, unnecessary, this remained: to be a good soldier. It was a proof of something.

He worked, he learned, and he came to be known as a good officer in the battalion. He did not have much to say. But he got along with the men; they liked him for the way he worked and got his hands dirty. The days came and went, he did the job. Yet he never felt right in this heavy battalion. He was restless for the other thing, that life with an infantry company: the elemental dependence of each man on each man—a life that was like the life of a hunter, in the open, the eyes alert, listening, moving, full of the unexpected. This was like working in a factory.

And then for three weeks, when there was sickness in the battalion, he was assigned to the Fire Direction Center, which was the brains of this factory. He liked this even less. It was in the cellar of a half-ruined house that had once been used to store cheese and wine: primitive arched vault-work made with big rough stones that looked as if they had been taken from a Roman temple. Here was the complex work-room, looking like a computation center for astronomers, where the nerve-endings of the battalion were tied up. It was a quiet chamber full of wires and phones and instruments and mathematician-corporals and officers, working over charts and maps and tables of firing data. Here the war was all numbers and grid sheets stuck full of colored pins. From the maps and charts problems of distance and deflection and wind-drift were computed, and coordinates plotted on other maps with slide rules and celluloid plotting instruments. Data for old targets were recorded and evaluated for each of the three batteries; new targets were plotted from information supplied by Intelligence through Corps and Brigade Head-quarters. Road junctions, supply dumps, bridges, possible troop concentration points—none of these had ever been seen by the men in this cellar, but for all of them firing data had been computed that could, on demand, result in their sudden annihilation. The maps and data of this Fire Direction Center were coordinated with those at higher headquarters so that, on short notice, fifty or a hundred big guns could be concentrated on a single target—say an enemy regiment forming for an attack—in massed fires. Mass production, a saturation of the market, invented and perfected by the technicians of the Corporation.

3

So they lived, from day to day, hands and brain coordinated to play a kind of blind man's chess with high explosive shells. It was a pretty regular life. The food was hot, now and then they got to put on clean clothes, and the mail came up regularly with the supplies. The worst that could happen was that they might be hit by counterbattery fire from the German artillery; but they hid themselves efficiently and the Germans never found them. Once, when they had fired almost continuously through the night, a gun barrel exploded and killed two men. But this was nothing more than an industrial accident. Otherwise it was not what most people think of as war; it was a more or less orderly excursion with big machines in a strange country, made exciting by the power of the guns and the prospect of movement, soured by cold and mud and homesickness.

One moonlit night on a road they heard an infantryman snarl and call them a motorized Boy Scout Troop. Well, it was more than that of course, but nobody pretended it was anything more than it was—a machine for throwing high explosive shells. In "A" Battery they were, mostly, a nice bunch of guys, and in the rest of the battalion it was about the same. They worked well together, and made themselves as comfortable as they could. The card games were congenial penny-ante affairs, no one trying to get rich. They liked the work—as much, anyway, as most people like their work; they had seen enough of the war in passing to know they had it good. A job—what the hell (they would say) if it isn't one lousy job it's another. A modest bunch, all in all—they dug their holes, fed and cared for the guns, waited for the war to end.

They were men with a trade and they were proud of it in a small way. The big guns were *their* guns, and sometimes, in the hot roaring excitement of a night's firing before a dawn attack, they loved these guns. The long barrels in their strong thrust and recoil, pumping shells into the hills. In these nights the gun crews let themselves go in a kind of lovemaking; rhythmically, blindly, they swung their bodies in the act of loading and firing. Round after round, in rising excitement, until the barrels were almost too hot to touch.

The officers didn't bother them much, they were more like technicians than bosses. So they had no kick coming. It was a kind of fraternal lodge or athletic club, the battalion; they had been together, almost intact, through North Africa and Italy. It had become a machine that functioned almost automatically. Most of the officers had gotten over their lust to command; they were satisfied to keep an eye on the machine and let it run.

Only the Colonel was a bastard, and he was too much the aloof executive to be an irritant. Periodically he would come down to walk around and around the machine, a cigar between his teeth, a cold eye probing every bolt and wheel, his hands clasped behind his back. Behind him, head cocked, came a scared lieutenant taking notes. He looked, he looked hard. Rarely did he shift the cigar to open his mouth. It was not that he was looking for promotion, it was not even that he liked to give orders. But he was an efficiency nut—it was *his* machine, *his* power in those guns, and he wanted it run right. He liked to see the wheels go round. In recent years he'd made a little money as a Chrysler dealer, but years before he had worked as a foreman in a Ford plant. He was still infatuated with the rhythms of the belt line. And then for years he had devoted two weeks in the summer and many a Thursday night to the National Guard, learning his profession. Selling cars was a business, this was a calling. The men he regarded as part of his equipment, given him so that he could fulfill what he thought of as a Mission. The guns—he too was in love with them; but his love was more constant and platonic, almost cold. So the Colonel was not an easy man to live with. But as they said in the gun crews, it could be worse.

5

When Lieutenant Freeman got to his battery he found three young officers—one from Purdue, a mining engineer; one from Yale, a good-natured fat man who sold insurance in Topeka; one from California, a tall relaxed redhead who had never, to listen to him, done anything but chase golf balls and women. Into this easy-going fraternity of quasi-gentlemen he made his way without friction. They did not, as so often happened, try to make use of the new junior officer. When they saw the way he worked they shook their heads and smiled. When he went on that way, they looked on in amazement. When he told them he would rather have gone to a light artillery battalion, they told him to get his head examined.

They asked him how things were at home, told him how long they had been overseas, and said they were hoping for some whiskey from Naples with the next load of ammunition. In their off-moments they held informal meetings of what they called The Celibates Club, recording how many weeks and months had passed since they had had a woman, and making plans for Rome. When he told them something of his life in Naples—seriously at first, then laughing with them as something like giddiness overcame them—they decided that he would have to go through Rome "untouched by human hands" if he hoped ever to become a member of the Club. He was glad to be with this bunch; after so many months of training, of working with earnest, solemn, competitive asses and prigs it came as relief. Even Walker, the engineer who was the Battery Commander, was an amiable human being.

But it rained, it was cold, and they had stopped moving. They were stuck in the mud of this valley of the moon as they called it. Boredom took hold of them, and amiability was lost in the slow-turning days of routine. No whiskey. The goddamned guns, the goddamned war—where the hell was it! They wanted to be moving again.

They were not alone. From other valleys came the hollow thump-thump-thump of other battalions firing. Then the low ring of the phone: the Exec on his feet: "Battery Adjust!" and the cannoneers groaning and swearing as they get up to stand carelessly by the guns. The commands come in a steady drone, the breech is opened, filled, closed. Sound and flash: and ten miles away the shells fall screaming like subway trains, the earth opens up, the air is alive with hot slashing fragments of steel—unseen and unheard by the men of the battalion. At a crossroads men clutch at the earth and are mangled by steel and concussion.

The Lieutenant did his job. He checked ammunition, he made sure of the camouflage, he inspected the guns and the vehicles. These things had their importance: a small order was maintained in the midst of a greater disorder. A job. He resigned himself to it, he lived by the routine from day to day. Was there a war? Where? This—the ritual of the twelve guns—was the only reality. This was a valley in the mountains of the moon; they were slowly turning through space; the rain fell; days became years.

He wondered about the men in the gun crews. Did they know there was a war? Did they know what it was? What did they want, what did they expect? They kept themselves to themselves; they trusted no officer. Dig your holes deeper, he told them. Watch out for trenchfoot. He tried to break through and talk with them as he had once talked with men in the infantry companies. It was not the same—they had their reticence to match the aloofness of officers they had known.

The machine went on churning, blind, precise, proclaiming its power. From nowhere into nowhere, throwing steel. Through the first month he would still sometimes turn and watch whenever the guns were firing, caught by the massiveness of their kick-thrust-blast-recoil, the flame spit around the muzzle—the shock, the exhilaration. That was the point, wasn't it, that the guns should go on firing? But after a month of it he no longer watched. The guns were someone else's job. He had his trucks, his ammunition, his kitchen to watch. Eat, sleep and keep dry. His only relief was in the letters he wrote to a girl in the other world. He hungered for her letters, kept them, lived in them. But she became an abstraction. He wrote to her more often, trying to preserve the sense of her.

2

On March 12 a New Zealand regiment fought its way up the impossible slopes of Monte Cassino to the German stronghold at the top. A German parachute regiment threw them back with terrible losses. The battalion in its valley nine miles away never knew of it. Their guns continued to gore the earth of the shattered mountain; but they never saw it.

They did not know it was there. They went on with their blasting like men working a quarry from a distance.

Now and then on the main road outside the valley the ammunition detail would see the infantry slogging along in the mud, the exhausted companies coming out of the line, the tired companies going up to relieve them. The supply trucks of the battalion would wait at the crossroads for them to go by. Lieutenant Freeman and his men would watch them, to get a glimpse of their faces. The foot soldiers did not look to either side; they stared straight ahead or kept their eyes on the ground. They passed and were gone. The artillerymen turned and drove carefully down the narrow dirt road into the valley, saying nothing, avoiding one another's eyes.

3

"OK. Break it up."

The Lieutenant elbowed his way into the angry circle of men at the number four gun. In the early morning light it had begun to rain again, after a quiet night. They fell silent, looking down at the moaning figure of the man on the ground.

"What happened, Sergeant? Who hit him?"

The sergeant did not look up. This was his gun crew. "I'm not sure Lieutenant. I wouldn't want to say."

"Goddamnit Lieutenant, I hit him, the lousy hillbilly bastard." It was Lecroix, the tough little musclebound waiter from New Jersey. "I just had enough of this creep and I hit him. If it wasn't me, somebody else'd done it. Son of a bitch, for a week now he's been sittin' around here and lookin' at us. Watchin' us. That's all the creep does is sit an' watch us. What's he want for chrissakes?"

The others broke in to agree. "It's enough to make you nutty Lieutenant. Every time you look around—"

There was a groan. Bowen was sitting up. The Lieutenant recognized him as the thin silent man who had worked with many of the ammunition details. On one occasion he had disappeared for an hour from the ammunition depot; no one knew where he had gone. They claimed he had been a sharecropper in Arkansas before the army took him, but no one was sure.

The Lieutenant moved closer to him. "Bowen, whatever it is you've been doing around here, cut it out. You hear me? You're getting on these men's nerves." He hesitated, uncertain of his ground. There was more to it than any of them were willing to say. "Bowen, you hear what I'm saying?"

Bowen looked up. His face was gaunt, almost emaciated. A long sad face. But the eyes were a peculiar golden brown, they seemed too strong and warm to belong to this face. There was a funny little smile on his face, as if he had been smiling in his sleep. Suddenly he frowned, and without looking at any of them began to speak.

"I am a faithful servant of the Lord. I have come here to be with these sinners in their trial. The Book says, It is the blood that maketh an atonement for the soul. They do not understand. But the day will come. A great light will be kindled on the eve. But first we must die with Him." He stopped. No one moved. They were listening. "Now we are in the darkness. He is coming and we are not ready for Him. They shall not drive me away from my flock. We are passing through the valley of death. We are here to serve his mysterious purposes. It is given to me that I shall see the light and that I shall lead them. My brothers, remember that it says, And many bodies of the saints which slept arose. We are among the saints. If we open our eyes on the day we shall see them arise." He turned his head slowly and looked up at them. "Now do you understand?"

They stared at him, then looked at each other. For a moment the spell that he had worked over them held. They listened for more. But he said nothing. With a solemn dignity he gathered himself to his feet, turned and walked with his head up through the other side of the broken circle.

6

There were quiet days when they had time to write letters. But from this valley what was there to write home about? Miles away was an enemy you had never seen. Here were the guns, the machines that fought the war. There, the cold mountains. Rain and mud. Holes in the ground.

The Lieutenant wrote:

This morning we had powdered eggs for breakfast, and coffee. Yesterday the same. This afternoon we're going to fire what's called a mission—that's when you fire on some target until it's knocked out, then you stop. The next target is another mission. It's all done with mirrors. The only trouble is you never even get to look in the mirror to see what's happened. Tonight we'll be firing on a schedule, to keep the Germans from using the roads. Maybe soon we'll move to another position. Another goddamn valley full of mud, but it would be a change anyway. How long can it go on? After a certain number of missions it has to end. Or does it? Who knows. We never get to see any of it. Even the big shots who are running it don't really know what's going on. They say they do, but they're only guessing. We're in the dark.

And then again (March 10, 1944):

What happens is you haul the gun into position and you get it squared away to fire. Then you get the camouflage nets up. Then you dig some slit trenches. Then you dig fox holes near the gun to get down deep in case the German artillery gets a bead on us. Then you dig a hole, a big one, to set the gun down into, and maybe build it up with sandbags or logs or whatever there is. Meanwhile someone else is digging holes for the ammunition, and maybe a little further back some more for the trucks and the other stuff. The trucks are enormous—they've got to be to pull these guns. Most of this happens in the middle of the night. No lights. Then between missions and taking care of the guns, you fix up here and there making it as comfortable as you can. Housekeeping is really what it is. You get all nice and settled down and bango, down comes the order to pick up and move. The men get pretty fed up with this. And then some lousy general comes smelling around and telling you to clean up and how to dig a hole. And then you sit in some godforsaken hole and never get to see what the hell is going on. A funny damn way to fight a war.

They sat on wooden boxes and wrote to the other world, to prove to themselves that something existed outside this valley.

April 1

Dear Eddie:
We're still here, in case you forgot, somewhere in Italy. Standing still. Yesterday we had some excitement you might say. There were some big shots making what's called a tour. Mediterranean Theater. Tour. Get it? You know, show business. Well the Colonel was worried as hell. It's a theater, so the generals take the big boys around and put on a show for them. It's great. Especially for us characters who are playing nursemaid to these big cannons. Anyway, early in the morning the Colonel rushes his ass down here to the batteries where the

guns are to see if we're behaving ourselves and if things are all neat and tidy like it says in the books on how to do it. The first thing that happened was we had the best breakfast we've had since we landed in this hole. This is supposed to prove everything is being done to keep our boys in the style they're accustomed to. And so nobody will make a stink when the important guests ask you how are things. Then they can go home and say how our boys are the best fed army in the world. Great. With that department store they're running back there in Naples, we damn well ought to be, even after they take their cut. Don't you believe those boys at the desks aren't making themselves a pile. Every guy here ought to get a couple of months off so we could go to Naples and do a little business, and then we'd all feel a lot better.

Well, the next thing you know we all had to get ourselves shaved and get on whatever clean clothes we can scrape up, and then get the guns and stuff polished up, and then dig us a new latrine. Man you'd of thought it was West Point. Someone said it was Forrestal who's the Secretary of the Navy or something and Patterson who's something in the War Department. Seems they made a real party out of it, General Clark and five or six other high class brass types and their valets and chauffeurs.

Yesterday we heard they were up around the command post of the Division nearest to us, only about two miles from here. This guy was saying they dined, and he meant dined, in real style and this general who commands the Division broke out the best he had, seems he had his trailer full of scotch and the best Italian stuff. I'm telling you this is one fancy war, if you get in the right circles. Then they gave out some medals and then they went over to some other CP and had a luncheon or cocktails or whatever the hell it was. I swear that's what the guy said, they had cocktails. You ought to see the way those bastards eat, I mean the brass and the rest of them. They say some of them keep a woman handy. Who knows. If I had a trailer like that I'd keep something more than pistols in it I can tell you.

Well, this colonel of ours was about as cool as a virgin on the big night. The bastard must of inspected every goddamn nut and bolt in the outfit, he was almost off his nut altogether. One minute he'd be screaming and chewing up cigars by the box, and the next minute he's smiling through his mustache to keep us in a good mood. Oh man what a party. The colonel had a spy out, one of his high class college boys, and this kid comes bowling back to say they were just over the next hill. Well, we got ourselves all straightened out like boy scouts and we waited. And we waited some more. Yeah, you guessed it, they passed us up, had to get back to Naples to a big dinner the boys had fixed up for them in some palace, with dancing girls, waiters, the works. Well the colonel he just stood around for a while like a guy's just lost an election. Then there's a mission come down on the phone and he starts tearing around in the mud like he's going to load and fire all twelve guns by himself. We didn't give a damn, it helped to break up the routine a little anyway. Christ it was funny though, us sitting around like some soldiers in a movie right in the middle of this godforsaken country. This place stinks let me tell you. What the hell are the goddamn generals hoping to get out of this broken down country anyway. Sometimes you get the feeling you're here for good. The asshole of creation. But when you see the poor goddamned infantry you can't complain. I guess they feel better up there now that the big shots have been around to dinner and given out some medals. Don't hand me any of that crap about feeling bad and you wish you could do something. Stick with that job, this is for the birds strictly.

Well I didn't finish the story. This morning we really had a time. Down the road comes this jeep with the Colonel driving himself and out of it steps two blondes about forty years old, all dressed up in boots and fur jackets and god knows what else. You should of seen the guys in the battery grinning like Saturday night in a whorehouse. The war went right out the window. Well they were no chickens but they were women and in this hole you get so you don't know one thing from another. One of them turns out to be a lady politician and the other one is taking pictures for some magazine. They congratulated us on being able to get in on the war and they said how sorry they were they couldn't and how they would stay if they could. In a pig's ass. Well the guys in the battery ran around like a bunch of horny monkeys being interviewed for a circus, and helping this babe take her pictures. We couldn't of fired a round if Jesus Christ himself had ordered it. Everybody had to get into the act. Give them half a chance and the whole outfit, including your boy, would have jumped them right there and then. Boy it was a big day, even the Colonel was all smiles. You've never seen two phonier women and everyone knew it and still we were sorry to see them go. I guess if all these important people are coming over for a look then something sure as hell is brewing in the good old Med. Theater. I can just see the politicians trying to figure out the next move. I'm not sure which one I'd rather have lousing it up, the politicians or the brass. Most of the guys have no idea what the hell we're trying to do here anyway. It's one goddamned mountain after another and those son of a bitch of Germans love to fight. Well that's the news if any of it gets past the censor. Say hello for me to any of the guys you see around town. Tell Sally Breitung if she's not doing anything she can come over here and cook for me. And if you see any of my old buddies from the composing room, ask them if they can spare me a post card.

Your boy,
Bert

2

So it dragged on, in the service of the guns. Eating, sleeping, digging holes, loading. Firing and feeding, the machine licking flame and roaring through the days and nights. No one ever smiled. Listlessness took hold. For the Lieutenant, as for the others, who had dragged themselves so much further in the train of the guns, the war had almost ceased to exist. He hung on to the one reality: to be a good soldier, to do the job—one of the few direct proofs of manhood, the way things stand. But in the hierarchy of the Corporation you are an employee, not a man.

Drugged by the routine. Sleepwalking: digging holes, waiting, firing, waiting—. But something was coming. They could smell it. There was more movement on the roads, trucks grinding uphill, tanks and halftracks clanking and roaring, moving up. The cold was breaking up. Something was coming.

Up front the patrols went out automatically, to die in the light of a German flare or to bring back some story, any story, that would satisfy the company commander, who could then satisfy the battalion commander, and so on up the line, saving their necks. All they wanted was to be let alone, the tired dirty reluctant common labor of the Corporation.

All along the front the two armies prodded and goaded one another, they could not leave one another alone. On the slopes and through the rubbled towns the infantrymen ripped and clawed at each other's flesh, tearing it, smashing the bone into the pink and dark red meat. They found out that the body of even a tough man is delicate, that it can be torn to raw chunks and smears of flesh in the flash of a hand grenade the size of a large pear. It becomes a way of life. There is nothing to do but kill. Or be killed. It's easy. One grenade thrown like an overweight baseball and three, four, five men are ripped through the guts by splinters of steel, pierced through the eyes to the brain, castrated—spread on the ground like sacks of meat, blood all over everything. This is easy, when they are tired, fed up with the never-ending attempts of others to kill them, stretched to the breaking point on the rack of fear. They are going to kill you; kill a few of them first. Make it worthwhile.

Follow me. Up out of the protection of the holes. In the open. Running. Through the teeth: Oh those bastards, let's get 'em. *Rock to rock, hole to hole, frightened, firing, running uphill, falling flat, then up again, fighting for breath, and down—a black hole in the forehead. Death by spray-gun, like flies. They fall flat, halfway up the hill, the fifty-six who are left out of a hundred and twenty. No one moves. Who's going to get up first and be an inspiration and be cut in half? Rigid on the ground, caught. Then mortar shells falling like a shower of pop-flies in the infield. Someone gets a direct hit and he is changed from a man with his bowels emptied into his pants to the stump of a man rocking, trying to get up, surprised in the end that this should happen to him. You're brave? No one cares. Alone here. Where is everyone? Where is the sun? You're dead. For your country. But now you have no country, and if you are one of a million dead in the war, or twenty million, who will count you as* one? One *man. One in a million. You are wrapped in a mattress cover, dumped in a hole—you become one million heroes. You were the replacement who arrived yesterday. Tomorrow you will be forgotten by men who are to die the day after tomorrow. Buddy. Don't believe it—nobody loves a dead man. Pity for the man who died young. But the dead man is always somebody else.*

Another one cracks, he lies shivering on the hillside, crying in a jag. He gets up yelling and goes stumbling downhill. Five seconds later his head is pierced three times, and before the dead body can fall it is slashed wide open by the fire of automatic weapons. He was from Chicago, name of Reilly—ever heard of him?

Ten men get back down the hill on their bellies. The rest of the story doesn't matter. Except that the next day these ten, whose names you wouldn't know, got up out of their foxholes tired and irritated, crawling with lice, thinking about a hot cup of coffee they couldn't have. Before they could eat something a company of tough methodical Germans came down on them. They turned savage, full of what is called the madness of battle. This means you don't care whether you live or die. They slaughtered the Germans even as they were overrun, until at the end there was nothing in this ridge outpost but a butchered pile of dead and dying men moaning to one another. A dirty gray morning, the sun just coming up out of the far mountains. They smelled bad, though they had not yet begun to rot. That afternoon the gravediggers came with stretchers and mattress covers and cleaned up the mess, and toward dusk the position was reoccupied.

3

Through the steel-cold winds of February, and the rain, and now in the warming up of March and April this is the way it goes. They crawl on their bellies toward Rome and the Germans give up one inch at a time, one hill at a time, blood all over everything. You don't count the months here. After a while you stop measuring your life-time, expecting nothing. No future. How can you measure it?—have I got five months to live, five weeks, five minutes? Can it be measured when in ten minutes of hacking and piercing two hundred men get the life ripped out of them? 200 x 70 makes 14,000 years of life. Count it. Wholesale: as if there were two hundred young men standing on a street corner and a light rain fell and when it was over they were strewn around like crudely cut pieces of meat that have fallen to the sawdust of the butcher shop. By the time the newspapers and the history books get to them they are ciphers, but if you catch them now in the final moment of life they are warm curved bodies, beautiful things, quick, all the parts moving in harmony. Measure it, the appetite that is in them; the force of the hands that would warm the bodies of women; the bodies of women that will starve for want of them. Beautiful things. And five minutes later caught in the meatgrinder. Every day. How do they do it? Why don't they quit? How do they make the muscles of their legs work to carry them toward it —into it? The joy of battle, is that it? Maybe for a few, but not for long, the first close scrape knocks them off that jag. The pull of the group? Yes, that takes them part of the way. And for the rest, they are numb as far as they can make themselves numb, as with an anaesthetic. Numb most of the time, resigned to futility; and then at times goaded to anger, snarling—through with life, eager to kill. One gets up and rushes and the others follow, glad to be moving, out of the hole, not to be waiting. A way of life, almost.

Terror. Men? No. No longer men. Animals surrounded by fields of fire. No way out.

Look—here on the map, eight miles from where the heavy artillery is dug in: Here is the first platoon of B Company, 331st Infantry, way up front near Cassino, weary. Tired, Christ they are tired. Dirty. Cruddy. They stink, their feet stink, everything stinks. They sneak in toward the smashed town (war is not open combat, it is waiting, hiding, sneaking, finding). One side hides, the other side searches in stealth, and when they meet there is a quick blast, one dies (or both) and the other moves on to die by a sniper's bullet at the other end of the street.

It happens every day: The platoon goes in past the German outpost, which holds its fire, down the street into an ambush of automatic weapons fire from all around the small piazza. They knew it was coming. They wither. They go down in bunches like subway riders, jerking and twisting as the bullets bounce off the pavement and gore big holes in them. The very air is screaming, whining. The end of the world. Those who live through the first blast fall flat on their faces and wait for the next. In pools of blood and urine. They wait. Trapped. But not Peters. No, Sergeant Peters had had enough. Maybe he's able to suspend his belief in his own mortality. He gets up and rushes that machine gun, straight at it; throws a grenade, falls flat near the fountain, gets up and goes on, shouting, firing the Browning Automatic Rifle from his hip as he runs. And the Germans, surprised at the sight of this crazy man (fascinated by the bold enactment of their own suppressed madness) hesitate, then fire badly,—and he kills them all with another grenade, all three of them dead around the gun. And then he stands over them in his passion —wild—and while the sense of immortality lasts forgets to run and hide himself, and is shot through the back of the head by a sniper kneeling at a window. But by this act the sniper is revealed, and in the next moment he is a dead man, a dumb rag-bag of a man kneeling in a window, still a perfect German soldier except for the black hole where one of his eyes had been. He falls as the muscles let go; he hits the street like a sack of old tin cans and sprawls in the peculiar obscenity of violent death. Faces are still pressed to the stone of the piazza. No one knows what has happened. There are the corpses, scattered in the design of the game. For the historians to piece together. The heat is still in the bodies. The sun comes up to warm them, to assist in their decomposition. But no one knows. And so it goes, onward and upward, inch by inch in terror, driven, numb and half-blind. To kill out of habit, gladly, for relief; and to force one foot after another toward your own death.

Finally, shrunken, a man can say: If I die then the war is over. Let it be over.

Die? For what? Everyone thinks he knows except the man who is about to die. Wars should be fought at home, as they used to be. Then we could all go out and watch with opera glasses, as they went out from Washington—ladies and gentlemen—to stand on the hills and look down on Bull Run. Watch closely: the shell fragments are smashing this man's legs to pulp, tearing a hole in one lung and ripping off one of his hands. You see? He's still breathing through a mouthful of blood, but he'll be dead in a minute. How would you like to be the guy who comes along later to pick up the pieces and stuff them into a mattress cover? Someone's got to do it.

4

This country of soft hills and jagged mountains, with pink and brown plaster houses on the flat, is the Abruzzi. It is nearly spring. A few birds sing. All you can hear is the bump and slam of artillery that seems never to stop firing. At night you can see the on-off on-off muzzle flash of the guns, their drum-beat echoes confused among the stony valleys. There on a hillside is one of the gored and splintered villages whose people, pacifists by nature, shiver in the caves where they hide until the war should pass, as others have passed. If the storm passes then the war will pass, it is only natural.

At night the lines of trucks grind uphill in the dark, no lights, with food and ammunition. In some places every muddy glen and gully and olive orchard is overrun with big guns—jammed hub to hub—and other heavy machinery, and the men, looking like factory workers, who work the machinery. Hidden in cellars and holes are typewriters and filing cabinets; the bookkeeping and accounting never end. At a road junction the engineers are putting up signposts to tell you where everything is in this confusion; there are other men endlessly running out wire that runs from switchboard to CP to OP to Division to Brigade to Corps to switchboard to the main office in Naples. Others are taking pictures of it all for purposes of record and advertising.

And a little further up in the mountains of the Abruzzi are the men—no longer men—who have not changed their wet shoes for a month and move in a cold dream; who push their lifeless bodies in the fight for ditches, for crumbling slopes, for a precipice where a mule would not go, for crags, for a rock to hide behind. Replacements come up—but only for the dead and wounded.

It is not like Agincourt where the impassioned knights and archers and crossbowmen swept toward each other to a measured beat, all in the open; where a yeoman on foot could win his fight against a prince on a horse; where men died one by one, each a separate recognized entity, not in bunches, sprayed by machines they could not see.

They talk about a "good soldier." But he is never good enough to outlast the machines that are to him what a spray gun is to a fly. All he can do is to hide, until the spray gun catches him in the open, or a shell fragment, like a meat cleaver, catches him in his hole. It is not much different from a slaughterhouse, except that here the slaughterers have become animals and turned on each other.

It is not what you think it is. It is not infantry sweeping all together across a plain, as it might have been at Waterloo or Gettysburg. It is small groups—patrols, squads, platoons —fighting in the dark, or blind, from room to room, door to door, confused. They fight another small group for a farmhouse, a ridge, a wall; they hide, they wait, they fire into the darkness; and in the end they fight for their lives because one group has to live and the other to die, they know no alternative.—No, there is an alternative: you lie down on your back in the hole and stick a leg up to catch a few slugs and go to a hospital and your war is over. But most of them are too far gone to understand this. When death stands looking down into your hole it is not easy to turn away, it takes will and imagination and the courage to live. And then, they need one another, they have begun to forget that there is anything else but this. Or they are cowards, men who cannot choose death, who cannot shove their bodies into a grinder, who have come to think: everything in this war is necessary except that I should die, because if I die then it is all unnecessary.

But this kind of thing is peanuts. Patrol action. Retail business in a butcher shop. Wait a little while. It's getting warmer every day and the ground is drying and the generals are eager to be moving. Toward that big day of the drive when the cattle will, at the sight of blood, gore each other to death in a stampede in the slaughterhouse.

The generals are impatient to practice their trade. They take the big view. The crusaders. Now—take one, two, three more strategic hills and we are ready to move. Business is business.

The infantry crawls from ridge to ridge leaving its trail of dead flesh; and is thrown back; and goes up again, a tormented animal, piling the dead on the dead and on the living; and they cling to the shattered mountain for no reason that they know. Get to the top and stay there: it is better to be above than below. They need no orders for that. The body knows it with no help from the brain.

Behind them the clumsy battalions of heavy artillery prepare to move house, displacing to stay within range. At night they are on the road, creeping forward, stop and go, almost bumper to bumper. In the ragged moonlight the men of the 501st Artillery Battalion saw that in the valleys were hospitals and cemeteries. It was getting very crowded, the dead and the living nudging one another on the roads, pressure building up in the narrow corridors through the mountains, machines packed into the level spaces around the mountains. Artillery battalion commanders fighting each other for a place to put their guns. The roads choked, traffic unable to move. Men became lost in these mixed-up nights, and equipment disappeared.

Among the fallen stones of towns and villages the corpses took their ease. Anywhere on earth the dead are at home. The sun warmed them. Now at last they were home. They looked straight into the sky and grinned.

Behind the trucks the big guns were dragged through the darkness. Inside the trucks the gun crews dozed. But Bowen, the man of God, watched from the back of the last truck, fully awake, mumbling to himself. "Now we are in the darkness. Why do the heathen so furiously rage together?" He watched for a sign. Many times in this night he repeated to himself, "Now we are in the darkness." For hours he watched along the road choked with machines and men. The moon went down. He murmured, "Let us die with Him." He prayed. The others slept.

7

This time they got a break. The new position was in an olive grove at the foot of a rocky hill that had once been green with olives. It was an odd corner, out of the way, no other artillery battalions nearby, almost peaceful. For the moment things were easy, just routine harassing fire and a counterbattery mission now and then. They hid themselves well; the German observers could not find them; nothing like olive trees for hiding. Each day the sun was a little warmer; there was not much rain. They could relax.

Above and behind them, on the hill, was another shattered village, stone hovels turned to ruins. The battalion had never before been so close to one. Above it the hill softened to more olive trees, massed into shimmering gray-green clouds, stepped up in terraces, pocked and scarred by artillery fire. Where the line of the hill and the trees broke in a small plateau near the top there was the church, the chewed half of a church.

At first there were no signs of life. But on the second day they saw a white ox wandering near the church, slow and silent and seeming very remote. Someone said, "Let's go up and get us a steak dinner," but no one moved, it didn't seem right somehow. The ox was so white. Up there it was at peace. "Agh, hell," they said, "leave it be."

If you looked up at the hilltop when the sun was setting, the war seemed far away. The men at the guns would often look up, watching the village for signs of life. It gave them something to think about. Up to now Italy had been nothing more to them than a desert, a garbage dump, an alien waste of hard mountains and mud and smashed houses, where ragged people wandered with their chairs and mattresses, a pot, a bundle, a child. Now some of the men could joke about the women and wine they would find in the village. But they were bad jokes, the heart wasn't in them. Between the guns and the village the hill was steep, and in some places hard with outcroppings of whitish rock, like skulls. If you looked twice through the field glasses you could see that what was left of the village was not worth a visit.

On the third day someone saw small figures moving through the olive trees between the village and the church. Watching the clearings through the glasses they could see a handful of kids gathering olive branches. They disappeared toward the church. The next morning—in what seemed an un-natural silence while their own guns were still and they could hear no others—they heard the church bell ring. It went on ringing. For months they had heard no bells. They looked at each other. No sound of guns . . . For a moment they al-lowed themselves one wild flush of hope. *The war is over?* But the bell was slow, mournful. Then a crash. Again. Again. Somewhere in the grove to their right the four guns of "B" Battery went on with the old song. And five minutes later they themselves were firing again into the unknown. The end-less mountains.

When the mission was completed the bell was still

ringing. It should not be ringing. The Germans might—. They were not supposed to be ringing bells. The goddamned guinzos, what the hell did they think they were doing!

The red-headed Exec had turned around in his hole to watch the church through his glasses. At the guns they saw the sergeant who was with him pointing, and someone yelled, "Hey look!" "What?" "Where?" Then they saw it. On a path that climbed zig-zag up the hill was a procession, a bobbing column of heads and above the heads three large shapes, like statues.

"Listen!" There was something like music, a strange slow winding pipe and the heavier beat of what sounded like bagpipes and a drum. Something primitive. But there was no joy in it; it was more like a death march. When the music stopped they heard another sound, a sobbing and wailing. And then the path came out into the open and they saw them clearly for a moment as they passed. About sixty of them. Some had their heads bowed and some had them raised, shouting, and their arms raised, pleading. The women were in heavy black. Behind the wailing was a steady chant that carried down to the guns on the mild shifting wind.

Every man was watching, in silence, the guns forgotten. Along the hill path there were some who followed on their knees and stopped now and then to beat their heads against the ground. And those big things, upraised . . . what—. Yes, a cross, and on the cross, Christ, larger than life in his nakedness. Then they were in among the trees again and only the Christ was seen, moving slowly above the olive leaves. The sun was up high now, it seemed to focus on the dead man riding his cross. You could see the blood.

The column dipped, disappeared, and then again was in the open, moving straight uphill, and they could see now the other carried forms—a Madonna in black on a pedestal, and behind her the carved polished wooden trunk of a saint riding on the shoulders of four men. The pipes took up the slow march. At the head of the column were men in white peaked hoods, one carrying a black cross, the others torches. Their feet were bare. All of them were barefooted. The children wore what looked like wings.

They moved slowly, stopping now and then. When they stopped some of the men prostrated themselves before the Christ and tore their hair. Then up, winding, lost among the olive trees, and out again, higher up. Now you could not hear them; but in the pantomime of heads and upraised arms their anguish seemed to be intensified.

"Battery adjust!" A mission. The tall red-head was shouting orders. They heard him and they didn't hear him. Their backs were turned to the guns. Their eyes were on the hill. No one moved. "Goddamnit, move, this war's not over!" He was bellowing. They heard him and turned without a word to the service of the guns. They looked back over their shoulders. The three large figures rocked and dipped once more and disappeared into the church. The people followed on their knees.

The rest of the day the men were quiet, looking up from the guns at the village from time to time, wondering, seeming not to hear the tangled echoes of the guns in other valleys or the thump of German shells that fell regularly on the road a half-mile away. It was a beautiful day, blue sky, lambswool clouds, the hills softening into green. Later in the afternoon they saw the white ox again, very close, watching them from a clearing on the edge of a terrace. Once when the roar of the guns had died they heard the sad pipes far away on the hill, but it was not until late in the afternoon that they saw the procession again. They were coming downhill out of the trees on a path that followed a ledge of the rocky slope less than a hundred yards above the guns. The men drifted back to the edge of the grove to watch them pass.

The Christ, the Madonna in her veils and the polished saint bucked and lurched on the steep path. The people were quiet, moving with their heads bowed, only the three mourning women behind the cross were crying. They went absorbed in their passion as if the guns did not exist. The black-haired angels twisted their heads to steal a look, but there was no playfulness in them. Four older girls carried velvet cushions held out before them. On the cushions were— what? The watching men strained to see. Hammer, nails, sponge and jug. The two pipers wore the patched capes of shepherds. The rest wore odds and ends of what had been Sunday clothes, black, except for the children, who wore white, and the peaked white hoods of the men who carried the cross and the torches. The Christ was crude and terrible— the feet, the knees, the dead hang of the head. The blood. No music, only a low chanting and the sobbing of the three veiled women. The men of the battery watched for a long time, until the procession had climbed to follow the path around the side of the hill and out of sight. Then they went quietly back to the guns.

That night and the next Bowen disappeared. Some of the men knew that he had gone, but none of them said anything. Before dawn on the two mornings he was back. He did not seem to need sleep.

On the morning of the day after the procession there was nothing to be seen or heard. They were busy with routine interdicting fire on roads and the German rear area. The ruined village was still, as if the people had gone back into hiding. At times there seemed to be some movement among the olive trees but you could not be sure.

In the afternoon the village came alive. When they had watched for a while through the field glasses passed from hand to hand they could make it out. With the help of the ox the men were working to clear the fallen stones; the women and children carried away baskets of the smaller stones on their heads. They worked steadily, rhythmically, until it was dark. In the battery that night they talked about it, wondering how long it would take them to rebuild it, how long it would take to replant the long gashes in the hill where the olive trees had been burned away by shell fire. No one had any idea how long it took from the planting until a tree was ready to bear olives.

They began to speak of the villagers not as *guineas* or *wops* but as *these people*. Every day they would watch the progress of the rebuilding. Soon they saw a few men putting back the stones of the broken terraces, preparing the ground for new trees. How many years would it be before the trees would bear fruit again?

2

The next morning they were ringing the bell again. The men at the guns thought they saw some of them climbing the paths to the church, but they weren't sure. They were sweating now as they loaded and fired and hauled ammunition. But no one complained; it was good to see the sun come up big and hot to drain the chill out of their bodies and to dry up the damp of the slit trenches once and for all. What a sun this was. Nothing like it, at least not in the northern countries. Even these rocky hills come alive with it. No wonder the Italians say that the sun is half a meal, and that it is the father of the poor.

There was green on the hills, and the first wildflowers. Almost overnight the big guns look out of place, all wrong. A scene for shepherds, for a bacchanal.

This was more like it. Everyone got a lift. Smiling,

cracking jokes, working with some of the old zest. Sunny Italy. It was almost a holiday. And a few days ago the whole country was like some gray corpse. It was a time to get busy and start to fix things up a little. Live a little better. The hell with it, even if they got an order to pick up and move tomorrow they were sick of the way they were living. From the wreckage of villages and towns they had picked up rafters, wire, pieces of pipe, chairs and tables, a sewing machine—all kinds of odds and ends—and with these things they set to work to make themselves comfortable. By putting a five-gallon can of gasoline inside an oil drum they made themselves a hot shower and got some of the dirt off. Things began to look pretty good. They even went back to kidding each other about their need for women; it had been a long time since that had happened. Rome, Rome, Rome. Man, wait till we hit Rome.

3

At the number four gun Simmons, the gunner, turned to the sergeant. "There he goes again. Son of a bitch looks like a turkey."

The sergeant looked around. "Who?—Oh Jesus Christ, again?" He stood up straight and shouted, "Hey Bowen, where the hell you off to—we'll be shootin' again in five minutes."

The tall thin man turned and looked back, hesitating as if he had not understood. "Just a minute, Sarge, there's something I mean to fetch out of my duffle bag. I got to have it." He shambled back through the olive trees to where a truck was concealed from air observation, and came back carrying his book.

Between missions he sat near the gun reading, mumbling to himself. In recent months he had kept more and more to himself; he had spoken only rarely in these months, and very little before that. Even when he was drunk he was silent. There had been a time when he had been good for a laugh among the gun crews, but not any more. They stayed clear of him. Some were afraid of him, though they could not have said why. He was ungainly and not very strong, but he did his job, helping to heft the big shell and ram it into the breech. For weeks now his face had been the remote mask of a man who is trying to remember some forgotten obligation. Now and then he looked up from his book to watch the men. They tried to ignore him, avoiding his eyes.

A week before, during a lull on the first warm day, he had disappeared for the first time from this gun position; later they had caught sight of him at a distance, walking bareheaded near the top of the hill. This time the Exec had seen him too. When they brought him back he told them he had gone to see a miraculous shrine some peasants had told him about. He had left all his money there. It was only right, he said, after all that has happened. He tried to take up a collection in the battery. They smiled and winked at each other and he withdrew into his silence again. Since that day he had said almost nothing to anyone.

And now again he sat hunched over the book, his lips moving as he ran his finger across the pages. The day was sunny and mild, a light wind played through the leaves of the olives. In the mottled ground-pattern of light and shade Lieutenant Freeman sat with his back against a tree, watching the man with the book. He had heard from some of the men of Bowen's disappearances in the night. Where did he go? What did he do? He could not rid himself of the idea that the man was not as simple as he looked, that he knew something. He wondered how he might approach him and talk to him. But he hesitated. The man was probably no more than a simple-minded religious nut. It would be awkward. Once you got him started he would never leave you alone. Yet the Lieutenant watched and wondered. In this void almost any strong voice would come as relief from the insane barking of the guns.

All that day, whenever he had a moment, Bowen read, while the rest of the men lay around with their shirts off, dozing, getting some sun, playing cards. It was Friday.

8

In this blue and purple April evening rich with the smells of earth, the men in his crew heard Bowen calling them. He was sitting on a bed of olive branches in his hole; his voice came up to them louder and firmer than they had ever heard it. Finally he was ready. Today was Saturday. It was almost time. "Hey you men, come on over here to me. Come on over, do you hear. It's time. Brothers, before it is too late, come to me."

They stirred in their sleep. He called again.

From the other holes complaints came back at him.

"Go to hell, deacon."   "Hey professor, don't you ever sleep? You stay up reading all night, you'll be late to work in the morning an' the old red-head will fire your ass."

"You hillbilly jerk, how'd you like to be the man who's shot out of a cannon? Shuddup, fa' chrissakes."

"You men better listen to me. We have come a long way. It's time. Before it's too late come over here to me. Otherwise you're going to be a sorry bunch of men." Someone laughed, someone shouted, "Fuck you, you creep." "Shut up." The sleepers tried to settle down again. But three or four men from the relief crew came over from the gun hoping for a laugh, anything to break the long waiting. They stood at the edges of the slit trench and looked down.

There he was kneeling, with the book open on a ledge he had cut into the earth. When he saw them he stood up and in a strong scolding voice said: "Now listen here, you men. Listen carefully. You know where you are? You are on a pilgrimage. You are standing on holy ground. Don't laugh. If you laugh you are damned. I said this is holy ground. Sacred ground. This place we are in is blessed, all of it. You men know how many saints have lived here in this country? Saint Francis, Saint Anthony, Saint Catherine—hundreds of 'em. And they are still here, they are with us, even if the likes of you can't see 'em. Don't you laugh at what I'm telling you. They are here for a reason. You damned heathen idolators, this is the luckiest thing that ever happened in your black lives. You have been chosen!—Now we are in the darkness, but we shall be shown a great light. Are you ready? You miserable fornicators, nothing but a bunch of card-playing drunks, you don't deserve to be saved, but I must try. The Lord works in mysterious ways. You have been chosen to carry his message to your people. You have been chosen!"

They whispered among themselves and tried to laugh at him again, but it was no good. Something about it wasn't funny. He saw them hesitate and pressed on. "Now you listen. I have seen the angel of death by the roadside and he has given me the sign. Listen carefully. He is speaking to us." He picked up the book and began to read.

"*Zacchaeus, make haste, and come down; for today I must abide at thy home.* And he made haste, and came down, and received him joyfully. And when they saw it, they all murmured, saying that he is gone to be guest with a man that is a sinner. And Zacchaeus stood and saith unto the Lord: *Behold, Lord, the half of my goods I give to the poor; and if*

I have taken anything from any man by false accusation, I restore him fourfold."

What was it, this crazy smile? They looked at him, and looked away, and looked again. "You men know what this is I'm reading to you? You know what it means?"

"Yeah, sure, Doc, it's the Bible. So what?"

"What you startin', a Sunday school, or what?"

"You buckin' for chaplain, kid? What's the idea?"

They didn't like the look on his face, but they stood there waiting; they wanted to see what was going to happen. What the hell else was there to do? It wasn't exactly what you'd call entertainment, but the skinny jerk knew how to read, that was sure.

Lieutenant Freeman could not get to sleep. When he heard Bowen's voice he came over to see what was going on. They did not notice him. He sat down on one of the guns and listened.

"Ok, Ok. If you're gonna read, read. We ain't gonna stand here all night Jack."

Bowen fastened the four men with his eyes. "All right, then listen while there's still time, an' cut out your damn wisecrackin'." His eyes were shining. He caught their puzzled eyes and held them. "All right." He read.

"And as soon as it was day, the elders of the people and the chief priests and the scribes came together, and led him into their council, saying, *Art thou the Christ? Tell us.* And he said unto them, *If I tell you, ye will not believe: and if I also ask you, ye will not answer me, nor let me go. Hereafter shall the Son of Man sit on the right hand of the power of God.*" Bowen looked up at them. They were listening, surprised. There were six of them now. Some of them sat down on the ground and waited.

"Then said they all, *Art thou then the Son of God?* And he said unto them, *Ye say that I am.*"

"You see," Bowen said. "You see what I mean?" They sat on the ground listening, undecided, looking at him now because they did not want to look at each other. And because he had changed, his eyes burning, his mouth smiling, so that they were not sure any more who he was. The voice too was strange to them; it was very low and sure. They did not ask him to go on, only waited, saying nothing, expectant. A few others came over from the guns to see what was up, and were caught in the air of expectation. One by one they settled down to listen.

Bowen worked his tongue around to wet his lips and went on reading, skipping to the parts he had marked.

"And as they led him away, they laid hold upon one Simon, a Cyrenian, coming out of the country, and on him they laid the cross, that he might bear it after Jesus. And there followed him a great company of people, and of women, which also bewailed and lamented him. But Jesus turning unto them said, *Daughters of Jerusalem, weep not for me, but weep for yourselves, and for your children. For, behold, the days are coming, in which they shall say, 'Blessed are the barren, and the wombs that never bore, and the paps which never gave suck.' Then shall they begin to say to the mountains, 'Fall on us!' and to the hills, 'Cover us!' For if they do these things in a green tree, what shall be done in the dry?'"*

He looked up from his hole. "Well?" And in the grip of his growing excitement he smiled. A terrible smile, like madness. They could only stare at him, then turn and look at one another. "Well?" He was expecting something. He was expecting them to go down on their knees. "Tomorrow! Do you know what will happen tomorrow?"

"Agh! You are damned!" His long bony nose was thrust up at them, his eyes insisted. He looked as if he might spit on them. They waited. They watched him. He knew something. "Pearls before swine!" He lowered his head slowly to the book and looked at it for a moment, sighing. Then he began again to read.

"And there were also two other malefactors, led with him to be put to death. And when they were come to the place, which is called Calvary, there they crucified him, and the malefactors, one on the right hand, and the other on the left." Bowen looked up at the hill that rose behind them, the sun's afterglow still lighting the broken church near the top, and then looked around at them from face to face. He read on.

". . . and cast lots. . . . and the soldiers also mocked him . . . And a superscription also was written over him in letters of Greek, and Latin, and Hebrew: THIS IS THE KING OF THE JEWS. . . . *Today thou shalt be with me in paradise.*" He read on to the end. They listened as if they had never heard it before.

He fell silent, smiling to himself. He turned the pages as if he were now alone. "Jesus, when he had cried again with a loud voice, yielded up the ghost. And behold the veil of the temple was rent in twain from the top to the bottom; and the earth did quake, and the rocks rent; and the graves were opened; and many bodies of the saints which slept arose, and came out of the graves after his resurrection, and went into the holy city, and appeared unto many . . ."

He stopped and his eyes moved from face to face. "And many bodies of the saints which slept arose—." His voice fell and then suddenly rose. "Do you hear? Do you see? Wake up from your sleeping. Don't you men see what is happening around here?" The sternness dropped from his voice, he was almost pleading with them. "If you all don't see then what's the use of you being here? What did you come here for? To sleep? To obey the orders of the devil? Listen, listen to what He said. Listen and you shall hear voices."

"Cast out the devils!" he cried. The long emaciated face was stretched tight. "Cast them out before it is too late."

His face was a hot iron. Suddenly he stopped and turned away from them. They did not move.

When he turned to face them again he was smiling, a man with a secret. His voice was quiet. "You men, you got to keep your eyes open tomorrow. You have been walking in your sleep. Sooner or later you're going to see." Looking around he saw the lighted eyes, the open mouths, and he knew that he had touched them. It roused him again. "In the name of God, brothers, you saw those people yesterday. Brothers! You saw them as clear as I did. You saw *Him*. Don't you all understand what's happening here? You saw it men, you saw it with your own eyes. You can't ever say you came over here for nothing. And now—"

"Tell us another, deacon. The one about the farmer's daughter." This one laughed loud and looked around for encouragement. But they all had their eyes on Bowen.

"Well, you saw it, didn't you brothers? With your own eyes." He paused. "Who do you think they are, those people? You think they're just some dumb hill people? You think they're a bunch of wops? Who do you think's winning this war, them or us? Who do you think? Take another look, brothers—this ain't the same war they tell you it is." He waited. They only looked at him in silence, listening.

"They are *His* people, brothers. They go with the cross. Where's our cross, brothers, why ain't we carrying a cross like them?" He turned and pointed into the darkness, toward the guns. "There's all the crosses we've got. The tree of life. Made of steel. The seeds of death. Crosses—we've got more crosses than anybody. Hah!" He grinned at them. "Steel ones. Yeah, laugh at these people and kick 'em in the ass. But you're wrong, brothers. You're going to see something. This is God's country. Holy ground, brothers. The day is coming. It is almost time. Tomorrow is the day. You're going to see. That was only the beginning, what you saw. Wait.

94

Maybe we don't have to carry the cross of death any more brothers. Maybe not. It depends. That's all. That's all, brothers. Goodnight. Goodnight!"

He laid himself down in the hole, pulled a blanket over him and shut his eyes. They stood still for a moment, waiting, uncertain, silent. Then they went back to their guns unlaughing. "Maybe he's crazy, but he sure can read that book." "You're damn right he can."   "He's crazy as a coot." "Yeah, only maybe he knows somethin', that boy."

"Agh, bullshit. That jerk is just another one of them hillbilly preachers. They're a dime a dozen. Strickly for the niggers."   "Yeah, OK, Kern, but anyway, who knows? Maybe he knows somethin'. Maybe. I'm sayin' maybe." "Agh, blow it you guys, let's get some sleep."

In the middle of the night a bright light flared out of the darkness of the hillside. For a moment it rose straight up in a column. The gun position was illuminated. And then it was dark again. Someone in the night crew went over to wake Bowen and ask him if he knew what it was. It had frightened them. But he was not in his hole.

2

The next morning, when his crew was relieved, Bowen slipped away up the hill, guiding himself through the olive trees by the sound of the bell that was ringing and ringing. No one saw him go. It was just after dawn. A strong sun was rising. With him he carried a can of red paint and a brush he had stolen from an engineer company, and a musette bag was slung across his back.

When he got to the church he got down on his knees. On his knees, erect, he crawled up the aisle. They were not surprised to see him, the people of the village. They were on their knees singing, rejoicing. They had brought the ox into the church with them. There was no priest.

They made way for him as he went toward the altar to kiss the feet of the resurrected Christ. The signs of mourning were gone. There were flowers and olive branches. Everything was illuminated by the sun that came in where the roof had been. When it was over they went out on the cobbled piazza in front of the church, crowding around him in their eagerness to welcome him. Their faces were lit with elation. Bowen gave them the loaves of bread and the cans of C Rations he had brought. They gave him a bottle of wine and thanked him through their spokesman, the man named Antonio who had worked for ten years in the steel mills of Pittsburgh. Then they gave him a small coral horn to put in his pocket, which was a protection against witches and the evil eye.

When they had talked for a while, Antonio took him aside and introduced him to an old woman who was the curer and knew more about the devil and his ways than any of them. She told him of the spirits that are seen in clouds and thunderstorms, of the clouds that become wolves and spirits and fight in the summertime, and of the lightning that is caused by the souls of the damned riding through the clouds. And she warned him about Monte Corno which is the devil's favorite place for his work.

Later he said good-bye to them; they cried, they kissed him and took his hand; and he went with Antonio and another man who were going to show him where the high flat rock was.

Late in the afternoon someone in the battery saw it. High up on the hillside facing the main road was the sign on the rock in big red letters: I HAVE SEEN THE LORD. THOU SHALT NOT KILL—and underneath, JESUS SAVES.

When he got back he had nothing to say. They watched him as he went about with his aloof smile. Only once he stopped and said to the men at his gun, "You men can stop worrying, you've got nothing to worry about now." He hid the wine from them. It was not yet time for the wine. He would save it.

Kern, the joker, caught sight of the red paint on his hands. "Hey corporal, give this man a poiple heart, he's bleeding." Bowen turned white and hid his hands behind him. He backed off, then turned and walked away, holding his, hands in front of him, looking at them.

3

If you looked carefully at the nearby hills on that bright Sunday you could see a few almond trees in blossom among the olives. A garden: the pink, the white, the silvery green. But even if they cared, the gun crews did not have much time to notice this. All through the late afternoon after Christ had risen the missions came down on the phone and the guns pumped shells into the opposing hills. First one battery and then another was firing. If you stood off at one side, at the right angle, you might see the shells begin their climb like four trained fish.

Just before dark, fire directions were relayed to all battalions from Brigade Headquarters for an important target that could not be reached by the light artillery battalions. It had been accidentally spotted by one of the air observers attached to Brigade: a large enemy troop concentration concealed in some olive groves. At their Sunday dinner the well-trained Germans had thought themselves protected by distance and the oncoming darkness and had disobeyed the commandment that soldiers shall not eat together but must spread out and hide themselves while eating as at all other times.

Circling absently in the small plane as if he had not seen them, the air observer had fooled them, making them think that his initial rounds were fired at a nearby hill. So that when he had adjusted the fire of one gun on the hill, and had waited while the Fire Direction Center was computing data for three battalions from the target data of the adjusted gun, he saw at last, to his delight, the massed fires of the thirty-six guns flash and flame among the olive trees. The computation had been perfect. The deception and surprise were complete. Over the radio he called back, "Range correct, deflection correct, continue fire for effect." The rest he couldn't see very well; he had been caught by small-arms fire and forced to climb. He did not see them stand and run from their meal in terror, but he knew he had them. Down came the hot rain of steel; up from the garden came the flame-flowers and the smoke-flowers.

At the guns they saw nothing. But the target was an important one. For twenty minutes the big guns consumed and spat shells until the olive wood ten miles away had vanished. The air observer went back for a look and reported the fire as having been very effective. And he was right.

Brigade telephoned congratulations to all battalions on a good job. In the 501st the Colonel suggested that the men at the guns should be told all about it. For morale purposes. There were some weeks, maybe months, of hard work coming. It was good news down at the batteries, proof of a good day's work. The cooks rummaged around and came up with something special for supper.

It was during that same night that Bowen began to work in a new way. Quietly he went from man to man, one man at a time, talking to whoever would listen. To one he would say, "For forty days He will come and go among us. We will see Him for the last time on the Mount of Olives, where He will vanish from our sight into the mist." To another he would say, "Why seek ye the living among the dead? He is not here, but is risen." Or, "A new commandment I give unto you: that ye love one another as I have loved you." Or he would come up to a man asleep in his hole, wake him and say, Listen, and recite the ten commandments to him. Night after night he did this. He seemed never to sleep. Seldom did he elaborate, but if he found a man who seemed to understand he would talk to him, would interpret, and answer questions. There were those who laughed in his face. There were others who feared him, and some who respected him for his passion, that they called his "sincerity." To the two or three men who were his disciples he told stories of the saints. As a young man, he told them, St. Francis had gone to war, as a man goes to the hunt. Then he would go no more.

4

The First Sergeant was a big placid bull of a man from somewhere in New England. He was the kind of man who could work all over his area as a building sub-contractor and still manage to keep a pretty fair dairy farm in operation. Nothing big either way, but solid. He came looking for Lieutenant Freeman back in the truck park at the foot of the hill. The Lieutenant took one look at him and almost laughed; he had never seen him looking like this. The man was in a hurry, he was sweating and jumpy. He made a couple of false starts, jumping back and forth.

"Come on over here where we can talk, Sergeant." The Lieutenant took him aside and offered him a cigarette. They walked up and down under the small shining trees.

"Lieutenant, no one else can talk to him. Maybe you

can. The men trust you Lieutenant. I think he'd talk to you—."

"Who?"

"Bowen, Lieutenant. Bowen. Something's wrong with the man. He's not right. If it gets to the Colonel there's going to be trouble." The Lieutenant tried to break in, but the big man wiped the sweat from his mouth and ran on. "He's going to throw the men off, that's what he'll do. They're jumpy enough the way it is. He'll get one of 'em alone at night, Lieutenant, and he'll talk to him, tell him all kinds of crazy things. Myself I don't know, I haven't heard it, but I hear the boys talking, and you know what he's been doing, running around loose like he was just along for the goddamned ride."

"That's all he does, just talks to them? Hard to stop a man from talking."

"But this man's a nut, Lieutenant, he's talking like he was Jesus Christ himself. Some of the men are going for it. Hell, it gives them something to do, you can't really blame 'em. Maybe only a few, but you can't tell. He's a devil, that man. He can talk, he's no run-of-the-mill hillbilly, don't kid yourself. They listen to him. Even the ones who laugh, they listen. They're getting rattled. You can't tell what he's going to say next."

They went on walking up and down under the olive trees.

"Listen, Sergeant, you mind if I ask you? Are you a religious man?"

"I'm a vestryman in the village where I come from. Do what I can, keep the building in repair and so on. Don't know that I'd call myself a religious man exactly."

"Ever see one of these itinerant preachers on the street? They like to talk. There's not much you can do. You don't have to listen."

"OK, Lieutenant. There's sense in that. But this man is going to make trouble, take it from me, and the sooner we put a stop to it the better. Talk is talk and trouble is trouble."

The Lieutenant stopped walking and looked back at the guns. "Maybe it's a good thing. Maybe they need it. You hang around here long enough you go dead in the head."

"The Colonel wouldn't understand that Lieutenant. If he gets on our necks there'll be hell to pay. We don't have to make things tough for ourselves just because this man's made up his mind to get religious."

The Lieutenant was silent for a moment. He bent over and tucked the leg of his coveralls into the top of his boot. "OK, Sergeant. I'll see what I can do. I'll talk to him."

"Thanks Lieutenant. Yeah, thanks. We've got some tough times coming up, we've got to keep the men on the ball."

5

The sun was not yet up, the morning air was cool on the flushed face of the tall man. He stood at the back of the truck, alone, the bottle of wine beside him. Close above his head was the faint whisper of the olive trees, in the distance was the rumbling of guns, but he heard neither. His trembling hands would not work to open the duffle bag.

"Bowen."

Startled, he did not recognize the voice behind him. His hands stopped working but he did not turn around. Who was calling him? Was he being called? The voice was low, it was gentle—. He stood motionless, feverish. Where was the voice coming from? From the tree above him? He dared not look. After such a night . . .

"Bowen."

His hand reached out, slowly, for the bottle of wine that stood on the steel bed of the truck.

"Bowen. It's me. Lieutenant Freeman. Where have you been?"

He turned, his long angular face working in confusion. The bottle of wine was in his hands. As he turned he hid it in one hand behind his back. His mouth moved but made no sound. Then the words formed themselves. "It is wine. It is some wine they gave to me. I gave them . . . something in return. But . . . it is not to drink. I cannot give you any to drink. It is . . . It was given to me."

The Lieutenant only looked at him; his throat tightened, in sudden fear of the unknown. In the exaggerated lift of his face the tall man seemed like a blind man. The Lieutenant fought himself for control of his voice. This man was not like the others. He wanted to reach him, to hear what he would say.

"Thanks. I don't want any wine. I want to speak to you." They were the wrong words, but he could find no others. "Where have you been? The First Sergeant has been looking for you."

"Where have I been?" He seemed to ask himself the question. His eyes stared straight ahead, as if he were looking at something that lay directly behind the other man. He shrugged and fell silent.

"Bowen, listen to me. I'm not here as an officer. I know that the men have been giving you a bad time." They stood ten feet apart. The other man did not seem to hear him. "I want to talk with you. I'd like to know . . ." He hesitated. What? he thought. What? What is it that I want to ask him?

Bowen held back. In the growing light his face was clouded over, his eyes were empty. He looked into the face of the younger man, then looked away. "I go away, but I return."

Suddenly he took a step toward the officer, the wine held out before him in both hands. "This wine . . . You see this wine? It is . . . wine." His mouth opened wide in an abrupt gasp for air. "It is not wine. It is . . ." He turned his eyes up and stopped speaking. His lips went on moving.

The Lieutenant heard the words, ". . . is drink indeed." He shivered at the sight of the uplifted face and turned his eyes down to look at the bottle that was cradled in the long bony hands. He did not know what to say. To turn and walk away and not see this man again, that was what he wanted. Yet something held him.

He kept his eyes on the bottle, not to have to see the face. Bowen was saying something. The voice was low and sweet.

"It is the blood . . . It is . . . It has been given to me. I have drunk of it . . . as He commanded. It is for this that I have come here. I have become one of them. They have raised me up. He is in me. It is the blood that maketh an atonement for the soul. Do you see?"

"Bowen, listen to me. They . . . I'd like to help you."

"Are they afraid? Are they afraid of the truth? Unless they see signs and wonders they do not believe."

"The people of the village, are they—?"

Without warning the other man moved, came up to him—the Lieutenant stood frozen—and embraced him. Through the thin layer of clothing he felt how thin Bowen was. The bones. He pulled back, the arms let go and he stepped back. In the first flash of the rising sun Bowen's eyes were very bright, as if he had been laughing.

"Yet a little while the light is among you. Walk while you have the light, that darkness may not overtake you. He who walks in the darkness does not know where he goes."

Sudden anger flashed through the Lieutenant. "For godsakes man, if you have something to say, say it, and to hell with this other crap."

Bowen glared into his eyes, then quickly softened. "You are like them, you do not listen. Listen! Hear me! Behold, I shall send my angel, who shall go before thee, and keep thee in thy journey, and bring thee into the place I have prepared."

They stood motionless, their eyes meeting.

"You do not understand?"

"No."

"In the city of our God, in his holy mountain."

"I don't get that kind of talk."

"I will tell you where I went last night."

"Yes. If you want to tell me . . ."

"I went up on the hill." He pointed. "I was watching Satan fall as lightning from heaven."

"What does that mean?" As he spoke the Lieutenant was surprised by the calm in his own voice, that matched the deliberate quiet of the other voice.

"We are on a journey. We will see many things."

"Yes?"

"In the name of God, Be thou opened. For you are the deaf and dumb!" He raised and shook the bottle of wine, turned sharply, and was gone.

6

Another beautiful day. With the sun on it this country is coming to life. The sunsets are big, full of flame and burning embers. In the morning light you can see the broken chains of mountains for miles, a few with the snow still on them. Somewhere on the other side is Rome. It's hard to believe there ever was a winter, or that some men died in these mountains. The mountains seem to stand so far above the noise and dirt.

Strange to think that the Germans are in there, hiding, waiting for us. They know how to pick their ground. They're in there, all set up, and we have to go in and dig them out, one at a time. They're tough. Some of the prisoners come in shaking like jelly after the artillery has raked them over, even when they've been dug in deep. They're terrified of our artillery. But they don't have much use for our infantry; sometimes if you ask them they just laugh in that arrogant way they have. It reminded us of those Afrikakorps prisoners we used to see working on the roads in North Carolina. To look at their goddamned sun-burned faces and the way they wore that peaked cap of theirs you'd have thought they'd just taken over the country. Well, they were the best infantry anybody's seen up to now—that much you have to give them. And in those mountains there are a lot more of them, just as good. If it was man-to-man, hand-to-hand, we'd never get them out. We've got to wear them down with machinery. It's a damned lucky thing they don't have our artillery. When it comes to mass production like an artillery barrage, we've got them. But it won't be easy. They're waiting in those mountains, the cagey bastards. Well, they haven't got long to wait now.

Listen. The bombers. Look, up there—so many of them you can't even count them. They look good to us. Once in a while even the Air Corps makes itself useful.

Today hundreds of our medium bombers passed over to plaster the German communication lines. They've been doing a job since the weather cleared up. These are beautiful days. You've never seen sun like this. The grapes are beginning to come on the vines and the roads are turning *to dust. Everyone is feeling a lot better about things. You get the feeling we're going to be moving. It's no joke being stuck in these mountains. The generals sure picked a spot to spend the winter in. Well, today is the first of May, it won't be long now.*

9

The long-legged Exec walked over to the number one gun like he was changing sides on a tennis court. Lieutenant Freeman was watching the crew strip down the breechblock. Orders had come down to see that all equipment was in perfect shape. The battalion had gotten four new guns from Ordnance in the past two weeks, to replace those whose barrels were worn out. He stopped for a moment to watch them work. They looked like kids with a new erector set. The redhead smiled; he felt good. All these men needed was a change. And it was coming. He strolled around the gun exchanging quips with the crew. Taking him by the arm he walked Lieutenant Freeman to one side, away from the gun.

"Hey Gil boy, looks like you get to go to the big revival meeting. Just got a call from Simpson—says the Colonel wants you as the morale man around here. Looks like we're about to be oriented in a big way. Some big gun is going to talk to the boys a few miles back. I guess they figure the reserves and the new boys back there need a boost for the big push."

"Jesus Christ, why me? I've heard enough of that crap."

"Why listen man, Colonel's got his eye on you for class historian, you're going to put him on the map when this is over." He laughed and nodded. "And like he says, you've got a way with the men, you're the boy to talk it up around here."

"To hell with that—"

"They want you to take one bright boy from each battery over to the lecture. The idea is, you come back and tell us all about it. Then we go out and fight like hell for dear old Fifth Army. Get it?"

"Goddamnit, isn't there enough shit flying around here without them going in for locker-room talks. Bunch of crumby prima donnas—"

"Yeah, but consider the Colonel's position. He figures his boys need a boost too; he's worried that the first time we get shelled real bad they're going to pack their bags and leave school. And listen, this is a great chance for an ambitious boy like you, you might even get invited over to the club for cocktails with the big boys. My god, a high-class character like you who speaks grammatical English, you might even get to be shoe-shine boy to some small-time general."

"OK, Red, cut the crap. I'm it. When's it going to be?"

"Tomorrow morning, in the dawn's early light. But no kidding, this might be good. They wouldn't say who he was—top secret—but it sounds like they've flown in some hard-fighting hard-talking brass monkey who's going to put the lead back in everybody's bullet. What a show in the old Mediterranean Theeayter, huh? Pep talks and everything." He wiped his brow with a long red arm and laughed. "Yessir, they must really have that Luftwaffe on the run if they're ready to put on some vaudeville right out in the open air. A regular frolic—." The other lieutenant wasn't listening; he was watching a man fifteen yards away—Bowen, with his book, the long finger moving from page to page. "Anyway—" He stopped and his eyes jumped to follow the line of the other man's sight. For a long moment they watched the concentrated curve of the bent back, the lips and the finger moving over the book. "Anyway—. Gil, are you listening? In the morning you take your four men and get over to Brigade Headquarters for a rendezvous—they'll show you the way from there. Don't forget to tell Berger to have a vehicle ready for you."

2

By the time the small convoy from Corps Artillery got there the next morning three sides of the bowl-shaped valley were black with troops. There must have been 100,000 of them, maybe more—but these things are hard to figure. Someone said they had two new divisions present, and a lot of replacements, and some reserve outfits that had been out of the line, and some beat-up infantrymen they'd scraped up from the hospitals—men who had been out of it so long they'd gotten back in the mood to live. Down at the bottom of the bowl was a wooden platform they'd put up, with a microphone on it and a couple of loudspeakers off to either side. It was warm, but not hot yet, with a fresh wind blowing down from the mountains. Everyone was pretty relaxed.

The big staff car was right on time; out of it stepped the big-bodied general followed by three other generals and some minor attendants. They moved briskly and things were under way in no time. One of the local generals got up to introduce the big one, and to listen to him you'd have thought it was an office boy introducing the president of U.S. Steel. Then the other one strode over to the microphone, almost brushing the office boy aside. He planted his feet wide apart and put his hands on his hips. The Boss.

For thirty seconds he said nothing—just stood there like the tall clean ramrod that he was and looked straight at them, first to the front and then to each side, pointing the heavy steel-gray eyebrows that showed beneath the three-star helmet. The only sound was the distant muttering of the big guns. He rocked once on his wide-spread booted legs, hitched his thumbs into the heavy belt of his pink pants and started to speak in short bursts. There was no warm-up. One minute he was talking and the next minute shouting like a man in a bar-room.

Maybe the Main Office wanted them to see what a real fighting man looked like. This was a beauty—not the big executive type, more like a cross between a circus cowboy and a West Pointer on parade. He was no reluctant speaker. There was a lot on his mind; once the lid was off he exploded.

"Men! You're in on a great show. This is history in the making. Remember that. We're here to show the world what kind of men they breed in America. Maybe while we're at it we'll improve the breed over here."

They roared.

"We've showed 'em a little fighting and a lot of loving. Now we're going to show 'em a lot of fighting and let the loving take care of itself. These people over here think they know all about fighting. Well Christ, they're fulla shit, as usual. They didn't know what a war was until we fought the Civil War. By god, we practically invented it. The Germans know that—where the hell do you think they found out about mobile warfare if they didn't get it from Sheridan and Jackson and the rest of those boys. We showed 'em how. And now we're going to give 'em the next lesson."

They cheered.

"All right men! I've heard them say in this theater that Italy isn't important, it's a side-show, it's a waste of time, the war's going to be won somewhere else anyway. Well take it from me, that's a crock of shit. The ass-end kibitzers who talk like that don't know their rosy red rectums from a slit trench."

They roared.

"Remember this, men! We've got Kesselring and a good-sized chunk of the goddamn German army tied up in this boot, and if we can get 'em before they run away and kick the shit out of them, the war's going to be half won right here. We've already knocked the purple-pissing guinea army out of the war, now we've got to do the same for their goose-stepping friends. This is a war and a tough one—men's work goddamnit—and if it were up to me we'd ship home every goddamned one of these fucking old women who do nothing but complain. It's an honor to be here, among men who are men, and any bastard who doesn't know it ought to get his ass kicked. Well, all right, to hell with that, we're here to fight, we've got to get to work."

He rocked back on his heels and slowly gazed up and down at the long rows of troops, who came right down to within ten yards of the platform. Here was a man, and a man who knew how to live in the field. In style. He was said to have the best set-up trailer of them all, with a whiskey supply that could not be exhausted. A fine figure of a man, well kept, well preserved. He had his buttons sewed on by his aide, who happened to be a Wac captain. She saw to his bed and board, all the little things. Could you bebrudge him that much? After all, for years he had gone as unnoticed as any railway conductor or mailman. Now he was the boss, a wise man. For a long time he'd had something on his mind, and now he was going to get it off.

"Men, this stuff we hear about America wanting to stay out of this war, not wanting to fight—we're going to show 'em it's a lot of bullshit. Americans love to fight, traditionally. Any American worth a good goddamn that is. All real

Americans love the sting and clash of battle. America loves a fighter, just like America loves a winner. We're Americans, we're here to keep America on the map. OK. America will not tolerate a loser. Hell no! Why should she, she's the greatest nation on the face of the earth. Americans despise a fucking coward. Americans play to win. That's why America has never lost a war and will never lose a war. The very thought of losing is hateful to a real American.

"Men, we're here in this goddamned broken down country to kill Germans, and any leftover sons of bitches of wops we happen to run across on the side. You're here to kill the bastards, remember that. Let's not get ourselves all screwed up with a lot of cockeyed ideas about what this war is about. That stuff is OK for the Section 8 Brigade. You're here to fight, to destroy the enemy. Don't worry yourself about anything else. If you do, you'll be dreaming along and some smart kraut who knows his business will put a bullet through your head. So keep your bowels open and your head down, and when the bastard sticks his head up, tear it off. This goddamn war is for men, you're here because you're men, not one of the lousy fairies who are sitting it out at home."

They tittered and roared and howled their pleasure.

"Get this straight now: You're not all going to die. Only two per cent of you right here today would be killed in a major battle. The man who uses his head will get through OK. Death must not be feared. Every man is frightened at first in battle. If any man says he isn't he's a goddamned liar. But a real man will never allow the fear of death to overpower his honor, his sense of duty to his country and to his manhood. Men! This is a holy war—more than any other in history. It's a crusade. We've got to win it!"

They cheered for a long time. He had them. He knew it. He was red hot with the excitement he heard in their cries. At this moment he would personally have led them up any mountain in Italy, right into the cannon's mouth, as they say.

"Now listen men! All through your army career you've bitched about what you call this chickenshit drilling, and discipline. Chickenshit my ass! That drilling was for a purpose. We want instant obedience to orders—you've got to be alert. If not, some sonofabitch of a German is sure as hell going to sneak up on you and beat you to death with a sock full of shit. You've got to be in there using your head or you're not going to last five minutes. This is no love feast, these fucking Germans know how to fight, they're one of the best trained armies any man has ever seen—you've got to hand it to them. They're men, not babies. OK. An army is a team. Remember that. It lives, sleeps, eats and fights as a team. This individual hero crap is a load of horseshit. The two-bit bastards who write that crap for the Saturday Evening Post don't know any more about real fighting than they know about fucking. Keep your head down, keep an eye on your buddy, and fight as a team. And that reminds me, there's been a lot of pansy talk about going easy on the local women. OK. But any man who can't fuck can't fight, and we're here to fight. Just so you know where I stand."

This time they mixed applause and whistling with the shouts.

"Remember—even if you're hit you can still fight. That's not bullshit either. Some bastards get a scratch on their ass they go yelling their heads off for an aid man. Stick with your buddy, keep pushing in there. You've got to be aggressive. Keep 'em off balance. Every damn man has a job to do. Every one of you has got to think not only of himself but of his buddies fighting there beside you, and of the big picture. Remember that. The big picture. We don't want any yellow-belly bastards in this army. They should be knocked off like flies. If not they will go home and breed more cowards. We've got to save the fucking for the fighting men. The brave man will breed more brave men. That's what we need in America. That's what the goddamned war is all about."

He rocked back on his heels while they cheered, surveying the valley full of men. His men. Bill Batchelor's men.

"We want to get the hell in there and clean the goddamn thing up. We've been sitting here on our asses long enough. And then we'll have nothing left but a little jaunt against the purple-pissing Japs and clean them up before the fucking Marines get all the credit. Like my old friend Bull Waley says, 'I hate Japs.' He said to me once that if he met a pregnant Jap woman he'd kick her in the belly. That's the kind of fight we need to finish this thing.

"Remember men! you don't know I'm here. Let the first bastards to find out be the goddamn Germans. I want to see them German bastards raise up on their hind legs and howl, Jeezus Christ! it's the goddamn Twelfth Corps and that sonofabitch Batchelor again!"

They forgot who they were and urged him on as if he were some kind of elected official, calling him by his nickname, ready to go with him, into the kill.

"There's one great thing you men will be able to say when you get home. You can all thank God that thirty years from now when you're sitting at the fire with your grandson on your knee and he asks you what you did in the great World War II, you won't have to say, I shovelled shit in Louisiana. Good luck men and God bless you."

They went on cheering until the command car was out of sight.

3

In the truck on the way back to the battalion the four men chattered and laughed in their excitement. The Lieutenant was cold and silent, they couldn't get a word out of him. It surprised them, they fell to whispering and shrugging at each other, and finally into silence. What the hell, one goddamned Lieutenant is like the next one.

Back at the battalion things were quiet, slow in the heat. Everything was in shape, ready to move. Only the guns were alert, their muzzles up, poised for the kill. The Lieutenant went over to the kitchen to get some lunch, but he could not eat it, he had no appetite. He went to write a letter and could not write it. Through the afternoon he said nothing to anyone.

The guns were quiet, the men sat around waiting. It went on being quiet into an evening so serene as to deny the very fact of war and of the professional soldier who had preached his crusade in the morning. Up above, in the village, they were putting one stone back on another, cutting them to fit, one at a time. Five hundred yards away in a deep hole under an olive tree the typewriter of the Counterbattery Section was assembling more data on German artillery positions that had been accurately located and charted and would be destroyed at the right moment. Later the cards were put back in the filing cabinet and the men went to supper. The clerks, the mathematicians, the executives, the common labor. Supper. Breakfast, lunch, supper. An order. A way of life. A job.

Christ, what I could do to a bottle of beer.

What this outfit needs is a good five-cent Coke machine.

You know what I dreamt last night? I was walking

on something nice and soft in my bare feet. I took a look. Women's knockers, a whole room full of 'em. What a dream. Man!

Rome. Rome Rome Rome Rome Rome. Rome sweet Rome.

The gun crews were lying around on the young grass under the olive trees, digesting their supper, exchanging dreams and expectations, trying to laugh off Bowen's last sermon. The Colonel had been called away to a kind of sales conference at Brigade Headquarters, to get his instructions for the big push. At a couple of the guns there were card games going. Some men slept; the ground was warm, a nice warm sleep.

Lieutenant Freeman's morale lecture didn't work out. At first Red Brock couldn't find him, and when he did the Lieutenant told him there was nothing to tell: just another general blowing off some steam. "There's nothing I can say to them. I can't do it."

"But why? Why not?"

"You know why? I'll tell you, Red. It was like listening to a punch-drunk old boxer who lives by working as a pimp and has a dirty mouth. If I thought that was all there was I'd go back to Naples and tell them I was declaring myself a conscientious objector."

"I don't get it."

"If you'd heard it, you'd get it."

"OK. OK. But the Colonel says tell 'em."

"Tell 'em what I think?"

"Tell 'em what's good for 'em. So we can finish it up and go home." The Executive bit off the words, and turned away.

He tried to tell them what the general had said; he ended by letting them see that he did not like what he had said. But they could not have cared less, the general was just another son-of-a-bitch as far as they were concerned, another boss. Yet the definite news that a big drive was on the way, this excited them—all they wanted now was to get going, to be moving, to arrive somewhere. Rome. That sounded good. Something to do, women, a drink, maybe something to buy.

4

Into this soft blue evening a red light goes up, drifting with the wind. At the guns they look up for a moment: it is familiar: a lighted meteorological balloon. Pretty. A red evening star.

Somewhere else technicians are watching it, gathering weather data for the computations that will assure the precise journeys of the big shells. Everything must be accounted for, even the tricks of nature; even the earth's rotation as the shells pass over it is taken into account. Just as in each new gun position a survey team must take precise measurements, to tie the guns into the map, orienting them to trees, hills, to any feature of the earth that will help the machines to their complete fulfillment.

Remember the old engravings of artillery pieces in the antique wars?—rushed here and there by the frightened horses, aimed by the eye and the hand, everything extemporaneous, improvised; until finally they are overrun, the horses shrieking, the cannoneers fighting hand to hand? Or even as late as the First War, when the French applied to it their exquisite taste and love of craft: the artistic aiming and firing of one gun, one shell at a time; one and then another one, marvelously precise, each target made, as it were, by hand. A personal matter, the work of man—the eye and the hand. Like the work of a baker, or of a butcher so skilled he ranks as a craftsman. Not any more. This is a branch of a corporation.

This is applied science in a mass production process. (In the corporation you are an employee, not a man.) Why waste time: find the target and smother it with a barrage: kill every living thing, leave no stone standing on another stone. That does it. Or even if you can't find the target—maybe there are some Germans in that village over there on the hill. Nothing to it: ten minutes' work and there is no village, and no Germans, if there were any. [That village was a living organism, planted deep in a thousand years of work and love, but maybe (maybe) its destruction saved the lives of two of our boys (who died anyway when they stepped on an unexploded mine in the rubble.)] How do you measure these things? In a war you don't measure them, period. This is the great achievement of the soldier-industrialist. They call it *massed fires*. It is a masterpiece of organized large-scale production. Close your eyes and let the machine run. It will surprise you. It will have its way.

5

There goes the red light, drifting toward the German positions. And under it eight tired men, an infantry patrol, climbing a hill in the dark, heavy with grenades and tommy guns, bareheaded because the clink of a helmet might give them away. They are out in the open, in the dark, looking for information. A routine procedure. Eight men, linked, who are used to each other's smell, who drink out of the same cup and have heard each other's secret prayers. For the rest of their short (one night? one hour?) lives, linked, frightened, unashamed, naked to each other. If they live to go home, will they remember what they have had of each other? If they die tonight, they will have had this much: each other, the love of the life of each other—guarding each other from the dark sur-

prises of this unknown slope, ready to fight for each other and maybe to die for each other.

One step at a time, in total silence, they go up the slope that has not been taken in a week of dying. The dead on the ground lie where they fell. Every five yards or so there is a foxhole and in each at least one body that had been a man in their battalion. They crawl around these holes of stink and stumble over the bodies of men who dared to leave their holes. The higher they climb, the shorter is the distance between the dead. They cannot make out the faces of the dead.

This is their war, one of the multiple small wars of dirty, frightened men that are like flute notes among the bass drums of the heavy machinery. Eight men—Carter, Paich, Blue, Zornig, Rivera—but never mind the names, just eight men at any moment from anywhere moving together in a sweat through a warm night, in need of each other. All that any of them has at this moment is the others—no war aims, hopes, expectations of reward or gratitude—only each other and what they will have to face together. Picking their way among the holes, the rocks, the dead; not knowing where they are or why they are here. They do what they can for each other, out of their elemental souls. They look up as the red light passes over . . .

Here, behind the big guns, the Lieutenant looked up from the checking of the fuses to see the red light drifting high toward no man's land. At this moment if he met the eight men he would go with them, gladly. To be out of this factory, this mass that did not move, did not see, only propelled steel into space that was abstract, that they had never seen—into nowhere, forever. Up there, the mystery: men walking through fire, at one, the at-one-ment of living and dying together. Each a separate man, not chained to the machine: one man and one man and one man, together. To be with them. To be moving, impelled by visible necessity, by love, by love of—each other. Through fire, coming to life—. Or so he saw it, dimly, his mind grappling with his heart: the rational young man grappling with the angel of his imagination.

Up there the eight men of the patrol made their feet take one step and then another over the dead ground toward their own deaths. Or perhaps they will choose to live. They might go only a part of the way, sit down on the ground for a while, and come back with a made-up story of what they had seen inside the German lines. Safe. One more day of life. The eight men were alone in the world. They had nothing to do with anyone else. Their aim was to stay alive.

6

Somewhere else, in the garden of an old villa, a general with charm and a profile held his head up and looked solemn for the sake of a photographer who had been instructed by the general's aide to take the picture from the *right* side—which was the general's more impressive side and clearly showed the stars on his cap. As the photographer worked with soothing words, the war correspondents held up their pads and wrote, and the general read his prepared statement (rewritten by his aide, a young lieutenant from a good school and a good family): "Our boys are not to blame for the slow progress of the campaign. The terrain has been very difficult. Morale is good. They know why they are fighting here. Maybe they do not like the discipline, the training and the rough life in this country, but they are proving themselves able to accept all this philosophically as they take on a disagreeable task, using the native ingenuity and self-reliance of Americans. The American soldier is demonstrating that if he is well equipped, well trained and gets good leadership, he has no superior among all the armies of the world."

After the interview the general's aide reminded the correspondents that the material was not to be cabled until after the attack was under way, and that clippings of the published interview would be appreciated. The general himself left his desk for the day, getting ready to make an appearance in a forward area where the morale showed signs of sagging. The plans were made, everything was about ready. He was as confident and as anxious as the oil-field engineer who has studied the ground, made his measurements and now can only wait for the machine to begin its searching penetration of the earth, to break through the unpredictable resisting layers.

7

Here in the battalion they were busy again with the ritual feeding of the guns. Now there was sun on them day after day, but the routine of their days was unchanged. They touched steel, they smelled gunpowder, they heard the guns explode in their heads. They saw nothing. They knew nothing. Like workers on a belt line, they were never sure that they had anything to do with the finished product. For a week they had prepared to move—and still they waited. They were fed up.

But the officers were engrossed; the Colonel had given them "the big picture." This for them was a profession like any other, requiring brains and good management. Efficiency, efficiency, the Colonel proclaimed. Production quotas. Precision work. The best outfit in this area. Yes, they were professional men, workers in a minor science, part of the great enterprise. Showing the world a thing or two. (The Colonel was making notes for a learned article that he would write for the Field Artillery Journal.)

At the open mouths of the guns it was something else; it was hard labor with nothing to show for it. For the young Lieutenant it was neither the one thing nor the other. It was a machine, he was tied to it; and he worked with his hands, hardly knowing what he did, to maintain himself as a man against the grinding repetitions of the machine. And he worked to give the war some shape for himself. But he could not make it come clear any more. Nor could he settle to the rhythm of the machine. Yet he went with it, like the others. His mind was filled with the steady pounding of the machine; it said to him: What the hell, go along, they know what they're doing, be a good soldier, do a job, and go home. Until he was numb and did not hear it any more. The trees, the night sky, the mountains—his eyes were dead to them.

One army is like the next, they imitate each other's methods, until the fighting becomes a contest of strength for its own sake.

And from that other world, from Anne, came the letters of purpose and hope and pride that struck him dumb. He did not know what to tell her. She believed. She had to believe. And he loved her for it. But what could he say? That it was a worthy corporation he worked for and he was glad to be with it? That it was nice to be safe? That he hoped for promotion? That the men fed the guns and hoped for nothing (as the fifty-year-old coal miner hopes for nothing)? Only to be done and go home and get another job? Home was their paradise. Maybe they were right. What was going to be done would have to be done at home, not here. Maybe after they had torn something down they would have the urge to build something. Maybe they would come back to it as to a new world, and start from the beginning. And Anne—

He wrote her letters to say that he loved her. He loved her. He loved her. As simple as that. But the time came

when he had to sit down and write to *tell* her, to tell her what
had become of him. He wrote:

> I came here thinking it was simple, a war, to make
> something clean that was dirty. I came here and I went to work
> in a factory. I live in a factory. I can't find out what's going
> on. Nobody seems to know anything. I remember you. I re-
> member what we used to say. But this is something else. Do
> you understand?

And he broke it off, not knowing what he thought,
or how it might be said. And then tried again, and again. To
explain. To her. To himself:

> Everything goes down, like a storm, the good with the
> bad . . . It's like being caught in a crowd and shoved . . . I
> work, I dig holes, I try to forget it . . . Like a flood that
> covers everything. And all the damned pitiful wreckage car-
> ried along with it. All you can do is try to stay afloat . . . It
> just goes on from day to day, like any other job. We never
> know where we are or what has happened until it's past . . .
> I tell you this because—

He wrote page after page like this; he carried the
letters for weeks; he never mailed them. He wrote others to
mail, V-letters full of love, needing a woman to press himself
to, to hold to; telling her this and that, and that everything
was all right. He knew what she needed from him—she needed
his strength, his belief. Something as clear and bright as her
war, the war she wanted (as others wanted it) as a way to
come clean, to begin over again. He did not know what to
give her. Her letters were full of eagerness, excitement, enthusiasms; the world for her was changing. Everything was
going to be different, new. In the Union they said . . . She
had left college, left home, gone to work in a factory, joined

the Union. She was becoming what she wanted to be; she saw the world becoming what she wanted it to be. Her family— a Good Family—and its confusions of wealth were behind her. She thought. She *knew*.—And this, here—what could she ever make of it, he wondered. If I told her that I had seen a man drive a jeep into a crowd of Italians because they didn't get out of the way fast enough, she would not believe it. She could not afford to believe it. One world. Another world. And another, and another. The living, the dead, the half-dead, the automatons—each in their own world. You can give away candy with one hand and loot the body of a dead man with the other. Four freedoms: to steal, to rape, to destroy, to kill. The first freedom they have ever known. Sprung from the traps of the cities and the farms, from the factory-prison and the farm-prison, from the endless work-weeks and the no-trespass signs—to the free territories of the war, the frontier, where everywhere is no man's land, where everything belongs to everyone, where there is no limitation on the kind of weapons used. If you want something, you can kill for it. If you want nothing but to kill, you can kill.

These were the things that came and went in his mind, formlessly, changing like the cloud shadows on the mountains. (At times there was no more than a drowsy numbness; he let it all go.) He tried to tell her these things (he talked to her at night, he shouted to her, soundlessly, above the shouting of the guns) but he could not give them form. Hot in the sun, he worked, to obliterate them. But they came back. He wanted to be honest with her, yet he could not tell her these things. He could not be himself with her. Slowly he was becoming a stranger to himself. She clung to her beliefs; they expanded; she went up, they carried her like balloons up and away from the shame and fear of wealth. He scraped his mind raw for an answer.

10

Toward noon of one flowering day there was a long pause in the firing. Lieutenant Freeman sat down near one of the guns on the edge of an ammunition pit and made small talk with the men. Like them he was stripped to the waist; the sweat was muddied with the dust on their bodies. One of the men asked Corporal Manzoni about Rome—what was it like. The small man turned and spat, insulted.

"But listen, Gus. You said your old man came from around there, so—"

"So how the hell do I know. I was born in Boston. OK? I dunno the first goddamn thing about this lousy country. OK?"

They let it drop.

When the lull in the firing continued, the red-head came over from his post behind the guns and made some joke that fizzled in the heat. After a few minutes of awkward chatter he took the other officer aside. They walked back into the deeper shade of the olive grove.

"Hey, Gil, what's up, what the hell is this strong-man act you're pulling, what are you bucking for, man? You're fighting a one-man war. Loosen up, kid."

"What the hell, Red, you've got to do something around here. I can't just sit on my ass all day like you and chat on the phone." He tried to smile as he wiped the sweat from his body with his hands.

"No kidding buddy, you ought to slow down. Save yourself, there's a big job coming."

"Listen, Red, if you work in a factory this is the way you work—right? What should I do, stand around and tell these guys what to do? Or what they're here for?"

"What do you mean, a factory?"

"I mean a factory, an outdoor factory. What else is it? Don't those guys over there look like guys in a factory?— Look, Red, why don't you stick to your telephone and I'll stick to my hauling and we'll all be happy. Or maybe you like it this way.—Oh, the hell with it, what's the good of talking about it." He turned and started to walk away.

"Hey, wait a minute. What the hell's come over you, buddy? For days now you've been glooming around all over the lot. It's not good." He waited and got no reply. "Whattya got, woman trouble? Fuck 'em all and cheer up pal, we're on the road to Rome. Pretty soon we'll have the krauts cleaned up and everyone's gonna have his own villino with hot and cold running signorinas."

"Let's forget it."

"Hell, man, aren't you the guy who was touting the local women? Come on off it.—Christ, you eastern stiffs, a bunch of worriers. Get the goddamn war off your mind, or whatever the hell it is, and you might learn something around here. You grab yourself a handful of signorinas, like grapes and you—"

"Why can't we treat them like they were human beings? Why in the name of Christ do we have to spit all over these people? To show them how strong we are, big strong men—? We blow the whole place to hell and then we—"

"OK, pal—have it your way, but the guinzos asked for it. And besides, the boys don't know what the hell else to do—they're not too sharp on foreign travel. What the hell you expect, a bunch of well-bred tourists? They don't have to like it, do they? OK, so they spit on 'em and feel better. You blame 'em? Every man to his own taste. Don't let it get you."

"But look—it's a lot more than that, it's—" He hesitated.

"OK—it's not nice. Forget it.—What I came over here for was to ask you about this guy Bowen on the number four gun. The hillbilly. Sergeant Moak tells me some of the boys think he's cracking up. He says you've talked to the guy. What's up with him?"

"He's all right. Just got religion. He's been talking to the people up there in the village. They've been feeding him on saints and black magic and the rest of that stuff. But he's no crazier than the rest of us. It's a kind of one-man revival. That's all."

"They say he's been drifting away."

"I don't know. He always seems to be around when he's needed. He's no dope. He likes the Italians, and the boys figure if he likes them he must be a nut."

"But they say—"

"Sure. He's got a bug. Something's bothering him. But he knows what he's doing. That's his business I guess.— Hey, look, one of your boys is calling you, maybe you've got a customer."

"OK, take it easy, and keep an eye on Bowen, will you? He's got some of the boys jumpy."

2

Waiting. For days it had been just waiting, empty, indefinite. Now it had become something else: tense, heavy, loaded with expectation.

The Lieutenant sat back against the tree and looked up at the sun through the olive leaves, rubbing the wet palms of his hands down the side of his fatigue pants. The strength of his body, its toughness, the heat pouring from it, gave him pleasure. He stood up, stretched, and went back to where they were moving shells.

The trucks backed and turned into the battery position and were loaded; the men swinging to the work, shouting and laughing their sense of release. The Lieutenant moved from gun to gun, truck to truck, working himself into another heavy sweat. As long as he kept working it was all right. But at times when there was nothing to do, when they waited, he fell off into sudden anger, and from there down into sullen apathy. And from this he would rouse himself and work himself to exhaustion, so that he should sleep.

There wasn't much time for sleep. This was the build-up. The ground was dry now. The roads were alive at night. Through the battalion ran currents of excitement, sudden outbreaks of laughter. They were cracking jokes, and it all seemed funny, whatever they said. Around the guns, at meals, during the night they giggled senselessly, and roared at old jokes. At times they could even get a laugh out of Bowen.

And then it came, before dawn of this May day. The infantry battalions moved up in the dark toward the lines of departure. The unknown soldiers, in silence. Here and there they concentrate, pick up their equipment, and one by one move off toward the familiar fields of their deaths that are always unrecognizable. This one last night of hiding and then
```
```

they will show themselves, in the open. *The field of battle—*
that turns out to be a sprawling formless landscape of fire, the
unknown, the end of the world. Over it they will crawl, hesitating, men and machines in tight knots of terror. A man moving into fields of fire is no better off than a hunted animal, and
he knows it.

Before they move out, a General Order comes down
announcing that the Allied Armies are now about to destroy
the German Armies in Italy. We have, it says, overwhelming
air control, and we outnumber them in guns and tanks. They
read it as they wait and laugh false laughter in silence, each
man's mind turned in to contemplate the vulnerability of his
body. Somewhere else, the minds of the generals are turning
in to consider the vulnerability of their reputations.

11

In these first nights of May the heavy battalions of Corps Artillery had been moved up on to the flat, as close as they could be gotten to the Front, and then had been hidden in one way or another. For four days they held themselves still, so that their positions should not be given away. On May 10 the 501st Battalion got orders to stock ammunition. Excitement cut through the men as a shark's fin rises suddenly to cut still water.

Around them in the valleys, the roads and trails were almost quiet in the day; at night they were congested as with new blood. The grinding of the trucks and the clanking rumble of armor tore up sleep. But by now they were too excited to sleep. On the evening of the tenth it was ready. They could feel the hush as it came down. Even the sporadic shelling by the Germans did not break it. Through all the artillery battalions the firing data and schedules had been distributed and plotted, gun by gun.

One thousand big guns stood as silent as war memorials. The men around them were almost solemn in their expectation. For a long time now they had stood still in mud and cold. Without women. Without any object. They were hungry for this night of animal violence with the guns, a kind of consummation. The whole of their power to be disgorged through these black muzzles. To smash a hole in a wall, to get out, to go.

The stillness held. By ten o'clock that night this ground made sacred by three thousand years of men's effort was restored almost to silence.

The infantry stirred restlessly in the advance outposts. *Now what?* None of it had been what they expected; it had been dull where it had not been murder. Dirty and cold. Lice. And now the days were flushed with sun and they wanted to live. And here they were again. Impaled on the point of death. Dumb fear rode their backs and crept like worms into their bellies. Here they were again. Waiting. What kind of act is this for a man, even an unknown man—plugging along in the mud month after month, watching your own blood mix with the mud, watching pieces of other men scattered in the mud when fifty shells come down out of nowhere, thrown more or less at random? Screaming steel; every nerve of the body screaming in anticipation. Impaled. Waiting.

Waiting to lift their shivering bodies out of the holes in the ground; to present these bodies as targets for hot chunks of lead and steel. Beautiful things, flesh and blood, the blood throbbing. To stand up and go forward in darkness to nowhere, to places where they have never been and do not want to go, to kill or be killed.

2

The night was electric with stars—and then, on the instant of 11 o'clock, there was no more night.

It begins with a solid roar, the overture. After the first bursting moment there begins an insane opera. Drums.

Flashing lights from the thousand mouths. A kind of idiotic fireworks music. The lunging-recoiling guns are the only performers, the dark comes alive with their long barrels sliding, howling, slashing the black air with smears of flame. It builds up and up, a great incoherent chorus, the guns getting hot, the echoes strangled in the deep-cut ravines, bouncing in the mountains until there are no more echoes, all lost in the wilderness of a new music. One thousand guns. (One of these guns can deafen a man, two of them can drive him insane.) All the hills are drums and the valleys are loudspeakers. The gods of the mountains do their star-spangled dance. Their dark bodies flash with sequins of flame.

There are no orders to give: the machines are fed and turned loose. Hour after hour they pump their shrieking seed into the air and from these, in time, the wild pointed flowers sprout and bloom in fire on the opposing hills.

Out of their renewed love of the guns the men worked hard to satisfy them. The far hills seemed to writhe under the shock of the incessant pounding, as if in the end they would collapse.

In the battalion everything moved as in a wild dance; the men swung their bodies to the rhythm of the guns, in growing elation. They were worshippers; the guns were the goddesses of fertility. But more than goddesses: gods and goddesses in one, double sexed, hermaphrodites. Opened, filled, triggered, emptied. In and out. All night long, in darkness.

Lieutenant Freeman worked with the ammunition detail, keeping the shells moving from their holes up to the guns. He worked like a man who has just become blind; living by what his hands touched, hearing almost more than he could stand. With the meticulous care of a blind man he worked at great speed. It began as another job. But it went on and on in the warm night, and he heard them at the guns

laughing and shouting and singing. Until the fury, the anticipation of freedom, the fervor, caught him, and he was hilarious with the others. He shouted and laughed, and the laboring
men of the ammunition detail who had no guns to worship
caught it from him. He began to sing and grunt the song of
the Volga Boatmen and the men sang with him, laughing, as
they heaved and hauled the big shells, the seed that made a
roaring garden of those dark hills.

And under the crust of those hills, the men who
have buried themselves for shelter, the enemy—? Who knows?
Only they could know, only they have ever had anything like
this done to them. Perhaps by now their minds have been torn
loose from their bodies and their bodies from their nerves and
they feel nothing. If there are any still alive in that garden. A
man who had been pinned down for eight hours under a
dentist's drill might have some faint idea of what is happening
there. There is no let-up. The intention is to destroy their
minds if their bodies are buried too deep to be reached. The
men who have planned it this way know what they are, the
Germans: they are firm with obedience, they are in love with
the job of soldier. But they are flesh and blood and nerves,
and they can be broken—if you have enough machinery.
They are not made to outlast the machines.

3

The sun is not yet up.

Under the dome of pure noise the infantry moves
out in broken lines, over the broken ground toward the trembling hills. The fire of the guns is sustained, crescendo, in a
rolling barrage until the infantry is very close, and then, by
the clock, it stops, sharp. The smoke lifts. The hills still stand
—unchanged, solid, as if they had not been touched. For a long
minute or more there is graveyard silence. Then, as the long

lines of infantry move close to the enemy hills, the remnants of the German artillery begin to fire into them. The Germans are like weeds. Some of those who live rise dazed and deaf from their beating and fight back. They believe in the work of the soldier. But others have become quivering masses of jellied flesh in their holes, sobbing, huddling. They are cleaned out by the purifying hand grenades, or they are led away to the prisoner compounds shaking like lunatics.

As the attackers move into the hills the Germans lock with them, fighting from rock to rock, hole to hole. In these broken entangled hills the big battle as the generals have planned it is over, split into a thousand small battles, each unit fighting for its own life, beyond the control of any general. There is terrible confusion. The infantrymen fall over each other on the unknown ground, they get lost, in the dim light they fire on each other as they prod and stumble into the ruin of the complex network of the German defenses. They break through here and there in jagged spurts, are trapped, pinned down. They climb, rush, fall, die in bunches. It is all fluid. No one knows. Here and there the crazed Germans counter-attack with precision and rip them up. It is wide open. Who knows where anyone else is, or what he will do. Miles back, the generals look at their useless maps and get on the phone and radio, trying to get control again. But it is not their war any more, the amateurs fight as they can. They feel their way, protect themselves as best they can, improvise against the unknown. Run. Hide. Wait. Sneak. Crawl. Fall flat. Get up and run. Where? Where is everybody? What happened?

4

The generals are telling the newspapermen that everything is going according to schedule, that losses are no greater than expected. That is, the Public Relations Officers are telling them; the generals are all too busy, trying to see in the dark. They are very anxious to get the main office moved up to Rome. Washington would like that. They hate to think that the British might beat them to it. An enemy capital—boy, there's something to fight for, huh?—complete with a big surrender ceremony on some balcony. Or something to show for their trouble, anyway.

At nine in the morning a history professor dressed as a Lieutenant-Colonel stands high on a safe hill and writes in his note book: "Victory is in the air and everyone's eyes are turned to the Eternal City. This will be a day in history."

At the positions of the heavy artillery battalions the men dropped exhausted by the guns, satisfied. There was no definite news yet. They had done a good job and now for them it was a question of when and where will we move. The lives and deaths of the infantrymen remained, for them, theoretical. What they saw was the fevered movement behind the battle: the trucks, tanks, tank destroyers, and men—the replacements—all moving northwest, moving up in long columns.

No one was trying to hide any more. It was a beautiful day. The dust rose from the roads in white clouds. Everything was moving. There was a crazy kind of gayety in it.

Late in the morning Bowen appeared out of the olive grove at the foot of the hill behind the battery position. In the excitement of the night his absence had not been noticed. Or if it had, no one had said anything. Glad, perhaps, to have him out of the way. There were some who hoped he would disappear and not come back.

Lying exhausted on the ground, dozing, they did not see him come. He walked up and down behind the guns, the Bible in his hand, his head erect, muttering through an angry mouth. He prayed for calm, for the full control of his voice.

"Thou shalt not kill!" It came out of him loud—a command.

The sound of his voice was the first they knew of his coming. They opened their eyes and swore to themselves. But no one moved.

"Sleepers awake! Wake up! Fools, listen to me."

The silence was unbroken. They hoped he would give up and go away. He walked slowly from gun to gun.

"Brothers, listen. In the night I walked on the hills. I was watching Satan fall as lightning from heaven."

No one laughed, no one stirred. They listened; they could not help but listen.

"Now let us pray for the dead." He paused and stood still, to look again at the men lying on the ground. "Are you dead? Have you been struck down by the lightning?"

Someone at the number three gun propped himself up on an elbow and shouted, "Go away you fucking bastard, we're trying to get some sleep!"

"The Book says, 'One of the soldiers opened His side with a lance and immediately there came out blood and water.' "

The silence held.

"You are at the gate of hell. You stand on the edge of the deep pit. You shall fall into darkness.—He who walks in the darkness does not know where he goes." He stopped speaking and waited for a sign.

"Awake from your sleep. Go down on your knees and ask the forgiveness of Christ for what you have done! It is His blood you have spilled!"

The blood roared in his head and for a moment his voice failed.

"Amen, amen, I say to you, unless you eat the flesh of the Son of Man, and drink His Blood, you shall not have life in you!"

As he spoke, a man ten yards away stood up with a gun in his hands and leveled it at him. It was O'Brien.

"Shut up! Shut up you bastid. Beat it. Go away or I'll kill you. I swear I will."

The others were sitting up to watch. Bowen let his arms fall to his sides. He did not move; his eyes shifted from face to face, as if to remember who they were. "Unless you see signs and wonders, you do not believe."

He stood looking at them for another moment. "It says, Thou shalt not kill." Then he turned and left them.

Later in the morning, and through the day, they fired missions on call from some far-away infantry regiment, or reinforced the fire of some of the light artillery battalions. For three days they fired and waited while the fighting moved away from them. They could not move; there was no room on the roads for them, night or day.

For eight days the infantry fought in the hills, eight days of wholesale killing without stint. At every turn in the road, from every blasted house the Germans fought back in their savage brilliance.

12

The heavy guns of Corps Artillery had begun to displace forward on the third day, and had by now all come up into advanced positions. The Germans were giving ground, and the artillery kept leapfrogging battalions and even batteries within battalions to keep the guns within range. The roads were like some great strung-out carnival. The good news had spread fast, a high wind of expectation had begun to blow.

On the ninth day the Germans broke and began their deliberate flight toward Rome. They fought back. They fought many rear-guard actions. They turned and ran. It became a chase.

A holiday. The lift of elation became like the release of drunkenness. The sun was shining. Even the infantry could feel its heat now. The Germans were running. Reinforcements were streaming up Highway 7. The push went on through the tenth night.

Around midnight a fresh infantry regiment moved out from Itri and rapidly led the forward division up Highway 7 through the early morning. They had trouble maintaining contact with the Germans. The artillery was left behind.

Far up ahead the leading battalion of infantry stopped every two hours and was passed through by succeeding battalions in order to rest the men. Out in front the 91st Cavalry Squadron ranged over the plain. The sun was very hot. The Germans were running all along the line. They pursued them through the ruined villages, eager for the kill. Even in this chase men died in droves. But they were moving and the dead were quickly left behind.

In ten days they had hardly slept, they were exhausted, and still the exhilaration of the chase drove them on. Communications were gone. No one knew where anything else was. Companies pushed on and fought alone, out of touch with their battalions. Units became mixed, men were separated from their outfits, fired on by friendly troops. Artillery fell short and killed its own. But they were moving and that was all that mattered. It was a break-through, a wide-open rush to finish it. A hunt, the prey in the open, running: You see him, then for a moment you don't see him, but you know you've got him.

Below Rome there were some fights around Cisterna, Velletri and Cori but the momentum was maintained, in the recklessness of pursuit. Again the dead were left behind as the living closed in to finish. The dead were left sunning themselves by the road. Beautiful days, clouds moving, billowing in from the sea to stand on the mountain-tops. Along the roads were Italians with shovels, filling in the shell holes that slowed up traffic. They looked up to watch the men from paradise go by. The grave diggers could not move fast enough. But their work was only temporary; the long neat rows of crosses were a thing of the future. The corpses were two days old and they had lost their friends; they were in the hands of strangers.

Where the planes had swooped to catch the retreat-
ing German columns the roads were garbage dumps: burned
and broken corpses of men and horses and machines. Along
the way the Germans had demolished the towns to block the
roads with rubble. Ahead of the infantry the engineers used
bulldozers to clear a path. Everywhere along the roads it
looked like hell with the sun on it. But it was warm and they
were moving. Everywhere, all along the line. It was good. It
looked like the end.

2

They came to Rome, the dirty tired men; they were
kissed and cheered, slept on the streets, and pushed on across
the river in the early morning. They were too late. The Germans were gone, only the rear-guards fought back here and
there to delay.

Later the generals arrived in the Eternal City, con-
templated the Tiber, and took their bows on a balcony. In a
few days the massed battalions of typewriters and office brass
would arrive to begin setting up the new Main Office, in the
convenient palazzi left empty by the defunct fascist bureaucracy.

It was spring. Even Rome was young again. People
were starving. In some places flowers wiped out the stink of
the dead. The pursued and the pursuers rolled north through
the ripening wheat and the vineyards of Latium, into the dark
isolated hills of Umbria, where the saints still possess the un-
worldly hill towns. The Americans didn't know where they
were and they didn't care. Yet when there was a pause in the
running and fighting they looked around them and were surprised by the calm beauty of this controlled landscape, the
richness of it. (They had expected only dryness and empti-

ness and poverty from the dirty wops.) And then forgot it all in the search for food and women.

On their right a small French army killed with traditional skill, in anger, to cancel the dishonor of 1941; and further east the British were plodding and dying in their deliberate old-fashioned way.

3

We thought we had them there for a while, with the VI Corps breaking out of Anzio to get them in a pocket, but one big general was dying to get to Rome before another big general (for the history books) and the next thing we knew the Germans were gone. They were too smart for us. In the middle of everything they managed to turn that big army around and get out of there, and hard as we pushed above Rome we couldn't lay our hands on them. But we went after them—even if the big brass no longer hoped to catch them and finish it, we did. We ate up a lot of ground chasing them, anyway. What marvelous clear warm days—the sun was like a bath, it made up for the lack of sleep. Not very good days for dying young—but when they're running and you're running after them you don't worry so much about dying. There wasn't much need for artillery now, even if they could keep up—which they couldn't, certainly not the big guns. They were way behind—someone had borrowed their trucks to keep the infantry moving up. There wouldn't have been any room for them on the roads anyway. Everything was moving behind us, bumper to fender, tight as a drum. In no time Rome was way back of us and forgotten. Up here in this clean rolling country there was almost no resistance for three or four days. Here and there the smart goddamned krauts would leave an 88 sited above a turn in the road to slow us up, with a truck

to haul it away when things got too hot for them. They made
it tough all the way. But we'd sure as hell broken through—
we were in the open.

4

    This 155 mm. gun battalion—the 501st—got a quick
look at Rome and then went into a rest area near Cesano for
three or four days. When their trucks came back from moving the infantry they got on the road again, leap-frogging batteries sometimes in a hopeless attempt to stay within range.
In these long hot days the war kept running away from them.
They would fire a few rounds into some distant village to
prove they were still in the war and then move on again, firing and moving up, hardly ever settling for more than a few
hours. When they could get clearance on the roads they
rolled in a tight column, a rod of packed power: the jeeps, the
trucks boring down the dusty roads with the big guns jog-
ging behind.
    The weather was fine, the country was fat and easy,
and the war—their war—had become a light-headed game, a
headlong rush as when a car is turned loose on a hill to coast.
The sky was ours, and there was no enemy artillery to worry
about. The men scrounged for wine and women when they
got the chance, but the way things were moving there was not
much time for either. Right now they didn't need them: they
were half-drunk with the sun and the unchecked power of the
column as it rolled through the hills. Nothing could stop
them; they rose to the blue and gold horizon of conquest and
climax.
    It might have been called the joy of battle, except
that for these artillerymen there was no battle. They had been
cheered as they rolled through Rome, and now they were
cheered through every broken-down liberated village along

the sunny road. They leaned from the trucks whistling and shouting invitations and obscenities at women and girls, laughing the conqueror's laugh at the men, throwing candy to the kids while it lasted. At times they had to pull off the road to let the new infantry and armor go through; then they rolled again through hills piled on hills behind hills that meant less than nothing to them.

So this is Italy, well well well.—Look at the loads those damn wop women can carry fachrissakes.—Why don't they wise up and learn something?—Hell you can't teach 'em anything, they don't wanna learn.—Christ, man, every time we dig us a slit trench we got better plumbing than these crummy wops have got.

Rounded hills; they went down and around and into the dark green of hills; down into a valley, narrow, opening at its far end to show a hill, a hill-town: carved, painted, inlaid; the ripe old stone, soft, and the delicacy of columns, arches, altars, bell-towers. Broken hills, and far-away mountains dipping and rising up through breaks in mountains. Months in cold hiding, and now they were through with hiding. They would come grinding to the top of a hill and see, far ahead, the dust rising where infantry columns wound their way for miles on either side of the glaring roads. Or through a village, fast, still smoking from its broken stones, dust on everything, quiet now, the bodies still lying twisted where they fell. Or the rubble like vomit—picking their way through it—where the planes had chopped and burned a German column. And down from the hills came the people of the villages, to take back these slaughterhouses and junk heaps that had been their homes and fields.

Rolling. The scenery shifted fast; every ten miles a whole new world. It was a cinch, a dream, this was the way to fight a war. Late June—the long warm days and the short warm nights. Italy unrolled for them—a paradise for those who could see it: more delicately carved and balanced, deeper and richer in its forms as they went north. A paradise for some and a dirty road home for the others.

The land was cut up by the criss-crossing hills into many small worlds of hills and valleys, each with its completeness of towers and churches and roofs and castles poised in the here and there of the clear distances. Castles and walls: relics of other battles, the wars of knights, the devoted armies of the city-states. Pictures—framed by the dark lines of cypress, the stepped-up curves of terraced hill, the puffs of umbrella pine; perfect arrangements, perfect control of the space—no waste, no discord. The oldest country.

From the trucks they laughed at it. They had to laugh. The big guns they dragged behind them were awesome, but they themselves, what were they after all, what could they claim? The fighting men had passed through; now they came, following, in the second or third wave, not far ahead of the uniformed carpetbaggers who would come with their files and their adding machines and their instruments (always the wrong tools in the wrong bag) of military government. So they laughed—elation overriding their doubts. Machine-men, servants—they did not see it. Maybe they were thinking of other things—a good meal, a room full of naked women, loot. Or of that other paradise of their nostalgia, the good old U.S.A. And a job. Whatever it was, it was on the way; they were moving, they were going somewhere, they were winning, they were not just sitting still, they were moving. The road, up and down and up; and the momentum of the machine, lifting them up, and in. To eat up the miles. To keep moving.

144

5

Some of the officers—with their college degrees—
knew Culture when they saw it. They got out their cameras,
to take some home. It became a tour—they watched it flow
along the road like a strip of color film, with the Colonel lec-
turing them on what to see. The Colonel was becoming a
connoisseur. He had listened with care to a Brigadier General
from an old Boston family who talked endlessly at Brigade
H.Q. about the ancient wonders of Italy; and somewhere he
had picked up an old Baedeker, to complete his education. It
startled him to be told how old things were; he became an
addict of antiquity. Never mind the details, only that it should
be old, very old. "This," he would say, "is something you
don't want to miss. The chance of a lifetime." There was
nothing he liked better than to bivouac around a handsome old
villa (preferably a villa of the Medici), and to hold court
among his officers, under the influence of the best wine avail-
able, on the green lawns. After a private half-hour with the
Baedeker (it was his secret source) he would come out to
them and announce, "Gentlemen, this house has Roman ori-
gins. It is two thousand years old. Think of it."

To Lieutenant Freeman the wide-open chase had
come as refreshment. He was quickened, made light by it. In
the smells of the summer fields, the deep colors of light and
flowers, the thick juices that swelled the world around them,
he was released from the restlessness that had held him sullen
and remote. He laughed. He wrote no letters. In the views
down tapering valleys to the carved perfection of other hills
(the hills in their warm green movement like women) he saw
grace, order, the means of life—after the death and disorder
in the massed mountains of the winter line.

One day as the long column of trucks and guns stood still for an hour in the street of a hill town, he saw Bowen moving down the line, and heard him say, "Taste and see that the Lord is sweet." And before he knew what he did he heard himself say, *Yes. That is what it is. Hell on earth. Heaven on earth. The earth is a paradise—and an inferno. Here. Now. Nowhere else.* On his way back Bowen was saying, "Blessed are the eyes that see what you see!"

With all his senses he ate and drank of the colors and textures and forms of this warm handworked earth, these ripe hills and valleys. And was nourished, moved in the blood, given back to sensation. And heard echoing in his mind the broken strands of Bowen's repeated refrain. *My flesh is food indeed and my blood is drink indeed.*

I go away, but I return . . .

For this is my body.

Be thou opened—

Taste and see that the Lord is sweet.

It was quiet after the fighting, after the delirium of liberation. The Lieutenant saw the tired smiles behind the hands that waved to them as they passed. The transfiguring smiles, the hardworking hands of all the liberated towns, that said, *We will make it new.* It put back into him some of the hope and belief he had brought to Italy—now tempered and sharpened. But hope and belief were of the head. The body, the heart, were half wild with the lust of movement, the wind cool through light clothes, the blood fired by heat and the shifting scene, the onrush into hills, and through to the oncoming towers of medieval towns, straight up, standing on solitary hills. The pursuit.

Hill to hill—through the densest design man has made on earth; sailing down hills into horizons hung with gold and dark green slopes. Green and gold tapestry of the Renaissance. Carved stone. Castles. Hill towns against the sky. Illuminations. The Past, coming toward them: processions of knights and ladies; falcons, dogs, attendants, horses in coats of gold; up the avenue of cypresses to the castle, gardens, on the hill. Against the sky that is still serene. To the top of another hill, to the climax of another sunset.

13

As they came up into Umbria they were firing more often. Here and there at some dark-brown medieval hill town the Germans made a stand to gain time. But on this July day it was very still. The battalion fired the last of its shells in support of a French regiment, and that night went into bivouac until more ammunition was brought up.

For this short holiday the Colonel looked around and found himself a small self-contained kingdom. It was a castle-village of the middle ages that had grown by accretion until now it was the center of a group of farms held by some nobleman in a semi-feudal arrangement. The big house was on the hill-top, commanding a bend of the upper Tiber and miles of green, brown, and yellow slopes that faded to dark rolling hills. There was not another village for miles. Somewhere on the horizon was the low flat isolated hill of Orvieto that had been sacred to the Etruscans.

In the distance they could see towns on other hills: the places where St. Francis renounced the world; where he was frequently favored with visions of the Virgin and the Savior; where Christ impressed upon him the marks of his wounds; where he was lifted from the ground in ecstasy and surrounded by a shining cloud; where he caused a spring of water to well forth from a bare mountain; where he rode in a fiery chariot; where the birds listened in attentive expectation when he preached to them; where he restored life to the child who had fallen from a tower of the Palazzo Spini.

Bowen alone knew these things; he moved in the living presence of the saint whose spirit saturated these hills. In the passion of his seeking he had gone into churches, he had asked questions, he had learned. He was inflamed with what he knew. All through the long march northward he had been pursuing the saints. He collected their words, their visions and their miracles. He had become a pilgrim; now he became a follower of St. Francis.

That fragile man, the clown of God, what would he think if he came one day and saw the machines of war among the willows and the poplars and the oaks of his tranquil hills. . . . Bowen knew; he was right about Umbria when he said that the trucks and the guns had no place here. After a little while in this stillness of streams and fountains there was no other place and no other time. The swallows came and went. This was all there was. The war was unreal, or it was over, if there had ever been a war at all. The surrounding hills, the small church, the presbytery, the school, the peasant cottages, the walls of the great house four feet thick—these were actual, here and now, peace; there was no need to go further. They settled down, and slept, and woke in the quiet evening to make what they could of it.

"Hey paesan, che vino?"

"Niente vino, signor. I tedeschi hanno portato via tutto."

"Bullshit. Go find the wine." The three carbines were raised to the belly line of the strong stout man in the moleskin vest and low boots who was the *fattore*, the chief farmer, the manager. "Vino. Subito, Jack. Move." The *fattore* shrugged and led them to the wine, a cellarful, in large barrels. The two *sotto-fattori* and two giggling girls (who were to be raped by thirty men) helped carry the wine from its hiding place, and the party began. It lasted all through these three days of rest.

The men had their orders: no looting, no rough stuff, etc., but enjoy yourselves boys, you've earned it. Then the Colonel settled back into the big leather chair to appreciate his conquered castle. Around him in the great somber room, voices resounding to the high beamed ceiling, his officers paid court and took their ease—his knights and pages. But it wasn't really a court, it was more like a club, an old established club with a grand piano nine feet long, paintings, sculpture, tapestries—the best of everything. There was a huge fireplace, taking up most of one wall, carved above with the family crest. They lounged and smoked and spoke of the best wines, the Colonel's gentlemen.

After brandy and wine had been brought from the Count's private stock (and paid for with cigarettes, to satisfy the Colonel's growing sense of honor) the Colonel lit a cigar and said, as he had said in other villas, "If this place had some real plumbing, I'd give 'em a thousand bucks for it on the spot." He was serious. He was dignified. The Old World, as he called it, had gotten a hold on him. Though he never did buy one of his castles, he did become something of a collector. Old silverware, jewelry—it was surprising what you could get for a carton of cigarettes. After he heard one of the generals talking about *legitimate booty*, he got to be insatiable.

2

The men had been seen to, everyone was right at home; they settled back into the big chairs (waiting for dinner) to hear what the Colonel had to say. The more he talked, the more they got to drink. He loved to talk.

The Colonel rolled the brandy on his tongue, looked around at the works of art to appraise them, and waited for his cue. Tradition called for everyone to keep quiet after the opening burst of conviviality while Captain Leopold, a lawyer and a bon viveur who had tactfully taught the Colonel a thing or two, steered the talk to where the Colonel was waiting with his opinions. These opinions flowed most freely on the subject of the British. If there was anything the Colonel didn't like about the war—and he liked almost everything about it— it was the British. Snobs, he called them. Imperialists. Don't pay their debts. Never pull their weight. Not to be trusted. Lousy soldiers.

The Captain set it up for him. "Isn't it getting a little tricky, Colonel, the way we're all exposed there on our right flank? The British aren't coming up there as fast as they might, are they Colonel?"

It was a routine that made some of the younger officers restless, but the wine was here, and the big chairs and the Persian rug—and anyway, where could they go?—to drink with the men? The Colonel wouldn't like that, and besides, the men expected some privacy in their pleasures. Lieutenant Freeman and the jolly fat man from Yale had thought they might slip away after a few drinks, maybe into the kitchen, but now it was too late for that. So they lounged and drank and half-listened and let the war go to hell while the Colonel picked up his cue.

"Damn right, Leopold. That's a danger. A real

danger. The Germans could slip in there on our right and give us a bad time. Roll us right back. There's been a lot of discussion about that at headquarters. But it's a risk we've got to take. Like the General says, the goddamned British will fight to the last American. They're being just too damned careful, as usual, he says. Fighting an old woman's war. Too worried about saving men, that's all they can think about. I've heard we may be moved up in a day or two to support these French troops who are fighting in the center. Damn good bunch everyone says—real aggressive fighters."

The Colonel went on with his lecture until the *fattore's* wife and the two giggling girls brought in the dinner. It was roast pig, with all the embellishments. The service, the linen tablecloth, the silver, the glass—nothing but the best. They assumed that the officers were gentlemen. Mixed with this naïveté was some folk wisdom: keep them happy and they will go away grateful and empty-handed.

3

They had only been in the place a few hours when Bowen painted his sign on the side of one of the peasant houses. I HAVE SEEN THE LORD. THOU SHALT NOT KILL. JESUS SAVES. Wherever they had stopped he had done this—and what could anyone say? But they had never seen him so grave and excited. For days no one had paid much attention to him; in the swift movement of the chase his voice was almost lost.

As soon as they were settled down in the gardens and orchards below the house he began to walk among them with his latest message, raising his hand for silence. Wherever he found them clustered around a cask of wine he lifted his face and said: "Hear what God says about the blood of his son. *The blood of Jesus Christ,*" (they were laughing and offering him a drink) "*His Son, cleanseth us from all sin. There is*

no salvation any other way. It says, *Without shedding of
blood is no remission.*" They were laughing—but not really at
him—and drowning themselves in the wine; he was shouting:
"Ye were not redeemed with silver and gold but with the
precious blood of Christ." They laughed and drank. He
thought they were mocking him and he gave it up.

He climbed up to the little piazza and across to the
church. It was locked, but a boy came to open it for him. The
peasants had heard of this man of God who did not drink with
the others, so that in the afternoon when he asked them for
word of their saints (he had learned a simple vocabulary of
religion) they were glad to talk to him; and when they heard
what he wanted they were glad to send the boy with him as
a guide. Around midnight, when the others were still singing
and fighting in the orchards, he took a jeep and drove with the
boy thirteen miles to Orvieto, a walled town, with walls like
cliffs, a kind of island in the plain.

The boy took him to the house of a priest who
spoke good English, the kind of English spoken in England
forty years before, when he had studied there. They talked
for a while, then slept, and in the morning went to the cathe-
dral whose intricate façade looked to Bowen, in his exaltation,
like an entrance to heaven.

Inside, wherever he went, he was a witness to the
facts of heaven and hell. As he stood before the great frescoes
(which to him were not frescoes, but the things themselves)
the old priest told him what was happening. In Paradise he
saw the tall male figures with grave features and serene, solemn
eyes—the choirs of angels—who dance and sing to the lute. Below them the naked figures of the elect look up in their rapture. It is serene and simple. It happens. Virtue is real. Paradise
is real. There are no false flowers, no softness of cherubs, no
rosy clouds. It is full of grace. To this man who has never seen
a fresco, who expects visions—this is no fresco but a vision.

They moved through the half-darkness into Hell. Here everything danced in an agony of attack and resistance, the mass of naked men and women snarled in the torturing knots of demons. Above them other demons are flying with the damned on their backs and hurling them down into the entanglement of bats' wings and writhing flesh. (But why are there angels with swords, watching?) There is still beauty in the human forms, and the fiends are not fantasies, they are real: lean dark naked men whose eyes are voluptuous with hate; their nails become claws, their horns are what you would expect. They are not very different from the men they torment. They are not very different, he thought, from the men I saw drinking in lust last night . . . They are a warning. A sign.

Slowly he moved past the great pillars from vision to vision, faintly muttering, followed by voices, of which one was the voice of the priest (who was forgotten), the priest who was now a captive of this strange man's ecstasy.

And here two angels of the judgment are hovering—big figures, strong, like blacksmiths—with the great wings of eagles, blowing the long thin trumpets. Beneath them The Dead are rising out of the ground, all naked in their original beauty, except for the few who are skeletons. By a painful effort they struggle from the ground that holds them, muscles tensed to obey the call of the trumpets. They are rising. Some have only their heads above ground, others are wrenching their limbs from the clasp of earth, and as each man rises free the ground closes under him. The ones who have risen stand and look up, some embracing in the joy of reunion, in innocence of their graceful nakedness—absorbed in expectation. Two of those who have freed themselves lean to help others to break from the earth; and one sits exhausted on the ground, unable yet to stand and join in the exultation. Bowen leaned toward them, tense in the completeness of his belief, eager to join them in this second birth. His hand was outstretched to touch them, to greet them. His voice rose to strike the vaulted ceiling. "Bow down Thine ear, make haste to deliver me!" The priest froze, and looked up to the shadowy heights where the voice echoed.

He stayed a long time, sweating in the mysterious light and shadow of these vaulted stone chambers. Before he left he had one last revelation: of the end of the world. Everywhere are signs of the end of things: the sun and moon darkened, the sun throwing chunks of fire, stars falling, temples and palaces tumbled by earthquake, mankind destroyed by fire. Great naked angels dive on extended wings to breathe shafts of fire into a crowd of condemned men and women. As they run in terror they look up toward the terrible air-borne faces. They hurry and stumble through a door, huddling together, men falling in agony, women clasping babies dead of the flame. A woman sneers as she dies. A young man presses the heels of his hands into his ears to shut out the screams and groans and the cascading thunder. Running in sudden fear and guilt they trample the stiffening bodies of the fallen.

As he went out into the sunlight of the piazza he knew why the war had to be. He knew why they had been brought here. The passage up through the mountains and the plains and the sacred towns was made of stages in a process of revelation. They would die so that they might rise again. They would—. But there were no more words; the words went up with him in flames; he was burning. The sun was burning. A warning of the wrath that was to come.

In the center of the square he turned once more to look at the marvelous design of the church, and raised his arms to it in gratitude. Then he walked to the jeep as an angel might walk. A voice said to him, Behold, I shall send my angel,

who shall go before thee, and keep thee in thy journey, and
bring thee into the place that I have prepared.

He did not say good-bye to the priest. He did not
see him, he did not know he was there. His huge eyes rolled
over the square towers, the somber façades of the town. The
homes of the saints, the angels. We have arrived, he said. It
is time.

The boy looked at him. The man from the other
world. He was very tall. He was—. Was he angry?

As they drove back across the plain in the warm late
afternoon (the orchards laid out as with a ruler, a ripe orange
light on the fruit) he abandoned his plan for ending the war.
The war was necessary. Many must die with Him, die young
and rise in all their vigor. The dead would rise, all together,
in their millions, at one moment. The saints would call them,
and they would struggle up out of the deep beds of earth, and
at the sight of them the guns would be silenced. But before it
was over they would all be awakened, the living, and they
would march, toward the throne where He waited. Ah, they
would be made to see.

Out of the soft wind, the power of the engine under
his foot—the jeep headed into the sun, his body all exposed to
sun and rush of air—the voice came back. He listened, then
stopped in the middle of the road to look in the Bible. Yes:
It is the blood that maketh an atonement for the soul. He read
it to the boy, who had the face of an angel.

They were moving west, the sun setting, getting
bigger, closer. Into the onrush of wind he shouted. "Blessed
are the eyes that see what you see!" But against the wind and
the oncoming sun his voice would not carry.

"See? You fool, what can they see?" Suddenly
angry, stiffening, he pushed the jeep as fast as it would go.
"They will see!" The boy was afraid. The jeep ripped the air,

as if it would finally obey him and leave the ground, rocketing into the wide red sunset.

The village when they got to it was silent except for the sobbing of the women that came from one of the cottages. A scream. A woman, the mother of the boy, came toward them across the piazza screaming. She stopped, to raise her arms in a plea. Bowen called to her. "Mother, come here. Madonna mia." She came and he embraced her, asking her what was the matter. She could only sob and clutch the boy. Bowen kissed her forehead and walked away toward the olive groves.

After the wine and the rape the men of the battalion still slept. The tops of the trees shone green-gold from terrace to terrace. He rushed among them where they lay under the olive trees, cursing, imploring. Some rolled over and swore at him; the rest were like dead men. "Awake you sinners. Awake. Before it is too late. You must listen. I have the word. I have seen." He rushed from tree to tree where they lay sprawled in clusters, shaking them and kicking them. "We are here to be judged. And to see. It is the day of doom, the world is burning. Now. Now—Now—Now! We are in the Garden. For this we were brought here. I have seen His Blood. I have seen Heaven and Hell. Brothers! It is the beginning of the end of the world. We must return and let it be known to our people. We must go into the streets and cry unto them, Sleepers awake!" (The sounds of voices—the priest, the saints, the voices of prophecy and gospel—were strong in him.) "Listen brothers. Listen. We are here, we have come up out of the valley of death onto the mount of olives, and we are here to be judged. To be shown. It is our test. We have seen, we shall be prophets unto our people who have not seen."

"The blood!" He raised a bottle and smashed it against a tree. The wine ran down to the ground. His hot eyes burned from side to side as he walked among the trees, slowly now. "Awake! Awake! Brothers, the angels have come and they are watching. Their trumpets will sound. Be ready. We are in the judgment place and there is a serpent among us who is hidden.—The saints are with us. We have passed through their land in cold and heat, we have seen men crucified, we have seen the dead and their wounds, we have seen the demons with wings. We shall see the dead rise, and they shall lead us." He stood still and raised his arms. "Oh my brothers we have seen the earth quake, we have seen fire, we have seen the palaces and the temples fall. We have sinned." His voice rocketed in the silence of the grove, against the gold line of sunset. "Now, brothers, it is time. Go down on your knees. Confess. Cleanse yourselves and drink of His Blood. I have been shown. We are watched. He is here. He has washed us in his blood; blood is his sign. I know it brothers, I have seen! Brothers!" He called to them as if they were at a distance, moving away from him. "Partake of his sacrifice. Share in the body of Christ. We are one body. Thou shalt not kill!"

One after another they began to lift their wild heads and look at him. He walked among them majestically, his eyes lifted, one hand raised in the gesture of benediction. "Blood is his sign. Blood. Why this great spilling of blood, for what is it meant? Why the rivers red with it, and the hills? Brothers it is Blood. We have bathed in it, we have been baptized into Christ's death, and we are made new. It is the sign. Arise, for you are no longer dead. For forty days He has come and gone among us, and now for the last time He appears before us. Ye who were far off are made nigh by the Blood of Christ."

They sat up silent and dazed under the faintly rustling trees to watch him, like men jerked from a nightmare that will not fade. His voice rocked and throbbed and shuddered to incantation; it went through them like knives. His eyes were big and hard, his face was a rock.

"We were not meant for soldiers. St. Francis is no soldier. The horse and the rider hath he thrown into the sea. I tell you I am no soldier. I am God's witness. I have seen. Jesus saves. We have come through the mountains for his sake. We have been brought here against our wills to be redeemed. We will rise from these graves and live with Christ in the body. We will return home with the message of love. We will be messengers. We will drive out the money-changers—."

Suddenly he smiled and raised his face to look up. "The war is over, brothers. Its purpose is served. We have seen, and we have died, and now it is over. All around us is peace. Peace through the Blood of his Cross. He tells us to go home. That is what He has said to me. We must go back down from the mountains, our time has come. Return brothers, give over and return. Let us put off the raiment of war. Let us rise!"

He ripped open his fatigue uniform from the neck. His body was pale and bony. "Let us cut branches of these sacred trees" (he broke off branches as he went) "and march with God's legions homeward, to bring the message to our people, who have not seen. They must be made to see. Let us deliver them, oh you who are more than brothers to me. For have we not died together, and will we not rise together in the body of Christ?"

He picked up a sharp stone and with a slashing stroke tore the skin of his narrow chest. "They must be made to look at the wounds. The blood of the covenant, brothers. Beware, tell them to beware what they do with the precious Blood of Christ. Unto him that loved us and washed us from our sins in His own Blood, be glory and dominion for ever and ever! Amen."

"Stop that jabbering you hillbilly bastard." Mersky,

one of the older men, sick with the wine and what he had seen in the night, pulled himself from the ground shouting and went for him. Bowen raised his arms to embrace him and the brawny man knocked him down. He stood over him. "You stop that crazy chatter or I'll kill you, you crazy bastard—." Bowen picked himself up and ran with a bloody nose, a scarecrow, very tall and thin. Mersky watched him go, then lay down again, muttering. In their relief they shouted congratulations at him. Even in their stupor they had been frightened. Bowen disappeared through the trees in the direction of the peasant cottages.

4

As the light was fading he reappeared on the steps of the church carrying a lamb in his arms and a knife in his hand. Its throat was cut and the blood ran over the remains of his uniform. He looked up and away to the sunset sky, another in a succession of miracles: orange and blue and green, crystalline. There was a breeze, cool and fresh. A last flash of gold light shimmered and jumped from the trees and roofs and the tower of the big house. Around the square all the shutters were closed tight. A peasant woman opened the door of one of the houses, saw him there and closed it again. Complete stillness. He was smiling, there on the steps. The lamb was warm and wet in his arms. He came down and began to walk toward the great house, trailing blood.

No one else saw him until he was through the courtyard and the door and into the great beamed room of the *club* where the officers sat over wine and cigars. They looked up from their supper to see the knife half-raised, the lamb hung around his neck, the head hanging. As he leaped over a couch he was shouting, "I am the bloody man and I have the bloody hand and I shall have revenge!" The table was overturned and someone was cut in the first lunge and screamed. They scattered and he went after them. A great Chinese vase went down and exploded against the stone floor. He caught and cut another. Another. No one would stand and face him. He screamed, "I am the bloody man and I have the bloody hand and I–" His mouth went on working soundlessly as he jerked against the bullet in his back. When the second shot hit him he collapsed and rolled over once among the dishes. The gun went on firing into him until it was empty. In the first moment of silence they saw Sergeant Mersky throw the carbine down in the doorway and walk away. There was blood all over everything.

14

Dear Eddie,

Just realized you haven't had a word out of me since way back in April sometime. You must of read about the big push here though. We've really been moving and seeing the world like they say in the recruiting posters. Boy what a show, better than the Fourth of July. And what a country. Don't let anyone tell you these Italians haven't got one beautiful country, I don't see what the hell they ever want to leave it for. Except maybe to get out from under these wars. Well I guess that's enough reason, they're really getting cleaned this time. Poor slobs, they don't know what hit them and nobody gives them a break. I mean, what the Germans don't steal from them our boys do. This is the greatest souvenir hunt since the gold rush. What these poor sons of bitches are going to do when it's over God only knows, they won't have a pot to piss in.

Well, clap hands, your boy has made the grade. No more calluses for this kid except maybe on the ass. I'm now what they call a T/5, it's a kind of corporal, at $20 a week, kind of a low grade mathematician. They found out I could do arithmetic—only took them two years and three months to find out—and that puts me up with the college boys who are the brains of this outfit. I never realized how damn complicated this whole business is. If you think we just shove a shell in and pull the string you're way off. This is more like building a bridge, only in reverse if you get what I mean. Well, when I see you I'll tell you all about it, and the way we're going here it won't be long now. Did I say brains? Well, OK, if you can call an adding machine that wears captain's bars brains. Strictly white collar. Ha Ha. Well you always said I was cut out for the better things in life.

The weather's been great, what a change from the mud and the crud back there in those mountains. You ought to see these sunsets. We've been pounding the shit out of the Germans from one mountain to the next, really clobbering them. You've never seen so many castles. Christ are they old. The real thing. I'm telling you these people know how to build them. Hell, we've knocked over at least a hundred of them that would make the State capitol look like a burlesque house.

When we get up to these places we've been firing at it looks like hell. You'd never believe what these big guns will do. All over the place you see these towns that look like what's left of the chicken after a hard-fought meal. And sometimes there isn't even the bones, not so you could tell. Hell it's a mess, I don't know, what are you going to do. A war is a war I guess. But sometimes you can't help wondering if sometimes these big boys with the brass just go ahead and bust up the place for the hell of it like a kid with a bee-bee gun shooting the milk bottles off the front porches. Well I don't know why I'm bothering you with this stuff except you told me you wanted to know what's going on over here.

Did I say mess? Boy, it's a lot worse than that even. Yesterday we get up to this big house where the Germans had been camping out and what the hell do you think, the bastards have gone and taken a shit all over everything. A beautiful place too, real old with gardens, and these SOB's have gone and taken a dump on the floors, the beds, in the kitchen, everywhere you can think of. Great. You'd of thought they'd use the toilets, the house was full of bathrooms, but no, when they got into a bathroom they let fly in the bathtub. Talk about the shit hitting the fan. And then they had to go and draw these dirty pictures all over the walls, they must be even hornier than our guys, and have they got filthy minds. Boy, you should of seen the colonel, was he burned up. He's got to be a big country house man, never passes one up if he can help it. Makes it kind of nice for us sometimes, I always did want to get a look at how the other half lives. Well, this time the colonel took one look and got the hell out of there. We had to set him up a tent in the garden. What a laugh.

The last few days or so we've been supplying artillery support for a French outfit they've got fighting here in the center. Man, can these Frenchies fight. That is, they're not exactly French, they come mostly from Africa somewhere, but they've got French officers and uniforms and all. They go in after these krauts like a weasel after rabbits. It's a pleasure to be helping these guys, I can tell you, they're real soldiers, the real thing. Just passing them on the road you can see it. And the damndest thing is these Goums, they call them, that they've got in their outfits, big colored guys from Africa, the biggest guys you ever saw. Christ you ought to see them, the size of them. We keep seeing them along the roads. They got this big arab thing they wear on their heads and they're really big and rough looking, and with these big wicked knives stuck in their belts. Boy it's a sight let me tell you, you don't know whether you ought to laugh or just run. We're sure as hell glad they're on our side. Real tough babies. They've got French officers, but officers don't mean a thing to these boys. It's all the French can do to keep them from screwing the women to death. They don't bother to supply them much, they just live right off the land. And fight, man the krauts are scared to death of them. They say they don't try to organize them into some kind of attack, they just get them up close to the Germans and turn them loose. It's murder. It ain't exactly human, but what the hell is around here.

They say we're coming up to a big town up the road called Siena, biggest thing since we hit Rome. If the Germans leave anything behind I'll get you a souvenir. Thanks for the news of Sally. Tell her I'll bring her a German pistol and a sword and if she don't write she's going to get the wrong end of both of them. And tell the boys in the composing room I'll send them all some filthy postcards, and tell them I'm faithfully carrying my union card so nothing can happen to me.

Your boy,
Bert

2

Aside from the fact that the Germans had loused up his villas, the Colonel really had nothing to complain about. The fighting was tougher—the Germans were making short hard stands from hill to hill as they backed up into Tuscany— and the Colonel certainly liked it better that way. The battalion was rolling again, there was still that hot smell of victory in the air, the weather stayed fair and warm most of the time. In among these small stone-housed hill villages the Colonel had gotten in some good work with the guns—some good *shoots* as he called them. No, he couldn't complain.

The fighting had gotten noisy again. There was more German artillery and the Allies were blasting with every gun they had all up and down the line. As they withdrew, the Germans were still blowing up the roads and blowing up villages along the roads to block them. After it got its orders the battalion moved up fast to support the French Expeditionary Corps in its drive toward Siena. They came up at night through the rich open Paglia Valley and made contact with the French near Acquapendente. And immediately they sensed a change. This was not the same war. It was the war of the French against the Germans, an older war and a fiercer one.

For months the battalion had been firing in general

support, adding weight to the fires of other outfits, behind a lot of different infantry regiments, and there had always been that remote, anonymous feeling about it, never really knowing who it was they were supporting and not caring very much. Not any more than the man who mines coal knows or cares who uses it, or how much he has to pay for it. How could it have been otherwise in this sprawling war of the argus and the centipede, when you fired at ranges of 10, 12, 15 miles into a void, on orders that came indirectly, through the big switchboards at Corps or Brigade Headquarters?

But now it was different. This was a smaller war, more compact, better defined—part of an old feud, man-to-man. The battalion was up close; the gun crews came to feel that the Frenchmen needed them, depended on them. Maybe it was because the battalion was more or less on its own now, working directly with the French regiments by way of forward observers. Or maybe, as the Colonel said, it was because of the way those Frenchmen fought. He kept saying, like the connoisseur that he was: "For a good steady workmanlike job of killing Germans you can't beat them."

The Colonel was right. With the French it was another kind of war, simpler and, as he said, more old-fashioned. They had no big supply train behind them: no refrigerator trucks, no sock-washing installations, no divisional gin distilleries. They had had no relief for months. They stayed in close, slugging like the bare fist of an angry man, to kill Germans and to hell with everything else. Most of the time they lived off the country, and they did not complain about food or cigarettes. And for them there was never any mail. The men of the battalion felt these things. It moved them out of their apathy, it gave them back their taste for the war.

It was not easy to maintain contact with the French. Most of the outfits around them would bed down during these short summer nights—but not the French. The momentum of hate and revenge would not let them stop. They fought like men who have known humiliation, like men who fight down from the hills to retake their own homes.

But here in the lonely rugged country on the Tuscan-Umbrian border they were stopped dead. The Germans were holed up in the hill town of Cofaridani. From the castle above the town they had one of the best views in Italy, with complete control of the road. During the night the French had attacked, taking their losses on the rocky crags and in the chasms as the Germans rolled grenades down from the walls of the town. A long night, and in the morning the Germans still held the town. Not even the Goumiers, the big relentless black men, were able to move. It was a fix. And to top everything, the Colonel had orders not to hit the old castle; it was classed as a national monument and therefore untouchable. This was where the Colonel started his raving about "the damned art professors who're making a half-assed war out of it." He blew up. "How the hell do they expect us to fight a goddamn war in an art museum!" And as they went deeper into this fragile province of churches and monasteries and cloisters and galleries and castles he almost forgot to hate the British as he cursed the Battlefield Art Commission for its meddling.

3

Later in the morning these dirty bearded smiling Frenchmen patched up their wounds and buried their dead and got ready to attack again. Here for the first time they asked the heavy artillery battalion for close support, and the Colonel sent Lieutenant Freeman—who knew some French—to direct the fire. The Lieutenant was glad of the chance: finally he would be doing the job of forward observation that he had been trained for. That need to be in the open, on the forward edge, had never left him.

He went up in the jeep with a radioman, along the deep-cut glaring road. Up close, he left the jeep and went on foot, and then crawling on his belly, up the broken slopes to one side of the town—until he was high enough to see a long way in this towering solitary country, melancholy even in this light of a summer morning. In the distance high mountains unfolding, some ringed with chestnut and beech woods, one bearing a huge cross at its peak. Again he saw Bowen for a moment, the upraised knife, the lamb—hurtling; then quietly walking along the tops of those far mountains; then arriving at some secret valley, the place that had been prepared for him. Unforgettable man. For a moment he lost himself in the calm of the mountains, the high places that were beyond the reach of war.

When he saw the French troops he forgot about Bowen and the mountains. These were men—something hard and clear about them. Close-knit men, spare, precise—no waste motion. A cutting edge. He liked them, at the first glance: the hard handshake, the straight look into his eyes, the smiling seriousness of men who know why they fight and assume that you know why you fight. The assured look of craftsmen; there was no fear and no numbness in them. They seemed to look straight down at their deaths and to say, If it be so, so be it.

On the way up to one of their battalion observation posts they congratulated him on the American artillery. They climbed, hiding themselves as they went, in mounting excitement. As they came up to the crag that was almost on a level with the town he was caught by the ardor of their hatred for the Germans. In the way they said *Les Boches* there was a purity of hate that made everything seem very simple. In its bright white light the blurred outlines of the war hardened sharply into focus. In the field glasses of the hunter—blurred, then adjusted—the clear image of the vicious animal, running. Pursue him. Kill him.

The Lieutenant checked his position with the young infantry officer at the observation post, then got the battalion on the radio. There was no sign of life in the town; the Germans were holed up, waiting, in the compact stone houses. He reached into the case for his field glasses, trying to control the trembling of his hands, and settled down to the job with pleasure. He was right there on top of the war, the whole power of the battalion was in his hands. For a moment he did not hear the level voice of the French officer, who was pointing out strong points in the German position. In the stone houses of the town were hundreds of Germans. But not a sign of them showed.

He checked the map again, took one more look at the sun-baked town, and picked up the telephone that would relay his orders back through the radio in the jeep to the battalion switchboard. (In the Fire Direction Center the computers waited with their pencils and instruments, and at the guns the factory workers waited, eager for something to do.) Quietly, into the phone, he spoke the necessary formula.

A rustling whisper high up, a silence—the first shell bored into the edge of the town. A roar: smoke and fragments, pierced by flame. The crust was broken. He adjusted the fire of one gun on the near edge of the town, then called for the massed fire of the twelve guns. The town went to pieces, cracking and bursting like a crate of eggs. The deep spaces of the houses were penetrated; light came in; the insides were forced out and up. It was as if the stones of the houses themselves were explosive.

Like a line of invisible pneumatic drills the succeeding waves of shells moved over the jumble of tile roofs. The Lieutenant lost himself, staring at the sudden eruptions; he had never seen anything like it. It absorbed him completely. Pure pleasure of destruction: it was in its way a terribly beautiful thing . . . The sound and the fire fused. Furious . . . A transfiguration. Continuing . . . effortlessly. Thunderstorm after a hot day. Release of all pressure . . . The sluggishness of the world broken by the explosive strokes. The town: it is— and then it is not. Something moved, quivered, in his groin, as if in response to a woman. A moment of wild delight, half suppressed—. And silence, with the smoke still rising.

The death of another town. Hidden in the hills, the people of the town watched it die. And the Lieutenant watched it, a lightness in him, and an up-rush of blood, as in a man who has created something.

Someone behind him was speaking in French and he did not know for a moment where he was. "C'est magnifique. Ah, c'est vraiment magnifique." And the others (he felt their shining eyes on his back) in excited laughter: "Oui. Oui. C'est formidable. Parfait. Ah oui. Magnifique." He went on watching as if he had not heard them—flushed with pleasure. Then could not resist, and turned to them. They were grinning at him, and moving to take his hand. And one held up a circle of thumb against index finger: appreciation and congratulation.

The high whirring again and the last twelve shells came down, blasting the old stone to dust, picking at the skeletons of the houses, splashing flame and oily black smoke. Into the phone the Lieutenant said, "Cease fire. Infantry ready to move in. Mission accomplished." He was thinking—feeling with his whole body—that to fight a war with men like these on a day like this, this is good. This is damned good. The blood still pounded in his stomach, up into his chest. He wanted to shout or sing. He wanted to go in and get a German with his own hands. The words of French came to him in a flood as he started to speak, words he had never used before in speech. They surrounded him, the Frenchmen, and shook his hand, and embraced him, calling him *camarade*.

They heard the fire of small arms and in their excitement forgot about safety as they climbed up on to the ledge to watch the infantry climb from their holes and begin to run toward the town. The Lieutenant watched through the field glasses; his body went tight against the impact, the spasm and fall of a man in the open. Up the broken rocky slope the tired men were crawling and dying and going on with their bayonets fixed from street to street, cellar to cellar, wall to wall. He stopped breathing—thinking: Have I done them any good? From the upper floors of the remaining houses the Germans were rolling grenades down on them. Some fell and lay still. And then they were into the houses, room to room, hand to hand. Out of sight. And it occurred to the Lieutenant that he had not seen any of the Germans.

Four hours later the dead town was theirs. They had taken no prisoners. And they did not stop. They reformed their units, sat down for a smoke and some wine, and moved on down the road into the next valley. The Lieutenant would have liked to go with them; he had orders to get back to the battalion. They were moving again.

15

For the next two weeks the battalion followed the French in the pursuit, pushing the Germans back and back through the sun-swollen paradise of grapes and olives and orchards and wrought-stone the color of honey—the stone of fluted pediments and carved moldings that were frames to hold what grew and glistened here. They hurried in the trucks over this holy ground, past arches of the Romans and tombs of the Etruscans; the ground worked and cherished for three thousand years. From the trucks and from the gun positions in the olive groves they saw only what they looked for. They were thirsty and they saw the grapes beginning to swell under the vine leaves in the fields on both sides of the road; they were hungry and they stopped to strip the pears and plums from the trees that stood near the road.

And every few hundred yards they passed through the quiet patient corpses waiting by the side of the road for someone to bury them. At first the men had looked down from the trucks at them, as if to pay their respects, but there were too many and they learned to keep their eyes straight ahead, to pass them by like so many squashed animals on a heavily traveled road. How else? The eyes do not really focus on the dead, anyway—the senses refuse to take hold of them, except for the defenseless nose, and most of these corpses had not yet begun to stink.

With the first few, the eye looks for traces of the beautiful fluid body that had been. But what can the eye find in them now—inert, rag bags, stiff and clumsy in the way they are propped and strewn by the sides of the road. The lids of the eyes are half-open in some, the mouths are agape, the skin of the hands is a hard cold white. They are unnatural. Only in the thick living hair of those who have lost their helmets is there a reminder of the hot life that has leaked out of the punctured bodies.

And it is summer and there are the grapes; and from up here in this hill town you can see the clear distances, in great detail: the near green hills and the far blue mountains of a strange country, those distant places that some who are alive today will never reach. The great spaces of unlived life, the unknown that will not become known. *He died so young. A pity. A pity. So far from home.* Strange to these living, and stranger to the dead, whose country this is not, yet who will become now a part of its soil. So far from home. So much heat in their bodies. Yesterday, if you think of it, they had names. Look at the dog-tags: Ford, Anderson, Schultz—each a separate man with a name and a number, a blood type and a religion, known to someone, somewhere; now nameless and unknown, ready to go into the ground, young men, young dead men, with no names that matter to those who pass, now or later; unknown soldiers. They went just so far on this strange road (ate one last pear) and no further; and never found out what was over the next hill.

Well, to hell with it, a man dies, what can you do?— the dead man might be you but it is always somebody else. So far so good. They were, anyway, goddamnit, moving along and it was a goddamn beautiful summer day, there was a breeze blowing in from the sea, and there—*There! Look! On the hills*—the strong lean towers of Siena. There might be women, if they should stop long enough. They've got to stop! For two months the French have been fighting up and down these hills and they are exhausted. And there *must* be women. Breasts, thighs, legs, bellies. Women. A piece of ass. Any god-damned thing.

The nights in this garden are decorated with colored rockets and the long orange streaks of tracer and the multiple lightning of the big guns. The thunders of the artillery never let up. The German guns are active again, and all day and all night the earth shakes as the Germans dynamite the factories and houses and bridges and roads. And in the daytime the horizon is marked with the huge hanging columns of smoke. Around Siena the German troops have gotten out of hand, plundering and burning. In some of the towns there are rapes of very young girls, and the peasant women wail at the loss of their cups and saucers. The Germans are stealing their tablecloths. The dead go unburied. All this where centuries ago war was outgrown, leaving the country in stillness and order. For centuries a steady ripening, as of an ornate melon, and now the melon in its fullness is pierced, cracked, spilling its guts, left to rot.

2

Lieutenant Freeman did not get a chance to work with the French again. But he could not forget them. Some battalions of light armored artillery from another sector had been diverted to give the French direct mobile support in their rush up this highway, and the 501st fell back again, out of sight of the fighting, to reinforce the fire of the light battalions.

He thought about the French, often and with pleasure, and remembered every detail of that day when he had been with them. The elation he had felt did not subside, nor the solid pleasure of the shells pumped into the town as if from his own hands. At moments when the guns were quiet and they were alone, he tried to tell Red Brock about it, but it was not easy. The French, he said, they don't kid themselves. They know what they're here for . . . He hesitated, it was from the heart, it was difficult to get hold of it. He went on, and as he talked it came clearer to him. They, the French, made nothing sentimental of it; they fought in a quiet expectation of death. It was not the first time. They accepted it as one of man's natural acts, they had expected it all their lives—part of every man's life is a war or two. They had no dreams to fight toward; there was only this solemn ritual of attack against the traditional enemy. Their war was not our war, as their world is not ours; it was only one of the small separate wars within the larger one. War only *seems* to provide common ground. But this did not, he knew, change the way he felt about the French. By the way they carried themselves, by their unerring passion they had inspired him—it was nothing less than that. From that day the war was no longer shapeless and remote for him. They had brought him to see that it was not "home," not America, he was here for. America was only another abstraction outside of the war. It was far away, it was at peace, it did not see *this*. What mattered was what was right here, under their feet, and if they were here for something more than for the sake of each other, then it was to restore some order to the broken world of Europe, to open a way for it, so that it might rise again into life, renewed.

And he knew too—somewhere in his elemental soul—that something of what the French felt about the Germans had rubbed off on him, some of their small clear purpose: to drive back the Germans, to kill them like mad dogs and have done with it. For the first time in his life he had felt the need to kill.

Some of these things he tried to explain to Red Brock; but for others he could not begin to find words. The tall red-head listened in his easy way, but he did not smile or joke as he might have done. He listened, closely, and was held by the intensity of the voice. As he listened he understood, but when the passionate voice had stopped, he lost it, running away from it, evading, denying to himself the fact of his understanding. There was an easier way, and he took it. The guns, the machinery, the pleasure of movement. He had never left the guns: their power had touched him, and nothing else. The role he had to play was enough: the Executive Officer. The Foreman at the guns. Employee. He did his job and waited to go home. At the end he said, "I guess that's one way of looking at it, Gil. I don't know. I'm not sure I know what you're talking about. A war is a war, always has been, always will be. What did you expect?"

3

And the Germans—what the hell was it with them? They were on the run, tired, beat-up, being forced into a corner from three sides of Europe, their cities blasted from the air. Then why did they go on fighting this way, mile after mile? Were they crazy? Hadn't they had enough—three full years of dying? Any other army would have shown signs of quitting by this time. Why not this one? Well, as a Prussian Prince said sometime in the 19th century: "It is the warlike spirit that decides, not the tactical form . . . The more developed the warlike spirit in the individual soldier, the greater will be the energy of the whole mass, and the less will be the influence of the tactical form."

And then this German Prince said something else. He said, about the general and the men who follow him:

"The general is the loved and respected chief, not a scolding, punishing taskmaster. When he addresses his troops (which he should do only seldom) all hearts beat faster. He must know how to touch those chords which produce a fine ring . . . They delight in his near presence and they are proud of him. He has rendered both the men and their officers susceptible to the inspiration which his presence, his glance, his words and his bearing must infuse into them on the day of battle, and which must result in a trebling of their efforts. If then, in the fullness of their enthusiasm, they ask him eagerly, 'Sire, where is it your will that we should die?'—then and only then has he succeeded in making the right impression upon them in time of peace."

And so it was: these Germans, now, were still asking this question. They did not ask it of the Führer; in these squalls and rainstorms of death he and all the other unseeing men who sit at desks are forgotten, and it is the army they fight for—for The General and for each other—the German Army whose invincibility they must prove. And no matter for what cause? No matter. The army itself becomes the meaning of their lives.

So they asked the question, from hill to hill and house to house: "Sire, where is it your will that we should die?" Town by town, street by street, until we wore them down with our heavy machinery.

4

And now they come to the heart of the ripe flower that is at the center of the garden. Into Tuscany, where there is the purest sculpturing of the landscape, the earth lifted in men's hands for thirty centuries and laid back in terraces, delicately, with respect. They come, the pursued and the pursuers, heavyfooted, heavyhanded, killing and dying steadily into this shaped and fertile world, under the luminous peace of its sky. They come with steel and fire and filth and blood-shot eyes. They crush, they trample underfoot.

What has a war got to do with this? The peace of cypresses against this sky. Can there be a war? Can they go on fighting over this ground? If they see it?—Look at it. The hills so gently rounded by the hands of men, the hillsides in-habited by trees, in a natural order, trees for use and cere-monial trees. The pines cluster to make shelter and quiet, the cypresses climb in dark lines to shape and hold the hills against the sky. The trees are used to organize the space to the human scale. And the man of this place, the Tuscan, comprehends his space, is at ease in it. Here it is a blue-green landscape, undu-lant, encircled by the crude mountains that are its limits. It is called a garden, but it is not a garden, it is not all gentle and tame. And the low solid farmhouses, honey-colored, deep-roofed, are not the objects of a garden; nor are the white oxen who swing up and down the fields. A garden would not con-tain these lines of force.

As the battalion column climbed to the top of another hill the young Lieutenant looked around, and saw it, and it seemed to him he must have seen it before, in a dream, somewhere. It was the perfect, contained, coherent world men dream about. It was as if he had been seeking it. Under the late afternoon sun it was ten kinds of green in its fruitful-ness, rolling away to the earth colors of the hill towns, broken by the dry stone walls of the curving terraces. It entered him, filling him, until finally he could no longer contain it alone. To the man who was driving the jeep he said, "Someday I've got to come back here." The man only looked at him and muttered something. They came to the top, and went down, into it, all the greens, the intricate design on the earth; and at that moment the Lieutenant wanted to break from the column of steel and to walk, to walk into it, and to keep walking until he was a part of it.

And again they were firing, somewhere below Siena, firing blind into nowhere from data supplied through a switchboard ten miles away. The sky above them, through the leaves of this olive grove, was as pure, as crystalline as anything they had ever seen. A high serenity. And where it came down to meet the treeline on the hill crests there was a great potential stillness; but the guns would not allow it to be. They made the houses shake sixty miles away. They seemed to be enjoying themselves, chewing the earth and spitting it out. Their servants worked hard to feed them, gladly. How could they help feeling good? The mornings were fresh and through most of the day a breeze blew in from the sea. And the Germans were still running.

16

The Germans did not try to hold Siena. Sixteen miles below the city they made their last important delaying stand along the Orcia River, and then pulled out. The French entered Siena early in July, raised their flag from the tower of the great Palazzo Communale in their ceremonial way, and left by the north gate to pursue the Germans toward Poggibonsi and San Gimignano.

A city of severe and vigorous elegance, Siena, of boldness. A people with a medieval zest, boisterous, who love the wild and solemn ceremonies. At the center a great piazza, a source and an outlet for the streams of life, shaped and hollowed like a sea shell; and here, at the living center of their world, these hungry and unbeaten people mass to cheer the pursuers as they roll through the town. And here the battalion of 155 mm. guns,—the Americans, the favorites, the open-faced smiling boys who look down from the big trucks not knowing if they come as conquerors or liberators or what. But what the hell, it's a holiday, one way or another—it's all sun and flowers and girls and music; and the roaring crowd pressed through the tight stone streets as if drunk, chanting their release, their hope. A carnival. No lights, no gas, no water, no doctors, no hospitals, no police, no government—and on they come screaming joy. What the hell do they expect to happen?

The battalion had a long wait on the north edge of the town, and the men slipped away in search of women, a drink, anything they could lay their hands on. The passion of this crowd had aroused them, had made their hearts move to the flap of flags and the brass of bands. They were the liberators; with their awesome trucks and guns they had crawled through the overflowing streets like floats in a parade, the swirls of laughing crying faces hemming them in—it had caught them at the throat until they laughed and cried, caught them and spun them around, to be touched by hands and lips, clutched in the arms of women; then left them quiet for a while, lumps in their throats and tears in their eyes. Today they loved the Italians, and the Italians were ready to do anything for them. Strong shining brave boys from the new world.

When the shouting was over the Lieutenant, like the others, wiped the tears from his face and went to find a woman, or a bottle of wine, or a bottle of wine and a woman, something to touch in the fever of this heated day that would bloom in the flowering flesh of the summer night. He went with his hands and his eyes alive, to embrace.

A hell of a fine town, layer on layer of its past piled up in solid stone; so that for a while it was enough to be walking in it, in the narrow cobbled streets of unexpected palaces, streets that were cut up and down, in and out of the three hills, the living nest of a great medieval city. Yet small—to be held in the palm of the hand. A street ending at a low wall, and beyond, the hills of vines and olives. And further, toward

Florence, the distances mysteriously illuminated—a revealed, jewel-cut perfection. A dark line of cypress, a pair of oxen, an old man with a basket of cherries. A hill village golden brown in the sunset, like some vision of serenity.

Or was it a mirage, this paradise? This completeness, that the hands longed to touch and to know. No—. He descended a wide stone stairway and came out into another piazza, a sudden opening, hot after the cool of the alleys, and there they were again, the Sienese, strolling as though it were a Sunday afternoon—out to see one another, to keep in touch, as always. Back and forth they went in their exaltation, heels beating on the cobbles. (Others, it was said, having no jobs to go to, had gone out on the hills, whole families, to eat the fruit from the trees, to sing, to make a holiday of their freedom, to sleep.) Seizing life by the tail. He stopped to watch them, the moving, burning faces—a people worth saving.

He turned to try another narrow street, to see the life welling in it, and there in front of him was the fading fascist poster on a wall. "Sea, do not give us back our dead, do not give us back our ships, but give us back our glory." And over it in red paint was splashed the motto of the Partisans: "Insorgere per Risorgere," Insurrection for the sake of Resurrection. His lips moved to speak the words, and he was speaking them to Anne. She would want to hear this. Tell her.

She came up close to him, in a café where he sat down to read again her last few letters. Full of her, full of a rosy hope, he dreamed over a bottle of wine, and the letters looked good to him. She seemed, in this life she made for herself in a factory town in Connecticut, to have found herself. The letters spoke with her voice, easy and warm. Her body was there, under his hands. A woman. She gave herself, she was there in the letters with a boldness that surprised him, in the flesh—with love and plans and an eagerness for what they would do together. Plans, hopes, a new world, etc. She was naïve, sure, but what did it matter? She was moving, exhilarated; there was a kind of awe in her letters that matched his mood—awe of the war, that mystery, that *experience*. And a kind of worship of him, her man in the war, partaking of the mystery. And he liked it, how could he not like it? She loved him. She was a dreamer? she simplified things? Well—good. She was a woman. The beautiful body of a woman, flowering, toward him, her eyes on him, proud of him. Warm. A woman.

He spent an hour with her letters, deaf to the noises of the street, and wrote one to her, full of the elation of the chase. And when he came out again to walk on the warm cobbles of the street his dream of her still enveloped him. In it he was sure, ready for anything. Like a boy at the moment when he comes out into the sunlight of the street from a movie that has quickened him. The war a moving picture, a drama; himself in it, and outside of it; the woman watching him, all her attention on him, needing him. The soldier, moving forward; a campaign; the pursuit; Italy, the ripeness of it, in the ripe gold summer; the war moving to climax; himself ready for whatever might come.

Walking in the last light, the afterglow, among the people of Siena, he was close to them, lifted by their great energy. The energy released by liberation: it flowed from them into him. As the night came on they stopped him and took him into their arms; they heard him speak their language, and could not do enough for him. Into the night he drank with them and sang and danced with them; and found a woman, young and ardent, who was his for tonight with no expectation of tomorrow.

2

When he got back to the bivouac he was lightheaded with wine and fatigue. He tried to sleep, but it would not come. Their liberation was in him: he wanted more of it, more opening of doors, floods of sunlight, people pouring into their streets. His mind and body were light and open, unresting, eager to be moving again. He thought of Anne again and smiled; it was as if she were with him. His blood raced in widening circles of joy and expectation; and at the center darkened to a pure lust for action. From the hills a few miles to the north the sounds of heavy fighting came down again. He lay on his back in the dark near the guns and listened.

He did not get any sleep but it didn't matter; in another hour the motors were grinding and they were moving again, toward San Gimignano and Certaldo. Through the intricate hills: more scenery, more art, more monuments and ruins; and the piled-up villages of deep-pitched roofs, the ripe tile green-gold in the sun. And all of it—carved and painted and inlaid—trembling now with the blast of the big guns; all but the fat round blue hills of grapes and olives. Old work of the hands, it is fragile—but it holds, against the shaking of the earth. Except where it gets a direct hit, it holds.

And by the sides of the roads, in white dust and rubble, always the resting dead men, waiting—tow-headed Germans, the big black men, Moroccans, French and a few Americans. Pretty complete examples of each: only here and there a head missing, or part of a head, or a leg. But the damndest thing of all was this nest of dead Germans around a punctured 88 at a turn in the road. There they were, dumped around the gun like broken dolls, and all around them this junk-pile of wine bottles and mattresses and blankets and women's fur coats. The truck that had been pulling their gun had been hit and all this stuff had spilled out: cameras, knives and forks, silk underwear, furniture, a typewriter, some rabbits and geese, traveling bags, pots and pans, silk ties (nothing but the best)—and all of it tangled and shining in the olive oil that had broken from its bottles. The battalion rolled by. *What a shame to have gone and wasted all that nice stuff.* There was even a painting.

3

Who said this was a small country? It seemed like years now that they'd been moving up and moving up, and where in the world was the end of it?

They came to a village where life had begun again, and on the remains of a house someone had written: *Ed quindi uscimmo rividere le stelle*—And then we came out to see the stars again. Nearby was an old man sitting in a doorway; the Lieutenant asked him about it. He said that it was from Dante. He smiled and took the young man's hand and held it, smiling. I am a shoemaker, he said. There are no shoes. But there are the stars, we see them now. And the grapes are good. Thank God.

Down the fat well-planted valley of the Elsa it went easier, the road running level along the slopes of these soft hills, the men in the trucks rolling, rolling, glad to be rolling. Here and there the batttalion went into position in an orchard to fire a few rounds; and the old squared-off towers of the hill towns made convenient aiming points for the orientation of the guns. The Germans were using more artillery again and the battalion was ordered to stay well back of the front, shooting unobserved reinforcing missions for the light artillery that was giving the French close support near San Gimignano.

Whenever he saw the strong sure Tuscan peasants the Lieutenant would ask them how it was going, and they would try to smile out of those calm brown faces, saying, *Che finisca presto*—May it finish soon. Never glory, or victory, winner or loser, hate or spite or flattery—only this, that it might be finished. The faces—those fluent human faces— they were worth everything. Sometimes it seemed to him that this was what he had been looking for all his life, the living grace of these faces, and the life in their bodies as they worked for what the earth would give them. For them the war did not have any real existence, it was unbelievable; they were too absorbed in recreating the earth, every year recreating it, feeling their way to it with their hands, never violating it—the same earth for 3000 years. It was a kind of paradise they lived in and they knew it, without ever saying it. They did not complain. They looked up to watch the guns roll by, then looked down again to the earth under their hands. He came to love them.

And so they moved, through the ripening terraced hills of summer, with nothing to think about, with pleasure in the movement. And just over the next hill, maybe, is the end of the war.

17

And suddenly they stopped dead. Along the fluid front it was all confusion. They waited, puzzled, listening to rumors.

Nobody seemed to know what was happening. Somewhere above Siena the Germans had suddenly broken off and pulled out. The French were thrown off balance, then began to move fast in the effort to make contact again. The light artillery battalions and the armor followed in a scramble; but some outfits, like this battalion of heavy guns, were left standing, not knowing what to do next. Higher headquarters was too busy to bother with them. So they waited. They couldn't just take off up the road—along these deep-cut snaking roads they were blind, vulnerable. They could not be sure, in any case, which way the French combat team had gone; they had lost contact with them in the night.

So here they were sitting in another grove of olives, a very nice position in a hollow, the guns ready to fire and the war running away from them. The Colonel chewed up a couple of cigars, went up on a hill for a look around, saw nothing, and got "A" Battery on the phone.

"Look, Walker, send Freeman up there, we've got to find out what the hell is going on. These Africans are getting the idea they're going to win the war all by themselves. Tell him to tell those Frog officers they got to keep in touch with us I don't care what happens. If this kind of thing goes on we're going to find ourselves in some hole where they'll blow the hell out of us. All right, you got that?"

Down in the batteries the boys had nothing to do, so they strolled over to the nearby pear orchard, stripped off all the fruit they could get their hands on, then moved over to where the plums were. They ate the best of the meat of each piece and threw the rest away; and ended by throwing what they could not eat at each other. A fruit fight, laughing and throwing, until they sat on the ground breathless.

A few hundred yards above them and to the left were the solid rectangular towers of the hill town, the hard crown of all these fruitful slopes. From other valleys—no one knew just where, or whose—they could hear the sound of guns. They asked each other what was happening. But it was another nice day and they did not stop to worry too much about it. Sooner or later some one would know, some one would tell them what to do. In the meantime they got out the cards. A big game, for real money. Everyone was watching Robinson, the man on the number three gun who had won over three thousand dollars since Africa.

Further down the slope, behind the guns, a peasant in shirtsleeves and a small round felt hat followed the two white oxen up and down up and down under the sun, stopping at the edge of the olive trees to wipe the sweat from his eyes. On the other side of the small river, down on the flat, was another village, more silver haze of olive leaves below the cluster of earth-colored roofs, more men bent over their vines, pruning. Closer to the guns the olive leaves gleamed and then did not gleam as the breeze turned them under the sun. A long slow summer afternoon. When it was quiet they could hear the singing of the cicadas behind the low voices of the card-players.

2

It must have been about five in the afternoon when Lieutenant Freeman got word of his assignment to find the French battalions. The Exec came over to where he was sitting under a tree and told him what the Colonel wanted. "This is a tough one, Gil. It's all in the dark, no one knows where the hell anything is. I hate to—."

"Look, Red, don't get solemn on me. I don't mind going. Hell, it's a relief. I told you last time—that's what I want. I can take just so much of this sitting around. OK?"

"OK, buddy, I'm glad you like it. Here's a real chance to get up off your ass; it's moving fast, you can't tell what you might run into." He squatted down close to the man on the ground. "Now here's what we've got in the way of maps. With luck you should find the Frenchies up in here somewhere." He ran his finger over the map and pointed. For a few minutes more they talked over the maps, the roads, the possible eventualities. "OK, it's almost five-thirty now. You ought to get going around seven. Let's go and eat."

After supper the Lieutenant got his field glasses and whatever else he needed and went over to where the jeep was waiting. They'd given him Chiarello for his driver; he knew how to operate the radio and his Italian was pretty good. The Lieutenant was glad to see him, he liked him about as well as anybody in the outfit. A tall, good-looking kid who seemed to know what it was all about. He was the only Italian-American in the battalion who wasn't always apologizing for his ancestors' poverty.

Just before they started down the dirt path to the

road the Exec came over with a tommy-gun for each of them. "Here, you guys, there's a war on." He fabricated a smile. "Now get out there and fight for the old 501st, y'hear? If you can't win it with these, give us a buzz and we'll see what we can do for you. And for chrissakes keep your eyes open, huh? We'll wait up for you. Arrividerc'. Take it easy."

He waved as they laughed and rolled downhill into a sunset that was like the meeting of heaven and hell. The cypresses on the hill crests stood up firm and glistening, black worshippers before the fires in the western sky.

Moving, cut loose, refreshed, the two men turned their heads to watch the sky change, cooling, crystallizing to jade. They said nothing, but each knew that the other was glad to be moving—only the two of them—away from the factory routine of the battalion. Sitting back there at the guns you got to feel stale, heavy. Here, in the open body of the jeep, its quick easy action, they were young again, alert, keyed to the chase—as if this were the first day of the war. And there was something between them: an instant liking, a quick current of wordless understanding. They went like two men who renew a friendship, who drive away from the tedium of their jobs for a weekend of hunting. Whatever remained between them of the fraudulent game of master and servant was left behind.

The dark silence of a grove of umbrella pines. Concentric curves of terraces moving past, up and down. And around to a cluster of abandoned houses, the shuttered windows, the deep overhang of the Tuscan roof. Soft interplay of hills, in and out, up and down.

"Beautiful country. I like it. I like the people. You born here, Frank?"

"No. Buffalo, New York. But my mother and father come from up north there, other side of the Arno, one of the hill towns above Lucca. Family's always been there I guess.

Still got uncles there, cousins, aunts. Sure would be nice to run into them."

They bumped along for a while, watching the map, and turned off into a side road that might have fewer craters in it. The jeep roared as it climbed, turned at the top and went down in a breeze into all these greens. In the last dark flaming of the sunset the greens were almost blinding, as if the sun were shining out of the earth itself, green and gold fire about to break through the ground. And everything hard and clear on the ground: columns of cypress, umbrellas of pine, twisted bodies of olive trees, the weathered stone and tile of the strong and simple houses.

The dense fecund presence of the land, the darkening hills, deeply shadowed, glowing like copper pots illuminated, so engrossed them that they forgot to see it as cover, vantage point, threat—the habit of fear broken in this sudden illumination, serenity, exhilaration of movement. The fullness of it, glowing and darkening. The fullness of the earth matching their own fullness, and the completeness of their devotion to it. No war, no death. A fruit coming to ripeness, the heaviness of it; the hand impulsively reaching for it, in nature. The elemental need to touch, eat, live on the earth as earth. The body of the land; two men entering into it; in it; deep in.

3

The light almost gone now, moving slowly, the road curving and curving; Chiarello talking about what he had seen, found, in Italy, his pleasure in it. It was himself, a part of him; he reaffirmed it, acknowledged it. *This is mine. This is what I might have been.* His speech quickening, then slowing as he felt the response of the other man, the depth of his appreciation; knowing finally that with this man—though he was officer, "white" man, "real" American—there was nothing he needed to prove. They spoke—in few words—of what they had seen, with love, their enthusiasms fusing and flaring up.

Silence, their words suddenly frozen in their mouths; slowing the jeep—hardly moving—to pick a way through this crowded section of the road. In total silence through a litter of dead men, a carnage-procession of dead men and dead horses. Bloated bellies. Garbage, with the smell of garbage— strewn in the pattern of flight. The violated bodies, unburied, in postures of tormented sleep. Complete disrespect for the body; the no-longer-useful meat left to rot. No rest: the insomniac dead.

The jeep backing and turning like some frightened animal, to find a way through the frozen confusion of overturned, burned-out wagons, caissons, guns. Horse-drawn artillery, an old-fashioned scene from another war. The two living men stiffened, turning their heads away. They stopped breathing. A river of stench between high banks, bordered by grapes and olives. They had to look, finally, if only to get through. The happening of it they could read in the remains. Pathetic (the dead are no man's enemy) to read in the ruin the moment of terror: the downrush of the fighter-bombers, their full bellies and screaming wings: the Germans with horses and harness and wagons trapped in the high-banked narrowness of the country road. Beaten and dejected sauerkraut eaters, gasoline all gone, plodding with horses and wagons, running for home. And the happy grins of the pilots, diving, to hammer them, see them run, send them sprawling.— Do you hear the crazy laughter? All on a quiet country road. Flashing bursts. Bursting flash of pink pulp. Dull burst of bone-punctured lung. Mouths spraying blood. An insane merry-go-round, the planes circling, screaming for another turn.

Slowly, through it; slowly, not to let the wheels of the jeep strike and squash. Not a word; they evaded each other's eyes. A yard at a time, in low gear, as if on tip-toe. All the way through to the end; quick change of gear, and out, fast. Speed for a hundred yards; a deep breath; breathing again. Silent, eyes pointed straight down the road. Forget it, forget it. Past. Forgotten.

Forgotten? That stench of death? Behind them, anyway. A clean quiet country road before them, winding, darkening. Silent, and the air damp and sweet where the banks are high.

Uphill, and down, and in the last light the grapes hang blue; sometimes close enough for them to go slow, reach out and grab a bunch where the untended vines straggle to the road's edge. "Wait. Hold it." The Lieutenant reaches and gets hold of some; they stop and throw their heads back to eat and drink. The grapes are not quite ripe but they taste good to them, cool inside and fresh in their dry mouths. With the motor cut it is very still, lonesome. The deep blue hills seem abandoned. No war, no peace, nothing living or dead.

They went on up and over a rise and almost head-long into a ragged man crouching to loot the dead. Absorbed, he had not seen them, but when finally he heard them he went down on his knees and fell hard to the road to join the group of corpses, to look like one of them. What difference did it make; they looked away. They went by him, past the anti-tank gun, through a half-ruined village. At the end of the street was a house, intact, and a smell of burning charcoal coming from it. They got no answer to their knock, and went on, watching the glow fade from the distant mountains; went in deeper, saying nothing, dark now, into the close-folded hills, turning, winding, with a cool breeze coming up out of the west, almost a wind, to heighten the pleasure of move-ment. The slopes off the road were closely wooded now, and in the slow penetration of interior folds of hill they got the smell of earth, of cypress and pine—all the senses alive and taking as they went, glad to be out, alone, exposed.

They were hunting and there was that excitement in it, an excitement of the body and the primitive part of the brain that belongs more to the body than to the mind. They let themselves go into the dark, drinking the peaceful air of the quiet-standing olive trees.

They were free, cut loose from the tight web of the machine and its domestic routine. The machine, the foreman, the boss, the boss's boss; Brigade, Corps, Army: centipede corporation—crawling mass; huge promiscuous heaving floundering trampling insentient blind brown bug that smothers, squashes, defecates, burrows as it goes. Worm that chopped to pieces moves on. Amoeba that changes shape, engulfs what it touches, and moves on.

Gladly they moved ahead into darkness, the two young men, past the ancient figures of olive trees, alive. They knew this relief: to be alone, to be oneself.

4

The sun was right down, but the afterlight hung on the hill tops. They moved faster, but with more care, still riding the wave of their release, more and more enclosed in the perfection of these terraced hills. For a long time there was no sign of war, only here and there the orchards stripped by some passing troops, branches broken and hanging. Or a house blown open, gaping, vomiting ruin.

On the road a velvet dark was unfolding ahead of them. And no sign of the French. No sound of guns. Nothing. A big shape, moving, surprised them—Chiarello braked the jeep hard. A cow—and they laughed their relief like two kids out late in the unfamiliar dark. A kind of hunter's camaraderie kept them going, buoyed them. They chattered and laughed.

Then another layer of darkness came down and they were quiet. They strained to see, afraid to use the lights. The hills closed in, hills folded within hills. And became mountains in the dark, and massed against them.

There was too much of the abandoned here, too much emptiness and soundlessness. Where had they all gone? Why no guns? They had been foolish and they knew it. They had gone too fast, too easily, expecting to find the French around the next turn in the road, or the next. They stopped at a crossroads, spread the map and turned a flashlight on it. Their eyes came up for a moment, met; and they saw there the fear that they were being watched.

"Where are we Lieutenant?"

The other said nothing, studying the map.

"Where the hell you figure we've got to Lieutenant?"

"I don't know Frank. Take a look—your guess is as good as mine."

They looked again, trying to trace the network of small roads back to where they had started. But the map didn't show all the roads. It seemed wrong, out of scale somehow.

"We should have found something by now, unless things have moved a lot faster than anyone figured." The Lieutenant lifted his head and looked around. "Look, they're sure as hell not behind us—let's give it another mile and figure it from there. We've got no place else to go." He smiled. "If that sounds OK to you Frank."

"That's OK for me. It's a lot better when you're moving."

They laughed, then were suddenly quiet; and in this first sign of fear came closer to one another. Chiarello pointed and said, "Look at that, fireflies. We're in luck." And they drove on in silence.

They crept ahead, feeling their way—until the moon came around a hill to surprise them. They had forgotten there would be a moon. It showed them everything, in an icy yellow light. Around a curve, moving faster with the moon, they swerved to avoid a German tank, a big one. The gun was long and pointed straight at them. But the hatch was open and over the opening hung the burned bodies of what had been two men, white-green in the moonlight. And near the tank were the bodies of three of the Goums, three huge black men, smashed and sprawling. It was a narrow road. The map did not show it.

Around the tank, looking back at it, they kept going. The moon did funny things to the landscape. The wind was higher, blowing the shadows—trees became animals and men, the shadows of walls were very deep. The vines came up out of their fields like bony arms, cold in the moonlight. You could see, and yet you couldn't see. And with the coming of the moon the silence was undermined by bullfrogs, whose echo announced the distant chorus of guns.

This cold yellow world of the moon was more lonely than darkness.

And in this sharply shadowed void the Lieutenant saw again the figure of Bowen, the lamb draped around his neck.

"Frank, what happened to Bowen, what did they do to him?"

Chiarello hesitated, watching the road. In the battalion no one mentioned Bowen.

"Nobody seems to know, Lieutenant. I wouldn't like to be the one to say. You know how it is. But sometimes he wasn't as crazy as he looked. Some of the boys were afraid of him."

"I know. But what—?" The other man cut him off.

"During the night he wasn't there. That was a bad night, everybody got too much wine. Maybe he was there, maybe he saw what happened. Maybe that's why he was so excited when he came around in the afternoon. I don't know. He started to preach, the way he was always doing. There was something he wanted the boys to do. I don't know Lieutenant, he sounded crazy as hell, but still—. Well, if he saw what went on that night he had a reason for going psycho. It was rough."

"Why, what happened?"

But Chiarello was concentrating on the road.

5

Another turn and they were surrounded by the crippled figures of very old olive trees. A clear moonlit grove. And then somewhere above them, cracking the glaze of the night, the short bursts of automatic weapons. Where? There. Above them, in moon-white silence on the hill, the exaggerated profile of high towers, squared and castellated, a medieval town. They were half-way up the narrow white road among the olives. A pot shot, from above. They swerved sharply to the side, jumped from the jeep into the ditch, and waited. Nothing. Listening. Nothing. Breaking the outline of the jeep with olive branches they left it and climbed toward the heavy walls of the town.

Through the huge arched gate they followed the narrow curving street, the houses high and dark on each side, the overhang of the roofs almost touching to shut out the moon. The rows of shutters and doors were closed; nothing showed, nothing moved; there was a smell of charcoal and olive oil and urine in the street, mixed with the damp stone smell of the old houses. They went one behind the other, fingering the tommy-guns, keeping to the shadow of the buildings. The street rose, dipped, passed through an archway, went down stone steps and opened into a big piazza, an indefinite space flood-lit by the moon. The towers dominated this space, big and cold under the moon. Somewhere on the other side some-one was speaking. Voices echoing, carrying. They stood in the shadow of this archway and watched.

In the piazza—maybe forty yards away—were twenty or thirty armed men. They were not in uniform. They looked like peasants setting out to hunt. They were sitting and stand-ing on a broad flight of steps that led up to a romanesque church—a huge winged creature in the moonlight—and they were arguing. Their guns were slung on their shoulders or across their backs, their arms and hands were moving in strong gestures. The two Americans listened to the voices echoing among the massive stones of the walls that formed the square.

"We're in luck, Lieutenant. Those guys are parti-sans."

For another moment they waited. "OK Frank, let's go. But don't wait to let them know who we are." They started across the moon-shining flagstones of the piazza; the talk stopped and the band of men turned to face them. Some of the guns were raised.

"Chi c'è?"

"Americani. Partigiani, voi?"

"Si. Partigiani. Ciao."

They came together and shook hands in the middle of the piazza. The two Americans were giants among these small men. For a moment longer some of the guns were held half-raised in surprise.

A burly, bearded man with a feather in his hat did the talking. They exchanged information, bit by bit. "Ma—da dove viene? Where do you come from? We did not expect you until tomorrow. You have come through the German rear guards. Why?"

Chiarello tried to explain. The Lieutenant looked at the circle of faces. He could not make out what they might have been. They might once have been anything—peasants, craftsmen, lawyers; one of them had the look of a priest. Whatever they had been, they looked like nothing but hunters now, men who had left the life of towns to hunt in the mountains and had never gone back. They had a leader, but no one of them was only a follower. On each face there was the confidence of a man who has made up his mind what his life is worth to him, and what he intends to use it for. They were not soldiers, as the Lieutenant had known them; they were not the operators of a machine. There was a more natural relation among them, face-to-face, as in a band of Indians. A unity, based on some passionate mutual concern. They stood on their own ground; they knew that ground, intimately, by way of their hands and feet.

The thickset man with the vigorous head and beard snorted and looked over his shoulder at the other side of the piazza. "And we," he said, "we have been fumigating this town. You see?" The Americans could see nothing but the broken windows and smashed shutters, the broken glass glittering under the moon.

They all laughed. The two strangers stood puzzled and uneasy. A voice from the back of the circle said, "Lupo— ask them if they can help us in the valley."

"Yes. Yes. We have an opportunity. It does not happen every day. A very fine target. Bellissimo. When you came we were discussing what we would do—but we are a small group here, there are too many of them, we were undecided. It must be done before morning—they will be moving. With your artillery perhaps . . . You have a radio? It is a very fine opportunity, a whole regiment . . ." Behind him they were murmuring in their eagerness as his voice rose.

"Where?"

Several of them turned and pointed toward the north. "There, on the far side of the hill. In the valley. They are there, we have seen them. They have stopped for the night. In the early morning they will be moving; there is not much time." The circle tightened, to hear what the response might be.

"Frank, go and get the jeep, will you. Get one of these guys to go with you and show you a way in here."

Chiarello took one of the partisans and left.

"We have seen the work of your artillery, Tenente. E magnifico. They are afraid of it, i tedeschi. They run from it. They—."

But what was that screaming? They turned slowly toward one of the streets that led into the piazza. Two men came dragging another who stumbled between them. He was still screaming, dragging his feet. They had to pull him across the big flagstones, his head hanging face down. What was it he was screaming? Only the words No, No, No came through to the Lieutenant. The others seemed to forget him as they turned to watch. They did not go toward the group of three. They waited. The three came closer and the cries bounced wildly from the thick stone walls. "No! No! I have done no wrong. Niente. Niente. You are my friends! You—. Giacomo! Aiuto! Help me."

Then the dragged man was quiet, letting his legs sag under him, his head hanging, as they dragged him forward, face down, one under each arm. The group turned in a semicircle, silent, to follow. He was dressed in a white shirt, well-cut gray trousers and delicate suede shoes, a man in his thirties with a magnificent head of black hair, bright in the moonlight.

The group moved, muttering and swearing, toward where the three had stopped near a row of shapeless bundles lined up at the side of the church steps. They were corpses. In the moonlight the captive's face was as white as the faces of the corpses. The pools of blood shone black. They moved together, dragging him again, to the other side of the broad steps where, on the big stones, were the naked bodies of three women. They stood him up here and one shouted, "Who are these women? Tell us, pig, fascist pig! Who are they?"

He stared down, the captive, and began to whimper prayers to the virgin. "They are friends of yours, pig?" "They are the virgins that you worship?" From all of them now wild shouts. "Chi sono? Chi sono, queste donne?" Who are these women? He shut his mouth and looked. He might once have known these women, but he had not done this thing.

He shivered and turned his face away. How could he say who they were? The faces had been made unrecognizable by the Germans, who had used these women when they occupied this town, and had mutilated them and thrown them away when they left. One man came up close, and under, and spat in the face of the captive. Another broke from the circle crying, to throw himself down at the feet of one of the corpses.

Out of the clamor came the bull voice of the leader. "Basta! Basta! There is work to be done. We are not here for speeches."

Nothing more was said. The two who were holding him let go and he fell, silent, to his hands and knees, his fingers clawing at the stones. They took a step back and the men standing over him raised the guns slightly and filled the white shirt with black holes. There was a final jerk of his legs. The blood ran out black on to the stones. They began to walk away. One man turned back with a shout to empty his automatic weapon into the staring white face.

The Lieutenant stood still, unable to move. He did not want to stand here alone, but he did not know which way to turn. He did not want to see their faces.

Someone standing near him said, "At first you do not know how to kill, but you learn." He turned. It was a woman, a young woman, dressed much like the others, in an open-necked shirt with a kerchief at her throat. Her face was clenched tight and her eyes were big with shock. It was a good face, the pure woman-face of this country, glad of its woman-quality, sure of it. She stared down at the shrinking body, the muscles of her thin face working—pain working against satisfaction. Her hand came up as if to touch the black hair with the life still crisp in it. Abruptly she turned to meet the eyes that were watching her. The Lieutenant looked into the darkness of her eyes, but he could read nothing there. She held for a moment, as if to compare the living face with the dead. Then she turned and walked slowly after the men. He watched her walk. She was no more than eighteen.

They gathered on the other side of the piazza under a sign that said TABACCHI, relaxed, sitting themselves down at the outdoor tables of the café. Someone went in and came out with two big bottles of wine. There were glasses on the tables. They passed the wine from table to table, raising the glasses in salutes. Above them were the arched windows of what had been a palace, with delicate columns. Set into the wall was the great crest of some branch of the Medici family, and above it rose the tower, without windows, only a few small openings to fire from, or to pour boiling oil on besiegers.

The partisans talked and laughed among themselves. One of them turned to the Lieutenant as he came up, and raised his glass. He spoke with care, the pure Italian of Siena. "Salute! Let us drink to this town. It has been made clean. It is fit to be lived in again." (He looked, as he spoke, like a musician or a painter.) He was smiling his satisfaction like the others.

The Lieutenant tried to match the smile and failed. He raised the glass, and drank, and tasted nothing, tasting the violence of the death he—. There was blood in the wine. He tasted blood. Alone, he sought a response in the faces around him. Nothing. Out of the snarl, the entanglements of three thousand years, things had suddenly become simple for them.

There was the necessity to kill, to destroy. To purify. And then they could start over again. In this fierce brilliance of purpose they could see everything, clearly. They could kill and laugh and drink and make love as they paused in their work. They were sure.

He drank with them but he did not know what to say to them. There was something he wanted to ask them but he could not get it clear. They were laughing. They who had showed him another kind of death, the separate identifiable death of a single man, who had been given a reason for his dying. He emptied his glass again and smiled at them. They did not see him—they were laughing and talking and showing their teeth. The vigor of their speech struck him and silenced him. His eyes moving from table to table, he looked for the girl, because she had seen what he had seen. She was standing near the door of the café; she had been watching him; he caught her eyes as she turned away. Had she been laughing with them, was she satisfied? He could not tell. She would not look at him. He watched her, to see what her face might show. But she held it closed, it showed nothing. She was a good-looking girl. He wondered about her. Her arms she held crossed over her breasts, the long fine hands clutching the shoulders. Had she killed someone? With those hands—.

6

They all looked up as Chiarello and the guide came across the square in the jeep. Immediately the talk stopped and they got ready. The leader stood up. "Francesco. Aldo. Lorenzo. You know the position. Go with the Tenente." There was a silence. The three who had been chosen got up and slung their guns. There was a lot of handshaking all around. Then the three went with the Americans in the jeep through the silent cobbled streets.

It was a small town, a maze cut into the hill. In a few minutes they were in another piazza on its north side; they had been climbing and now they were almost to the crest of the hill the town was built on. Out of this piazza they climbed a steep ramp-like street that went up past the moon-filled arches and columns of a small palace, then turned at a right angle and continued to climb up a narrow road walled in by cypresses that grew close together. The Italians did not say much; they rode tensed forward in expectation. They knew the ground foot by foot; they carried their weapons as a craftsman carries his tools.

Near the top of the rise they stopped the jeep where the trees ended and Chiarello hid it among some small pines. The Lieutenant and the partisans left him there with the radio and went ahead with a phone and some wire that would be their connection with him.

They climbed another fifty yards and the path ended abruptly. They were on the furthest edge of a high ridge that formed the northern limit of the town and looked down on the next valley to the north. The ridge was in the form of a crescent, a kind of high amphitheater that hung over the valley beyond, its center merging with the wall of the town and its wings extending out over the valley on either side of the town. They crept out along one of these wings a little way and settled themselves. It was as if they sat in one of those boxes in a theater that hangs almost directly over one end of the stage. Three hundred feet below them a thin mist snaked its way up toward the narrow end of the fan-shaped valley. Somewhere on the valley floor beneath the mist was what they had come for.

But the moon had gone down and the Lieutenant could not tell where they were or what it was like. The Italians were close to him in the darkness, whispering among themselves. They were up high, on the edge of some steep decline—that much he could sense—with only the deep bowl of darkness and mist in front of them. He did not want to ask them questions, it was their party. What he wanted at this moment was a good look at their faces; he had no idea what they looked like beyond the fact of their quick-moving gun-bearing silhouettes.

They crouched down here among the scrub oak. One of the partisans pointed toward the valley and whispered, "Ecco—they are down there. We have only to wait for the light." One of the others whispered, "From here one could paint a fine landscape. Una bella vista. È vero?" They laughed. The Lieutenant smiled and thought they were smiling but he could not really tell. He looked at his watch. They had about three hours to wait for the light. He picked up the phone and checked his connection with the jeep. Chiarello had already made contact with the battalion. There was excitement in his voice. "I gave them the coordinates off the map like you told me Lieutenant. They're all hopped up, they can't figure how in hell we got up here. They can't wait to hear what we've got."

"Tell them it's a Panzer Division with Kesselring himself. We don't want them holding back on us."

"Listen Lieutenant, if you told 'em it was only one guy with his pants down they'd let go with a hundred rounds they're so excited."

"OK Frank, keep them that way and keep your fingers crossed. I think we've got something. You'll hear from me."

18

The four men sat on the ground waiting, silent, looking into the blackness of the soft deceptive night. The warm west wind blew harder now. In and out of the wind the aroma of cypress; and nothing that they could see or hear.

Four men. Three men of this country and one foreigner, a man from an army that had come to fight in this country for reasons that were now abstractions. The weak and the strong, here acting together. In other places they had seen it otherwise, these three and this one: had seen the Americans in clumsy arrogance saying to the men of this country: We are stronger than you are, and you're goddamn well going to know it. You lose, we win. Get that straight. You goddamn wops.

Here on this ridge it was something else. The defeated were undefeated, fighting their own war in the spaces that the greater war had not filled. The stranger had watched them kill not in the crude clumsiness of rage, or in fear, or mechanically, but with the cool skill of men pruning trees. They were not drunk with it; they were deliberate and insistent. They had no big machines for killing—they had not much more than their hands. They worked with discrimination, as craftsmen. The Lieutenant was reminded of the French infantry he had seen—for them it was never a game.

It is like that with all the Europeans—the Germans as well. They take it seriously. It is never a game, played on impulse. Once begun, they keep at it, through pain and boredom and terror. For the good steady workmanlike job of killing—with a taste for the close-up, the knife, the bayonet—there is nothing like a European. War—like death—comes as no surprise to them, it is only an extension of their lives, a traditional necessity, what they had always expected. For the others, the strangers from the new world, each war was still something separate, special—the unique experience: secret adventure far from home, another life—a way out of that tedium of acquisition that had become a way of life. The Europeans have come beyond this, knowing it with such intimacy, from birth. To them it is the familiar: one war and then another, continuing.

And yet in these partisans there was something new; they did not simply acquiesce, they *made* war. Men of intelligence and energy, they had made a choice with their eyes open; they came up from the grave of their slaughtered country to fight another kind of war in their own way. Not plugging along the roads in the mud, to find relief in the occasional pleasure of destruction. Not moving blind in corporate masses to manufacture total destruction. They fight out of the need to live, to uprise: in small groups, to clear the ground, to cut out the diseased parts of their own bodies, to destroy a malignant growth with the knife, with fire. Pruning, for the sake of new growth. To atone. To bleed. But more than that: to rise again from the prison that had become a tomb.

It was there, in the serious dark faces of these three, in the intense forward pitch of their bodies. Waiting for the light, intent, with the eyes alive. And the stranger watching them, trying to make them out in the dark, with a kind of awe, never having seen anything like them: their savage concentration, the involvement of the whole self. The sure quick movements of the body and the head, charged with energy.

Some of these things the Lieutenant thought as he sat with them, some of it ran beneath thought in wordless images, making something move in him, rousing him. Disturbing him, because they were so sure, and in the face of their certainty he was not sure.

Between him and them there was not that simple understanding that exists among men who fight together. They were ready to fight alongside him, and yet they seemed to withhold something. They were content now to be silent and to wait, to neglect the things that lay unsettled between themselves and the stranger. But for him it was not enough. There was something he wanted from them. And the wind blowing in forty miles from the sea—it was up now, strong, giving them the cover of its sound so that there was no risk in speaking.

2

So he would have spoken, if he had known how to begin with them. They were somewhere beyond his reach. He would have laid a hand on the arm of the man next to him, if he could. But he was unsure. He stood up, walked to the edge and looked down. Nothing. He walked back and sat down again. He tried to see their faces but could not.

Of the three, two were middle-aged and one was young. The oldest, the one they called Francesco, might once have been a doctor, or a teacher. Out of the dark he was speaking:

"You like our country, Tenente?"

"Yes." He turned on his side to face them, though they were no more than dark forms of men. "Yes. It is very beautiful. I cannot tell you how much I like it." His Italian came slowly, in formal rhythms. There was more he would have said but the words came too slowly.

"It was most beautiful. When we have made it beautiful again you must come back to see it."

"I have thought many times of coming back."

"You have learned our language. In America?"

"No, here, in Italy. Your language pleases me very much. The sound of it . . . I do not speak it well enough."

"But yes, you speak it well enough for a beginning. Not all your soldiers speak it as well." He was smiling faintly, in resignation. But the Lieutenant could not see his smile. "Ah, but they have no need to speak it, eh?—They are strange men, your countrymen."

"It is true, they do not learn—. But that is the way it is with soldiers. They do not want to be here, they—."

"Yes, it is true, Tenente, but—. Why do you hate us in this way? Why?"

"No—. It is not that. It is not all of us who . . . They do not hate you. They—They do not understand."

"They hate us. We feel it. Even when we fight at their side . . . Yes, they will make use of us, they will send our men on their most dangerous patrols. And then they will spit on us." His voice was quiet, precise—but even in the darkness the other could feel the strong movement of his mouth, the eloquence of his gestures. "They do not want to understand. They do not want to look at us. Only to believe that we are a poor and cowardly people. They spit on us, Tenente." *Sputano*. The word itself carried insult. But he spoke in sadness, not in anger.

The Lieutenant grasped for words. "It is because they do not understand what is happening in Italy."

"They do not know. Nothing. They do not know that we are fighting the fascists and the Germans all over Italy.

They do not know that we fight the Tiger Tanks with our bare hands in the streets of Milan. They are not told this. We fight to redeem ourselves. But what do they care. Why do they fight? Why is it that they are not able to care?"

The others had said nothing. Now Aldo, the young one, was speaking. "It is why our people said Yes to Mussolini. He said to them, The world spits on you, but with me as your leader they will learn to respect you. And in that he was right. He was right."

"He was not right, Aldo. No. But he knew we had had enough of this contempt, of this humiliation. You understand, Tenente? And he made use of this knowledge. The Italians are not a warlike people, but for this they went to war. For respect." He stopped and drew breath. "And now we fight, we partisans, because we have been dead and in hell and we must rise again in order that we may live."

There was a pause. They waited for the Lieutenant's reply. But he had none.

The older man went on. "It did not happen as Mussolini intended it, but it has happened in any case. It has begun. We are beginning to respect ourselves again . . . Do you understand? We will make something here in Italy, Tenente, that the world must respect. Even the Americans . . . There is great strength in the Italian people—and it is not the strength of the soldier, but another thing. We will take this strength and free it from the hands of the exploiters and we will make a new country. A new life. More new than America—."

The young man broke in. "New! You understand? Because first we will make it clean. We will destroy—. You understand? We are not afraid. As you have seen it in the piazza—." His voice throbbed in its heat and rose to strike again.

The third voice, silent until now, stopped him with one word. "Basta!" Enough! Making a sharp silence.

From which the older man went on in his controlled urgency. "The Italians have suffered. They have learned. We have learned! We have been down as low as men can get. We have been humiliated. But we have learned something. And now—."

He stopped speaking. His breath came fast,—the silent man, the one they called Lorenzo, had leaned over to grip his arm, to cut him short. He said, "Francesco—we are not here to talk."

But the older man was not finished. "We are like the drowning man who has gone down twice and has then, by willing to live, found his strength. He frees himself of fear. He rises. And he saves himself. Himself! Do you understand?"

Lorenzo spoke again, still with that remoteness that was almost indifference. "Perhaps for the Lieutenant it is not an easy thing to understand . . ."

But the Lieutenant did not feel the cold breath of the untalkative man, so moved was he by their hope, their passion. So much moved that he could only say, "Yes. Yes. I understand—. I—" and rake his mind for words for the exhilaration he felt, for the rush of blood. Like the blind man who opens his eyes to see, and sees; and shouts his new vision, only to find that those who are with him are deaf and cannot tell. Words came in an uprushing like bubbles from the blood, hot; and evaporated . . . He knew no way to match their passion, or to respond to it.

They expected no response from him. He was an American. He was the outsider against whom they could test the sound of their hope, of what they had learned. And there was the need to hit him with it, to see his surprise. They did not expect him to understand.

The older man was speaking again, a fluid streaming

of words. "The Italian people are builders. Craftsmen. They
have been wasted. For the sake of money. Of paper. Their
reality lies in their hands, in the work of their hands. We have
been prisoners here. In our own country. You understand?
Prisoners. Not only with Mussolini, but for a long time before
him. We have spent our time quarreling among ourselves—and
submitting. Allowing ourselves to be wasted, to be eaten, for
the sake of a few who have lived off our flesh. Masters and
slaves. Servants who were glad of the chance to be servants.
Agh—we have been blind. Servants of men who did not believe in their country or their people. Great landowners. Cor-
rupt fox-hunters. By what right?—But we have learned. There
will be no more submission. Now, already, hope has begun to
rise among us, in the midst of ruin—and the energy that comes
with hope. Such energy as Europe has not seen in five hundred
years."

His voice had been rising, insisting, a cry of defiance.
And now he steadied suddenly and said, "We are ready. We
have made plans. We are together, even the priests and the
communists have come together—, not Rome, not the ruin and
the lust for power, but the priests who are of the people, who
work with their hands." He paused for breath; his voice fell.
"Lorenzo. This man. You must not think badly of him. Listen,
I will tell you about him, you must understand. He is an architect, a good one, who has never built a house. Nothing. When
he was young there was no work for him, and when he was
older he would not work for the fascists—. But soon he will
be able to work. We will build. We will waste nothing."

"You think we are crazy, Tenente?" It was Aldo,
who had been a railway worker. "You think we only know
how to talk—?"

"No. I like what you say. I have needed to hear it.
It gives me—. I did not know these things. Lo credo. I believe
it. I understand it. Yes. Lo credo."

"When the Germans came we were like the others, Tenente. I did my work on the railway. It was all I knew. And then we escaped to the mountains, and we have lived together, and we have come to understand. Many thousands of us. We have talked about these things, and we have agreed. We know what is necessary. You will see . . ."

The two voices, the older and the younger, hammered the darkness with the strong rhythms of their belief, and the Lieutenant listened, stretched out on the ground; listened and sought responses that would make them see that he was with them; grateful that he had been brought to this place to hear these voices, that filled him like music.

But the one called Lorenzo was not with them; he had turned away and sat apart. Once more he had tried to stop their talk, and had failed, and walked away. Now he came back and sat down again close to the others. "You will excuse me, Tenente. I am glad that you are here with us—there is work we must do together. But I must say what needs to be said to my comrades here. They are wrong to talk of these things to you. You cannot be expected to understand them. You have not seen what we have seen. You come from a place where people cannot understand these things that we have come to understand. In Rome and Naples your military government, your—Do you know what they are doing? Agh!" He spat on the ground. "My own brother, he is in New York. He knows nothing. He has become like a child. He makes money. I want to laugh. In a letter he wrote to me, he told me, I am a man here, I am making money. Do you hear? He is making money. Money. Is that what a man *makes* in your country? Is that the way—?"

"Lorenzo, you are not fair to the Tenente. He is not to blame—. He is interested. He is with us. È simpatico."

The other shrugged and turned away to the edge

of the steep rise on which they waited. He looked into the black space of the valley, impatient for the light.

The professor went on. (What is he, the Lieutenant thought, if he is not a professor?) "He is an angry man, our friend Lorenzo. He is afraid—."

They heard him move, a growl in his throat—and he was saying, his voice harsh, piercing, "I am afraid, Tenente, that your leaders, the stupid vulgar men of your military government, do not understand the Italians. I am afraid that they will go on spitting on us. To them we are dirty irresponsible beggars. They are going to teach us a lesson. Yes. I am afraid that they will try to strangle us before we have had a chance to speak. They would like to make us over in their own image —as in Rome and Naples and wherever else they have come with their cans of spaghetti. Agh! Their pleasure is to rule over us. To teach us. Hah! To be our teachers, eh Francesco? From the new world. Our teachers. But we are not interested in your way, Tenente. Your kind of freedom. What you *make*."

He stopped short, breathing heavily. "What is it, your liberty, this word that you speak as if it belonged to you? It is the right to do whatever does not harm another. That is what you mean. Which means to do nothing for the general good, which is the same as to act against the general good. But it is even less than that—it is the freedom to loot and steal, and call it profit. But to make profit is to steal. To buy cheap and sell dear. It is war. Your country is always at war, it has no peace. And the idea of a just price—you have never even heard of it." He got up and walked away, then came back and stood over them.

"We were blind once, like you, but now we see. The waste, each man grabbing what he needs to live, and then more, because he is afraid of starving and so he can never have enough. That is a war, each man against every other man. To grab, and to defend himself by wealth from the grabbing of others. It is disorder . . . preying on one another. And calling it freedom. In a poor country we cannot afford that kind of freedom, that waste. We will not live like cruel children. No. We are finished with it!"

In the darkness his mouth, the force of it, spitting, the explosions of his eyes, could only be felt. And they were felt. The air around him was charged with his heat, the vibrations of his anger. The Lieutenant listened; he listened as he had never listened. The words reached him, surrounding him, piercing. The downbeating wave of words caught him and spun him around and pushed him down into disorder: a wave into a waterfall into a whirlpool. *Where am I? What do I believe? What can I say?*

He said nothing; listening. The voice—low pitched, softening—moved in the darkness, circling; moved the clear round sounds of the Italian; repeating—with variations; the heart beating in the voice; the voice expanding in larger and larger circles. *Uomo. Montagna. Ponte. Battaglia. Lupo. Fratello. Risorgimento.* The sharp consonants, the wide-open vowels moving in pulsations of anger and belief; moving, encircling.

The fine-pointed energy of the man, the voice. The knife-edge; the trueness of it. The open assertion.

My God, here is a man—.

On the long swelling wave of the voice the Lieutenant was lifted, high—and dropped. The voice rising, breaking, exploding.

Under the force of the voice the Lieutenant went down, slowly turning over; went deep down, and came up far from where he had gone down. The voice had stopped.

In the silence the resounding of the words created an order, as music creates an order. The war, its disorder, was replaced by this order. Like music the words of the angry man buoyed him, gave him back the will to believe. That they could go on from the war to make something new. That the dying was worth something. He believed it. It repeated itself in him like a song. The words sang themselves over to his own music, singing in the blood, in the bones, in the nerves, in the mind. Echoing from the bottom of his soul, his own song sounded in him.

He listened. Strength welled up in him with which to confront the strength of the Italians. They remained sitting in silence.

He thought the silence was for him, for his reply. The uprising of hope in him made the words erupt from him. "No. You are wrong. I believe as you do. But in this you are wrong. It is the same in my country. The war—. There has been an awakening. They believe. Things will be different. It has begun. The war—." But what could he say, against the resounding of that other music? That voice rolling in on him, over him. "In America—." His voice rose, fell, fell away in him; from earnestness into nothingness in a vertigo of not-knowing. Did he know anything about it? Had he not floated without question all his life? From sea to shining sea. A democracy. A new deal. A big country. I am an American. Opportunity. America is this. Or that. Jobs. We are going to—what?

They were listening, waiting. He began again, but the words turned on him. He was not ready for this: since Naples he had impressed his mind to the service of the machine. He had gone along, for the ride, the movement, the sights—like any tourist. In search of other worlds. And here he was—almost without the power of speech. And yet there was something he would have said. Dimly the song echoed in his head. How did it go? My country—. He wanted to shout at them, to tell them it was not as simple as they thought. But it was dark—an alien darkness—, and he was not sure where he was or where he had come from; the darkness was everywhere around them and strangely quiet, and he could not see their faces. He wanted to tell them. But he could not form it—he had been numb and passive for too long, one of millions, an employee of a corporation.

"My country—you do not understand it." He spoke into the darkness, without strength.

The others held to their silence, having said what they needed to say—satisfied. They shifted on the ground to get comfortable, content now to wait for the light. They had learned their patience in hiding.

The Lieutenant moved around in the darkness, he could not sit still. He could still feel the sureness and heat of the voice in the darkness, in this silence; and he could hear, somewhere in himself, the faint intimations of another voice—his own, yet not his own—and what it might say. But it was not enough. He wanted them to know that he was with them; he wanted them to know that he knew why he was here. He wanted to tell them that he loved their country—and to free himself, in the telling, into an ardor like theirs.

He shifted to fit his body to the ground but it did not feel right to him, he could not settle himself to wait. It was not his, this ground. It was theirs. As much as he had come to care for it, it was not his. He was uneasy, with nothing to say; he could not believe that they were not waiting for him to speak.

In some sense a soldier must know the ground he fights on—and of this place he knew nothing. And of his own place—what was there that he could be sure he knew of it? Now. What, beyond the facts of an army that was, for a time without limits, his whole life now? Home—it had become part of a dream, a fantasy, for him as for the others who fought only to go home. To go back. Against the clear lines of these men's hopes it had all the irrelevance of a dream. And what, finally, is there to say about a dream?

It was not his, and these men were not with him, and he did not know where he was. The night dragged on. Embedded in this night, in its silence and formlessness, he came to feel in its darkness that he was nowhere, that the night itself was a place he had come to, that these men were of the night, that it had nothing to do with him.

No Man's Land. The words stood up in his mind like an electric sign advertising a movie. He tried to make himself laugh at them. Yet they stopped him cold, he went on looking at them, extending the moment of fear. The fear came and went, like the pulsations of pain.

Before he knew it he was listening for any sounds the others might make, asking himself, Do they trust me? And answering, No. Were they smiling together there in the darkness, knowing themselves to be the stronger? He came to feel that he might as well be alone. They were making use of him. They did not take him seriously. He was only another of those who fight aimlessly to go home. He listened. He heard an arrogance in their silence.

When the light came, where would he be? Maybe they had gone too far forward. Maybe there was some hill there above them in the dark, occupied by the Germans, who at daybreak would be there, on top, looking down at them. (Hasn't this all been too easy?) In a little while he was sure that they were being watched—somewhere above them were hunters who hunted the hunters. What did the sound of the wind conceal?

The partisans spoke a few words to each other, but too low and quick for him to understand. Then another long silence. And then the voice of the older man, asking, "What is it like in America, Tenente? We have heard so many things."

Instantly the Lieutenant began to speak, not knowing what would come. Here was one at least of this other world who wanted to know.

"It is hard to say. In my country—. There is so much of it. In a new country there are many things that might happen. Nothing is fixed. In a way your friend is right. We have been through a bad time. But it will be better now. Something is happening—the war—people learn. They speak to one another. Even strangers. There is something they want, there is something they expect from the war. Not just to go back. Something new. It is not only in your country that it is happening." As he spoke his hopes flowered, like tulip bulbs coming to life out of darkness. From the bottom of the well of his mind up came refreshment. "You can feel it. Everywhere. People coming together, asking questions, listening. When we go back it will be different. We have learned something . . . Like you."

"I have talked to your soldiers," Lorenzo said. "They are not all so sure as you are. They are not sure that there will be work for them. That is all they think about—that, and their contempt for us. And the others—. Remember, the war has not touched them in America. Nothing. *Niente*. Not a scratch. Not one city."

"Yes—. No. You are wrong. That is too simple." In the act of speaking, on the edge of anger, he found certainty. "The war has touched everything. Everywhere. If I could tell you . . ."

"We are listening."

"Then I will tell you." He said it with heat, pushing against the sharp edge of the questioning voice that made him uncertain even as he began to speak. "America is still new. It is something unknown to you. There is a freshness. It is open, full of possibilities. We are only at the beginning. There is something—. It is not easy to understand."

"Some countries," Lorenzo said, "age faster than others. Already you have become old and fat and tired. And now in the war you eat much and the fat comes . . ."

The Lieutenant turned from him to the older man and spoke quickly in pursuit of certainly. "It is wide open. Anything can happen. There is great energy." He made the effort to believe. He believed. He insisted and they listened quietly.

The heat came up in him. He found words. He told them of the Unions and of the changes that had come in the thirties. The fights that had been fought . . . once and for all. It would never be the same . . . The hard thrust of their challenge had thrown him off balance. But now he moved closer to them, speaking steadily. His hope—his song—was as strong as theirs. And yet—. It did not take shape as theirs did. He wavered, and then insisted.

Lorenzo was saying, "No, I have seen something else. I have seen your soldiers. I have watched them. They do not know where they are, or why they are here. They are without thoughts. They have no idea of themselves as a people. A formless mass—. Europe does not exist for them. To our women they boast of a job that pays much money, and of cars. They want only to prove to us, by force, that they are better than us, that we are conquered and that we must beg from them—. That is their great pleasure, that we should cringe and beg and offer them our women—"

"You are wrong. No!" The Lieutenant flared up with a force that surprised them. "You are wrong. You are full of bitterness. These are half-truths. You cannot understand my country. You are buried under your own history."

They murmured to one another. The interplay, the heat of it, was suspended in silence, in waves that moved back and forth between them, the three and the one. He waited, but they said nothing. He went on speaking, climbing the steep sounds of his own voice that urged him on, seeking footholds in the shifting sands of his mind, slipping—. He could not stop: by the sound of his voice he knew who he was. But it was all uphill. He would see for a moment clear particles in the sand, but always they sank into the morass before he could grasp them. Yet his voice was charged, it held them, and he went on, trying to break the darkness with it, trying to locate himself by it. "Soldiers are all the same. Away from home— Something is coming, change—   After the war—   My country—." Heat that gave rise to a kind of luminosity, and held them listening.

But in the end it was not much good. He had talked too much. And it did not answer the question they were asking (without ever using the words): Who is the stronger, you or us? The weak and the strong. Always the need to make a comparison. He knew of no way of saying to them, "You do not have to prove anything to me, I believe you." And yet, as he talked, they went on trying to prove it. What did they think he was? Couldn't they see he was with them?

A ledge on a steep hillside. Four men. Below them a lake of darkness in a valley. For them—the three—the known; for him, the unknown. For him too much darkness, too much time, too many words. A morass. The night had begun with pure motion, the jeep moving in and out of the hills. And now it had come to this, to talk, not knowing if he himself believed what he said to them. What was he trying to prove?

In motion it had been simple: the impulsive body taking over from the mind, taking the burden of decision—the body alert, eager, freed of the static routine. First the pure motion, up and down hill; then the darkness coming, and fear with it, making another kind of excitement; then the towers on the hill and the mystery of the dead-silent town, the precise vigor in the killing of the man in the white shirt, the dark climb to the vantage point, the rapture of their expectation, their resurrection—. And now this talk, having waited too long for the morning; in this confusion of words to be sitting here looking down into the dark valley, not knowing what the light would show. The waiting was too slow, too deliberate, too much a calculation. There was too much of stealth in it. And probably by morning there would be nothing in the valley anyway. These partisans were overeager, they exaggerated. A latin fault, wasn't it, this flair for the dramatic that went with their courage? Like something from an Italian opera, he thought.

For what seemed like hours the night was very still, as if they had somehow broken through the circle of fire and left the war behind. As the wind shifted it carried the song and the cry of birds, and then changed again to bring the droning of frogs. But later they could not hear these sounds: somewhere the war had begun again, or it had re-encircled them, and seemed to spread toward them until they could hear the chatter and rumble of guns behind them and on either side. And from the north, toward the Arno, came the sporadic boom of the demolitions as the Germans left monuments of rubble for the Italians to remember them by.

On the horizon a great pyramid of flame roared up. None of them knew what it was. It might have been the death of Florence. (The days and the nights were full of rumors, of sudden immense eruptions.) The partisans could not take their eyes off it. The flower. Florence, the center of their world. Their faces tightened. The flames fused into a pillar of fire. They said nothing.

The Lieutenant watched it burn, and it gave back to him that sense of the chase, the Germans running, destroying as they ran. Soon now it would be over—. And as the fire faded and the circle of darkness was complete again his mind jumped back to the living black hair of the dead man left behind them in the piazza, the white shirt open at the neck. The suede shoes. Who was he? And jumped again to the face of the girl in the piazza who had watched him die. *At first you do not know how to kill, but you learn.* Her face became the face of the girl in another world who wrote letters. One who had seen it all, and the other who had seen nothing. And the other, the wife of the hanged man in the street of Naples where he had lived, where the lamppost was. She had been like a wife to him and he had almost forgotten her.

The uncertain sounds of the war seemed to move with the wind all around them, now closer, now further away. This ridge on the far edge of the hill town—an island in a sea of war. Other islands, volcanic, hidden in the sea. From their eruptions, tidal waves, to sweep over this island. And below, in the valley—. For the first time it occurred to the Lieutenant that the valley might be full of men, that there might be thousands of them. Germans. Perhaps the partisans had understated it, so that he should not hesitate. They were fanatics, they would tackle anything. He was up against an unknown, like the hunter lost in a jungle.

Why, you stupid bastard, he thought, what are you trying to scare yourself with? Relax. They know what they're doing.

But as the night deepened to its final darkness there came moments when he felt more like a hunted animal than an armed man. He held the tommy-gun in his lap, and from time to time he gave the line of the telephone a tug, as if he half expected it to have been cut. He thought of Chiarello alone in the jeep on the other end of the line. And of the battalion, where the night crews sat waiting by the long guns, safe, miles away.

There was the sound of heavy breathing, an alternating rhythm. Two of the partisans slept.

19

And then the crying began, much louder than the distant guns. It was somewhere below them in the valley. It was a very young child crying and crying and crying. A child? A lamb? It went on steadily, rising to them. Sharp and clear, as if very close, and then far away. The sound of fear.

First one and then the other of the sleeping men was jerked from sleep.

"What is it?"

"It is a child?"

"A lamb."

"A lamb?"

"Yes. Down there. When the people of the valley went into the hills they must have forgotten him."

And yet it did not always sound like a lamb. It might have been a wounded man.

"It will be light soon. A half-hour, no more."

They looked at their watches.

They were silent, on edge, seeming to strain their eyes for the first hint of light. It came, leaking in over the hills, dissolving the night. The crying went on. They peered down into the valley but they could see nothing yet. They began to be able to see one another's eyes.

The Lieutenant did not want to ask them again what was down there, how many. So he said, "How did you find them?"

"Find them? Who?"

"Them. Down there."

Francesco answered. "What do you mean? They were there—yesterday evening. They destroyed the bridge at Castelnuovo and came from there along the road. We saw them from the hills. We—"

Lorenzo broke in. "L'uomo è cacciatore."

The Lieutenant did not understand. "Man is a—?"

The long somber face of the architect had begun to brighten with anticipation as the light began to come. He smiled, repeating. "L'uomo è cacciatore. Capito?"

The Lieutenant picked up the words and went over them one at a time. "Man—is—a—"

"Cacciatore." Aldo raised his gun and moved it like a man tracking a bird.

"Hunter? Ah. Si. Capito. Cacciatore. Man is a hunter."

The three faces were smiling into his, nodding, amused at the surprise they saw there. Or was it confusion they saw, and the remains of fear?

Francesco said, "It is a saying we have in our country. È vero, eh?"

The Lieutenant looked from face to face, and smiled with them, suddenly liking them again, glad to be with them. He felt better, as if he had been lost and now knew where he was, and why he was here.

Man is a hunter. These were hunters, these three. Yes. And there was strength and simplicity in the unity they formed together. They were sure of one another—and sure of something that they could make together. Hunters on a new frontier.

The Lieutenant was caught by the sound of the words. He spoke them again, "L'uomo è cacciatore." And the others said, Si, Si, and smiled their agreement. They accepted him as a hunter like themselves. They were men, each of them was the substantial figure of a man, with his own face, his own voice, and they knew—. The thought came to him suddenly: That he would rather fight the war with them than go back to the battalion. And that he could do it, if—.

And then they realized that they could see one another clearly—too clearly. There was light. They threw themselves prone on the ground and lay still for a moment. Then they crawled through the brush on their bellies to the edge and looked down.

They could see nothing. Higher up, the sun—still hidden—had edged the outlines of the encircling hills, and on the slopes the gray-green of the olive trees looked like great folds of moss rolling down. Below them the valley was deep in mist, that moved in swirls as it broke up.

The Lieutenant raised his head to look around. The ledge they were lying on curved out over the valley to merge with the slopes on its western side, to their left. The town was piled on the broken hilltop behind them and to their right. Almost directly behind them, along the small climbing road they had followed, was the wall of the cemetery, the monuments white behind a screen of tall cypresses. Further back the high square medieval towers stood up close together, dark and severe in this light. Where the ledge curved back to merge into the steep bluff at this edge of the town the old castle stood, a miniature of the great gothic palazzi of Florence and Siena, complete to the strong slender tower and the castellations. Where they lay, the ledge projected from the hill over the valley like the boxes in a theater that hang over one end of the stage.

About a mile away, across the valley to the east, was the line of hills that enclosed it on that side, terraced and cultivated below and bare higher up. The valley was almost a semicircle at this end, narrowing in a funnel-shape as it ran away toward the interleaved hills that closed it off to the north. From this part of the ledge, as from the town, a steep incline ran down to the valley floor, perhaps seven hundred feet below.

The mist below them was moving fast now, thinning as the light wind drove it up the valley. The four pairs of eyes pried at it, and as it broke open to show patches of olive grove they came up on their knees, forgetting concealment, breathing hard with their mouths open. The lamb was crying desperately; they were not listening to it now. The sun was not yet up over the eastern hills but there was pale green light in the sky; and there were holes in the mist as it opened and closed. They caught glimpses of a large country house, peasant cottages, some wagons and what looked like a long open sports car. Down there it was still closer to night than day, the mist absorbing the light. Nothing moved. The young partisan rose to one knee. "They are gone. We have lost them." He swore.

"Down, you fool! Lie down!" Lorenzo grabbed him by the ankle.

The lamb went on crying, seeming to call to them; and they looked for it, though they could not hope to find it. They were not sure that it was a lamb. The mist opened for a moment, and closed again. Again it sounded like a wounded man, out of control.

Something moved among the olive trees behind the old villa. The Lieutenant, kneeling, leaned back to pull the field glasses from the case slung at his side. He raised them, waiting. The mist thinned . . . He thought he saw a large white ox, still hitched to a plow, alone. It waited, in absolute stillness—abandoned, a figure meant for a sacrifice. It waited for the plowing to begin again.

The partisans went down flat on their bellies again, side by side, as the light increased. They had no glasses—but from the edge they stared down, tensed forward as if they would tear at the mist with their hands. The Lieutenant lay down beside them, still searching the mist through the glasses, saying to them: "A villa. An ox. A car."

The older man said to him, "It is a Medici villa." He was cooler than the other two, his voice still quiet and controlled. They could begin to see details of the house—the low delicately balanced mass of a Renaissance country house: the great iron gates, arched windows with columns, and the columns repeated around a central court; the ripe tiles of a sharp-angled roof. The great stone shield that was the Medici crest. Rising and dipping around the house, the shallow slopes of olives and vines. A fountain, a balustrade, box hedges, statues. The open loggia supported by slender columns; the deep-shading overhang of the roof. Everywhere, ripeness.

There was sadness in the way the older man said again, "A very old house, Tenente." The other two said nothing, stretched forward in search of something else.

There was no color in anything yet, only blacks and grays. A solid dark line of cypress separated the house from the row of peasant cottages and the farm buildings. A gray stone wall. A well. A statue. A garden. Serenity. Established. Rooted. Carved and fitted to the ground. Enclosed—a world of its own.

The Lieutenant moved the glasses, to find the ox again: its great white stillness held him. He swung them slowly in an arc, searching the ground—.

And they were there, dim bundles of men sleeping on the ground under the olive trees. When the mist opened he could see them. But the partisans, without glasses, could not see them. He moved the glasses over the grove. They were men. It surprised him. He had not believed in the end that they would be there. Under every tree. Here and there he could see feet sticking out from the rolls of blanket. The Germans. He felt a quiver in his groin. He said nothing, watching them. The men under the trees still slept. Nothing moved. Around them were wagons, German army wagons. And not far away, horses. And near the house the long black sports car. One of the horses rolled, kneeled, stood up. Listening. (Was it the crying of the lamb he heard?)

The partisans were talking among themselves, making what sounded like quarreling sounds. Side by side on the ground. He could feel Lorenzo's body next to him, tense, expectant. He turned his head and passed the glasses to him, saying, "Ecco—i tedeschi. Sotto gli ulivi." Lorenzo turned to him and looked at him in surprise. He raised a hand to push back the wave of dark hair from his forehead and began to say something; and stopped himself. *The Germans. Under the olive trees.*

The glasses were passed from hand to hand, then given back, with looks of satisfaction and congratulation. They said nothing as he began again his searching of the valley, but he could feel their impatience. It was like hunger. They were watching the valley floor again as if there were food or women there that they must have, now. The Lieutenant did not like it. He did not want to be hurried.

The sky was very clear, and now the brighter light began to come over the hills, catching and glistening on the wet upper surfaces of trees and houses. The Lieutenant went on playing the glasses over the valley, trying to control his excitement as he began to make calculations. He had the map on the ground in front of him. The glasses formed circular frames around the objects in the valley, making small still-lifes in great detail as they picked out pieces of equipment, mess tins, pieces of clothing hung on the trees. It was a ragbag assortment, the bivouac badly organized—the German discipline was beginning to go. They were sleeping too close together under the trees, more like refugees than soldiers. Probably they had thought the olive trees to be sufficient concealment, and they were almost right. Anyone looking down from the town would not have seen them, they were visible only from this oblique angle made by the projecting ledge. And beyond that they must have thought themselves protected by the rear guard positions, for this night anyway. They seemed to have broken their flight abruptly and thrown themselves down in their exhaustion. It was a resting place, a temptation—it would have been that to any soldier who had been on the run for weeks. It was green and soft and settled, a place that seemed to lie beyond killing or being killed.

The wagons—. They were loaded as if these were some kind of wealthy refugees, with treasures grabbed here and there at the last moment. Even in their flight they could not resist the chance to loot, to make a profit. To cover their losses. Or was it to the further glory of the Fatherland? The usual stuff—mattresses, blankets, fur coats, silk shirts, odds and ends, leather suitcases, a steamer trunk—anything. What was strange was that there was no sign of a weapon.

A cock crowed. The Italians moved restively on the ground, their eyes gripping what lay before them, as if to keep it from moving.

The Lieutenant got his mind back on the job. He felt their impatience, their eagerness for him to begin. But he was not ready, and he did not like to be rushed. He made the effort to be deliberate, checking the map against the ground, checking the coordinates on the map again. He reminded himself to ask for one or two smoke shells to begin, and to shift to air-burst afterwards because ordinary detonation fuse would plow too deep into this soft ground. By the use of time-fuses the shells could be made to burst just above the trees and spray downward like a shower of hot knives. He made what rough measurements he could on the ground, so that he would be able to adjust the fire quickly after the initial round and bring in the massed fire of the battalion before they could disperse.

He worked slowly. Something held him back, some dim uncertainty. But he worked. He checked the map again, and the lay of the valley.

He felt good. The night was over; it was going to be a beautiful morning. The night's fear was gone, and the confusion with it. He knew what had to be done. He knew how to do it. The unknown of the night was becoming known piece by piece. Below them the valley was spread out, still dim and vaporous like some Chinese landscape. They were on top of it—it was like holding it in the palm of your hand. It made him feel light and strong. His eyes, very sure and alert, moved to grasp the pieces, to assemble them. To form the outlines of the target.

He worked deliberately, making his calculations. The big shells were not to be wasted. They were watching him, intent, beside him—their excitement still feeding his own. They were hard, concentrated, their heads thrust forward. Waiting. He glanced at them for a moment and smiled to himself. He would show them something—.

Lifting himself slightly he looked around at the hills above the valley, pink and gold with the first flush of light. It was very still, very beautiful. He turned his head and said, "È bella." He said it in a sure slow voice, to let them know that he was in control, that he knew what he was doing.

At first they did not seem to have heard him. Then Lorenzo replied, "È bellissima." But they never took their eyes off the house and what surrounded it.

He went on searching the ground, so that he should miss nothing. He had not slept but he knew that he was functioning well—his body quick and his heart beating steadily against the earth, with the hunter's alertness. His eyes adjusted to the slow change of light. He did not need to think now: as he assembled the pieces of the target his tightsprung mind worked with the body, as a part of it, merged in action with it, as in the act of love. The good hunter; he becomes a part of the natural world; he lets the body take over, and it knows what to do.

And yet, underneath his mind, or whatever part of him was registering these things, something in him was disturbed. Off center. Something was not right. It was like the uneasiness of a man who has taken a wrong road, and half knows it, but goes on, trying not to care.

2

The lamb is crying again. Its cry pierces him and sends a shiver through his body. But this passes. He goes on with his deliberate search of the valley. To find out what is down there, how many, if there are others in some other place further away from the house. He wants to do this thing well. They are watching him. He must do it well. But there is no hurry. He had worked hard to learn this skill—and he was going to show them something.

He cannot find the lamb (if it is a lamb)—the valley shifts and changes in a confusion of darkness, mist, and light. Enlarged in the glasses, half-veiled: the house, the farm, the olive trees. The ox. All as if abandoned. Then were those men he had seen? Still nothing moves. But a cock crows, and again, and again. And it becomes easier to see now. He lies loose on his stomach, his elbows propped before him, moving the glasses slowly, point to point, taking his time. Hesitating. Go-

ing on. The valley is criss-crossed with paths, where the culti-
vators of the ground have walked for three thousand years.
Many of the paths lead toward the house, which is one with
the ground and grows out of it. It is all worked out in time,
from the Etruscan house with its high color down to these
muted shades of honey. The land squared and terraced—all of
it made with the hands. Through three millennia, until it is
worked deep, the work of man become a part of nature. It is
formed, it grows; men are born out of it, to take its form.

And now the blunt mechanical hands of the Germans laid on it. The thought disgusted him.

There is a faint radiance on the mist as it rises, on
the olive leaves and on the deep protecting angles of the roofs,
the green-gold lichen color beginning to come in the tiles.

At the center a sharp movement and the stillness is
broken. Through an arched doorway of the house a German
officer comes into the arcaded courtyard, moving in that stiff
angular way they have, in the close-fitting uniform. The uniform is dirty and torn, but the hands holding the stick, the
clipped thin head on the tight neck are tough and assured.
Through the glasses he comes very close; it is almost as if he
could reach out and touch him.

Around the corner of the house come two sergeants
in jack-boots, each carrying a small sub-machine gun. There is
no ceremony but there is obedience in their stance. It is a style,
they know how to play the parts. They get their orders and
stride away toward the olive trees below the house. The
officer takes a quick look around, turns to look at the house in
the half-light, and goes back through the doorway.

The Lieutenant goes on looking at the house, surprised—surprised finally that they are men, and that they are
there, under his hand. And that they do not know he is here,

above them, watching. This is the hunter's pleasure: the seeing without being seen. They are so close, and so sure of themselves. A smile broke on his face. He kept it to himself. But—. The smile faded as he made the soldier's automatic calculation: If they see you they will try to kill you. You have seen them first. Now hide yourself.

And with this he knows himself to be alone, as any soldier is alone confronting the concealed gun that no one can protect him from. In this suddenly remembered chaos of hiding and seeking and the blind flight of shells his body tightens, in subdued panic.

Someone was tugging at his sleeve. Lorenzo. In this light he seemed a total stranger. He seemed very happy, like a man wildly in love, and yet with a shadow of anger over the glow of it. "Tenente," he was saying. "Guarda. Look. There, up there in the valley. The bridge. They will destroy it. They must not do it. They are beasts, they have been destroying everything."

The Lieutenant looked at it through the glasses— a big concrete bridge. It explained why the Germans had stopped here for the night. The Lieutenant turned to reply to him, but he had gone back to watching the valley, like the others. Three hunters watching their prey; in their faces, in the forward thrust of their bodies, the tension of total absorption. He watched them for a moment, puzzled by the fierceness he saw in them. Then he remembered what he had seen in the night: that there was something they wanted that was beyond anything he wanted. Lorenzo's mouth was open and his teeth showed, clenched, large and white. It was the mouth of a hungry animal in the fine head of a man. An animal about to eat his kill. When he had turned in his anger to speak there had been a flame in his eyes that was something else than the exhilaration of the hunter. But the Lieutenant did not know what it was. Dimly he saw that they wanted something he did not want—something that was beyond him, something that he did not know existed.

But what did it matter? They were waiting for him. He had their respect; he was satisfied now with that much; a pride in what he was, a good soldier. He was in control. They were counting on him. They would be grateful for what he did.

He reached back, took the field phone from its leather case and cranked it. He told Chiarello to get the battalion on the radio, and to call back when he had them. "Tell them we've got the whole goddamn German army in a box." He gave him the coordinates of the target from the map.

The Italians were watching him, glad to see that he was acting at last. He turned to them and smiled and their fine faces sparkled for a moment. They went back to watching the house. The Lieutenant remembered that he should get some idea of how many Germans there were and how much of the ground they covered. At the battalion they would want to know what kind of target it was. He tried to estimate how many there might be, but it was not easy in this light.

Through the glasses, little by little, he could begin to make them out more clearly, dim shapes of men beginning to stir among the trees. They were everywhere. The sergeants were moving quickly through the rows, shouting and kicking at the men still rolled in their blankets. Already they had slept too long.

Some of them were up now. They moved slowly like men who are tired or reluctant. The mist on the valley floor had soaked them; it would be a long time before the sun would come up high enough to dry them. There were others who sat on the ground, half dressed, pulling on their shoes and lacing them. The sergeants seemed angry, only half effective in their urging. They were using sticks to prod the men still on the ground.

3

On all sides of the house there were signs of movement, half hidden in the trees. In the gray light under the rags of mist there might have been two hundred of them, or a thousand. There were eight or ten horse-drawn wagons, maybe more. But no trucks. They must have run out of gas.

They would get up and urinate against the trees, then reach into the bags hung on the branches for something to eat. Some of them went over to pick fruit from the other trees, eating where they stood, spitting the pits. Eating one after another. Here and there they passed a bottle of wine among them. But they seemed to pay little attention to one another, saying almost nothing. Drifting here and there . . . Strange, the way they were taking their time. Cocksure confident bastards, the Germans. Take what you can get. If they had to leave this country they'd strip it clean first. And yet, in the slow way they moved, they seemed like sick men. There was no pleasure in it. They did not seem to care one way or the other.

They were bringing the horses around the house, to the wagons that were drawn up near the line of cypresses. The wagons were loaded high with the profits of the long retreat—the contents of a dozen large and small villas. From the direction of the farmyard other men were coming, bareheaded men, carrying geese and chickens, throwing them into one of the wagons that was already alive with wings and beaks. Behind them came others who carried a lamb, calves, a few pigs. The confused protests of the animals made them laugh; but the laughter was weak, and fell away. They lifted the animals up and in, to where a man stood ready to tie their legs together. Around the edges of the courtyard the sergeants stood watching them, more like guards than non-commissioned officers.

The Lieutenant watched them work, forgetting for the moment what he was here for, interested, again surprised that they were so simply men, nothing more. The hard relentless Germans, fire, massacre and rape behind them. At this moment they did not even look like soldiers. Only the sergeants seemed to be armed, the short black tommy-guns cradled in the crook of their elbows.— One of the officers came out of the house struggling with a large valise. A sergeant ran over to help him lift it into the long open sports car.

They were muttering on the ground beside him. It was taking too long. They were whispering, loud, and he caught enough of it to know that it was meant for him. "There is enough light." "Of course." "What is he going to do— paint a picture?"

At that moment he saw the ox again at the edge of an olive grove, untouched. Even in the gray half-light he was white, massive. Dumb, still, waiting, the eyes in the huge head seeming to see nothing. He was hitched to a plow—motionless. The Lieutenant did not hear the phone ring. Lorenzo nudged him. He picked it up and for a moment did not know who it was, this voice that was telling him the battalion was ready. He hesitated, unsure what to do next. He heard the voice on the phone say, "What about it Lieutenant, they're waiting." Then he realized that he himself had been waiting for an order. There was no one to give him an order.

For months now he had functioned in the rhythm of the machine, remote from anything but the need to feed the guns and clean them and fire them. *Them*, the great animals

whom he served. Watching them propel steel into some remote place that was never seen. The target. He was looking
at it. He was pressed up close to the target, it was moving
under his eyes, he could almost reach out and lay a hand on
it. He had been part of a mechanism, and now it was miles
behind him, waiting. He was not there, he was here. Waiting
for what? Time ran away, leaving him in a void. He went
numb, his mind droning, empty, in complete lassitude. He
fought against it . . . His attention dissolved, he could not
focus it. He could not make himself believe that any of this
mattered very much.

"Lieutenant, you still there? I got the battalion, Lieutenant, they're ready—."

The voice was familiar, it brought him back half-
way to himself, almost clear, knowing that he would get no
order, that there was not much time, that he was operating the
machine now, controlling it. The master of it. And that *was*
the target. But still he hesitated—. He brought the phone up to
his mouth and said, "Tell them to wait a minute."

He fought against the trance-like drift of his attention. It was going to be a beautiful day . . . He watched his
hands rise to take hold of the binoculars . . . the hands seeming to act on their own. He felt the cool solidity of the binoculars in his hands and raised them to his eyes, to see the valley
again. It was very peaceful . . . the early morning stillness
. . . the ox stood motionless on the half-plowed ground.

As his eyes began to take hold, to penetrate the dim-
ness, the war began again. He listened. Somewhere—it was
near, it seemed to come from just over the hill behind them,
on the other side of the town—artillery was firing. They were
88's, German guns covering the withdrawal; the machines beginning another day of routine killing. Then there were more
—it was hard to tell where—echoing from the surrounding

valleys. So that this valley became a separate world, holding its own peace . . .

"Tenente, there is not much time." He could hear the words vibrate in the throat of the man next to him, a sound close to anger. He kept the glasses to his eyes as if he had not heard. They were coming together down there, coming from all sides, they seemed to be everywhere. He had underestimated them. Too many. So close. *Will they see us? How will we get out of here in broad daylight?* Fear flashed through him.

He turned himself on the ground and looked back up toward the towers of the town. In the ten seconds since the phone had rung there had come over him the absolute certainty that a sniper was sitting behind one of the windows up there, watching them. There was the flutter of panic in him again—more like a hunted animal than an armed man. Except that an animal knows the ground he is hunted on, knows where he might hide, knows, even, that there are certain limitations that control the hunter . . . that it is some other creature he is pursued by, and not a machine . . . that in a corner he might turn and fight, face to face.

Down below they were piling the loot into the wagons. The sergeants with their tommy-guns were shouting at them, hurrying them, uneasy.

At the moment of killing or being killed each lone man comes to some bright consciousness of himself, of the central living self, of the menace to this self. He stands apart, isolated from the encircling mass. Out of the numbness and chaos this much comes clear: the vivid longing to live. To survive, no matter what. To be a living thing. In this moment he knows what he wants. He fights to live. He will do what he must do to live. Fear is the goad.

There was nothing left to do but to do the job. To be doing something—. Ten miles back they had loaded one gun, it was charged and ready, the shell in the tube like a live thing—a tension of readiness. And he wanted to see it, to see the shell hit and bloom in the valley, to know that the battalion was there, connected with him. The valley and the encircling hills were hostile. He knew something about them now, but not enough. Their threatening was a pressure on him, worse than the darkness of the night. And worse than that was his fear of the fear in himself. He wanted to see the shells come, to blot it out.

He picked up the phone again and told Chiarello to tell them to fire the first round. He heard the radioman chuckle his pleasure and relief. Then there was nothing to do but wait. Over the phone he heard Chiarello say, "Number one on the way—"

And it came almost before he knew it, a soft shuddering whine over their heads, then silence, then, far up the valley and to the right, a white puff on the hillside, a sudden flowering, almost soundless. It was so white. He remembered that he had asked for smoke shells—they would be easier to spot.

It rose, a remote smoke-flower in the quiet valley, and the sun tinged it pink. It was not bad for a first round fired from a map. It was about five hundred yards to the right and a thousand yards beyond the house. It might have landed on the reverse slope of the hill, lost, and he would have had to start from scratch. Now it would be easy. Now he knew what to do, he could take hold and bring it in. This was his skill; his eyes jumped to make the measurement. Good judgment. You do your job and everything is all right. You concentrate, and everything falls into place.

On his left the partisans were murmuring their satisfaction. They were almost singing.

Here and there in the valley the cocks were crowing.

The Lieutenant was poised, like a man with a hammer—he held the glasses ready in one hand and the phone in the other, concentrated on his measurement of the space. A question of numbers. Precision. Into the phone he said, "Five hundred right, one thousand over." As he waited he was plotting the probabilities, seeing it as a diagram: the guns, the angle of elevation, the range, the deflection. He glanced down at the house. They were still stripping the fruit from the trees, still gathering and piling loot, heaving it up into the wagons. In among the small hills and depressions of the valley floor they had not seen or heard the first round. He felt himself beginning to sweat. The fear was broken. The body and the body's simple mind were taking over, freeing him into a timeless concentration of his self in the work. It was a big target. All he had to do was to get a bracket on it with this one gun, then call in the massed fire of the twelve guns. Smother it.

The second round was still long, over, but much closer. Methodically he spoke into the phone, asking them to bring it down 300 yards and move it 100 yards to the left. This was good (he shifted on the ground to make himself comfortable)—the eye making good in its judgment, the ritual formula of command coming automatically; he was getting the old kick out of it. The proof of skill, the marksmanship— in the end this was everything. A simple pleasure. The three other hunters were turning to smile and nod at him. That was good, that made him feel good. He was out of practice but he was doing all right. A glow of pleasure all through the body. The thing was in his hands and his hands knew what to do with it.

As he worked it was almost as if there were no longer a war. He was caught up in the habitual motions, the small satisfactions of the work. The job. From step to step. No war aims, no big objectives—they had nothing to do with it.

War breeds its own necessities, its own habits and momentums. The rest is superfluous.
So the Lieutenant works at this careful placing of one smoke puff at a time. A man with a hammer and nails. The eye and the hand.

The third shell falls about one hundred yards back of the house. The white smoke rises. Harmless smoke. But he begins to feel the power of the machine in his hands. As if with his fists he could smash it all, everything that was down there. His senses anticipate fire and the shaking of the earth.
The Italians say something to him, but he does not hear them. Into the phone he tells them to shorten the range by a hundred and twenty-five yards. Almost as an afterthought he looks through the glasses and he sees them, the men in the valley. The target. They are still there. They are men. They are running. They are in panic, some frozen and some running. Some run for the trees and some for the house. They know now that they are the target. They know the ways of this machine. Terror breaks among them. They are only men.

But with all the wild movement they seem to be making no sound. Some of them are running in circles, with the stiff jerky motion of a silent movie. And then the fourth puff of smoke rises just short of the house, and they know they are trapped. The bracket is established. They cannot run fast enough or far enough. One man stops to cross himself before he runs again.

The horses rear up screaming, twisting in the traces. Then they are running, the wagons bouncing and swinging, the stuff spilled in long tangled skeins. The captive geese and the chickens and the lambs and the pigs are shaken loose in a scrambling of wings and legs. The officers have come out of the house and stand dazed, yet braced, in the courtyard. One of them runs to the car, stops, and runs back into the house with the others.

The three partisans are up on their knees, shaking their fists and shouting down into the valley. The white smoke from the last shell drifts up and away. Near the house it is very quiet. The smoke shell has left no mark. Everywhere men are running, one way, then another, running back. Each alone. They have no holes to hide in. They are worse off than ants. Someone is going to step on them and they have no hole. Some throw themselves flat on the ground. They know that the machine is in motion, has found them, and will not be stopped. Only the ox stands in perfect stillness.

The Lieutenant could not take his eyes off them. Into the glasses they came up very close, they were running straight toward him—yet in their insane contortions they were not altogether credible.

The Italians were on their feet now, bellowing from their stomachs, shaking their fists. They raged and spat their obscenities. One of them picked up a stone and threw it. Lorenzo swung the tommy-gun from his shoulder and turned a wild spray into the valley, screaming, "Pigs! Traitors! Fascist pigs!"—dwindling to a snarl. "Where is your *Duce* now?"

On the phone the Lieutenant could hear Chiarello asking for the next command. The battalion was waiting. On the other side he felt first the heat and then the spasmodic breath of the man who was shouting in his ear. It was Lorenzo, the thick voice screaming, "Now! Now! Finish it. *Subito.*" The last word became a command. The Lieutenant picked up the phone and said, "Deflection correct, five-zero short, fire for effect."

The binoculars were still up to his eyes. A man ran into the circle made by the lenses. He could see his face, his mouth working. He was wearing a helmet that he had put on backwards. It was like a pot on his head. He stood still and threw his hands up. There was no one to surrender to. He went down on his knees. He prayed. The Lieutenant dropped the telephone and gripped the glasses with both hands. He saw the man. One single separate man.

There was something wrong with it. This man. He saw something he had not seen before. He moved the glasses quickly, looking hard at one and then another, following them where they ran. These men, their faces breaking up—what were these men? They were not Germans. The helmets— They were Italians. Italians. With German officers. Being moved north, to labor, to do the dirty work. Unarmed. Disarmed. Not much better than prisoners. A labor battalion. Ditch diggers. Road menders. Hod carriers. Bricklayers. Men who made terraces. Slaves in their own country. They were unarmed. They were tired, dirty, afraid, driven. Driven.

They were alive. Italians. Living men. Warm and alive.

The sun. Their sun. Is up. Is rising. The sun that is the father of the poor. Alive under this sun. Their sun.

The sun has caught them. It is up and rising. The sun shining on the green leaves of the valley and on the old stone of the house—.

They are not like the insect life of armies. Even in their terror they are not. They are whole men. Warmblooded.

The Lieutenant turned to face the three Italians who watched with him. They would not look at him. They knew. They had known. Had they known all through the night?

Ten miles away the machines of the battalion were in motion. The Lieutenant was no longer in control of them. Once in motion the machine will have its way. It is the man who works for the machine. He becomes linked to it, part of its movement—as when a car driven fast infatuates the driver with a need for speed. And those who go along for the ride. He was caught in the alternating rhythm of fire and load and fire—the guns' obscene searching of the ground for the living flesh . . . Now he waited for the machine to have its way.

It was very still. They ran wild in the valley, in circles, unable to help one another. The wind blew their cries away and up here on the ridge it was still, the stillness of early morning. It was less than a minute since he gave his last command. All around the tight ring of panic the sun opened the valley to serenity. Many of them ran for the house.

Many were running nowhere, in smaller and smaller circles.

The voice on the telephone was saying, "Able on the way . . . Charlie on the way . . . Baker on the way." But the Lieutenant had dropped the telephone on the ground.

Nor did he hear the shells pass over. He had the glasses up to his eyes, and he watched, everything. He could not stop watching. His eyes would not lie to him. He could not turn away. He tried to make himself believe that what was going to happen would not happen.

In the final moment of silence none of it had anything to do with him: he was the remote spectator. It was a mechanical process. He waited to see what would happen when the high explosive shells of twelve 155 mm. guns burst in a concentration. His mind moved like a fish into deeper water, pursued and pursuing at the same moment: to eat and be eaten; light and then dark, its pattern changing from moment to moment. Deviously: pleasure and horror circling head to tail.

The sun was up over the hills. It was all clear. The glasses held them framed: they ran in and out of the circles but they always came back. Smaller and smaller circles.

In the instant of the shells hitting the ground the stillness was unbroken. Quietly the balls of fire became pointed splashes of fire—. And then the roar, and then the dark whorls of smoke. And the earth rising, as if it were itself explosive. The earth spurting into the air, hanging for a moment, falling back. And in this rain, falling, fell pieces of men and trees and animals. The earth shuddered and seemed to go on shuddering as if some delicate equilibrium had been disturbed. The roar echoed in the valley. More shells followed and the earth belched, heaved, lifted itself in convulsions; then more, and out of the black spray the torn half of a man rose higher than anything else.

The shells kept coming, carefully seeded in rows over this part of the valley, dispersed in a formal pattern. Up and down and back again. Inside the network of explosive fires the hot steel fragments cut like razors. The men were not swallowed up all at once, as in the fairy tales. They were not snuffed out. They did not quietly disappear. One by one, rooted to the ground by concussion, they were chopped to pieces, as if with an axe. But not the quick precise axe of the headsman, or the butcher. The axe of the madman. Except that here there was not even the madman to confront. Or any man—only this chaos of blast and flame and the screaming chunks of steel. Out of nowhere. The men did not die as men. On the edge of death they became *things;* and then they became chunks of meat scattered in the rubble. But first, in the intervals between the waves of shells, those who still lived were given time to think. To think—or to listen to a voice in themselves that said: In ten seconds, in five seconds, in three seconds, in a moment I will be killed, I will be dead, I will be nothing.

And the Lieutenant, who was so close he could almost have touched them, who was on top of it (in the glasses they were almost as large as life) saw everything. He was on his knees looking down. He could not close his eyes or turn them away from it.

And one of the Italians, the professor, whispered to himself, "Cosi sia." So be it. And hid his face. And Lorenzo shouted, "Why do they not stop now? It is enough. Basta. Basta."

Even here, above it, the concussion, the reverberation were terrible. It seemed that the walls of the valley must break open and fall in.

But it went on. The men ten miles away had found work for their machines and were glad of it. They were beautiful machines, beautiful to watch in their smooth thrust and recoil. The coupling of the men and the machines, the rhythm of their play, back and forth, was a great pleasure. They were in heat and they had not yet been satisfied.

The shell bursts became other shell bursts, a wild blooming of fire. The seed planted, blooming instantly, seemed to scatter more seed. In a moment, the cycle from birth to death. And again.

One man at a time, each one a separate man running for his life (or flat on his face, eating dirt), they died in terror. The life was hot and thick and stubborn in them, and it was gouged out of them. And the torn off pieces of the men and the trees and the animals went into the air, spinning. And in the eyes of the Lieutenant, who saw everything, they fell slowly back to earth.

The field of death heaved and erupted in spasms under the red and orange bursts, even after the last man died. The Lieutenant, stretched flat on the ground, rigid, felt the shock, the tremors, run through his body. The dead men were chopped smaller. They were tossed in clumsy acrobatics. In the heavy roil of smoke and dust and blood the big splashes of flame flashed on and off.

It might be said that it was like a volcano, like an

earthquake, a tornado. But it was not. It was not like anything in life. And then, like a cloudburst, it was over, and all up and down the valley it was blue and pink and gold shining on the warm browns and grays and green-grays of the stone houses, the trees, the low hills—all of it figured and intricate as a persian rug. What a view—and far away, the mountains, the untouchable mountains. The valley was perfect in its stillness, like a new rug, except for this one place close under them, where the last smoke and dust were clearing to show a burn. There it was all torn and scorched, beaten down, gored, pocked.

The olive trees and the almond trees and the pear trees lay torn and scattered, where they had not disappeared. Except for the front wall and a row of beheaded columns, the old house was gone. The vineyards were gone. The terraces were broken and spilled down the low hills that rose from the valley floor. The earth was blackened and raw. Here and there it seemed to be steaming. Nothing moved. There was nothing to prove that there had been life here.

And all around the burned place the green life kept pushing up out of the ground, glistening now as it met the oncoming sun.

The body of the Lieutenant went tight, convulsed, and he sat down on the ground, something in him twisting until it broke; and he went down, falling, toward death. His hands gripped tufts of grass that they had torn from the earth. He was falling, as in the falling of a child's dreams—but now he was taken further down than he had ever been. And lost some part of himself as he fell. Some part of the day passed while he stayed there, far down, gone from himself.

And when the sun stroked him and forced his eyes open he could not remember what he had done. It was as if he had tried to kill himself and had failed, and still did not know if he were glad or sorry that he lived, or why he had tried. Or if he lived at all. Knowing only that he was cold, so cold that he took the shine of the sun for snow and imagined himself to be in a sleep of death, freezing to death. And this, this valley, was the dream of peace before death.

How strange that there was no war here. There was no sound of fighting, only the long ripe valley with a radiance on it. And at the far end of the valley, perched in miniature on a cross-cutting ridge, a village of white houses, pure white cubes, around a white church.

He stood up and looked around at the silence and the fullness of the day. The three men were gone. Where? Who had they been? What did they look like? He could not believe it. Any of it. It had not happened. There had been the night and the talking with three men and now he was here alone in this green and yellow morning. And he was looking down. Down there the earth was broken and scorched and cold like a piece of the moon. It was from some movie. It was the scene from twenty years of books and movies. War was not like that. It did not happen that way. Not any more. Yet it was there, a smoking rubbish dump, a fire-scorched corpse in a garden.

In his daze he told himself that it did not have anything to do with him. It was not the work of the guns. No sign of life. Where had they all gone? He picked up the glasses from the ground and raised them to his eyes to search the burned-out place, to see where the men had gone when they ran out of the field of fire. He explained to himself that they had escaped. There was no sign of them.

Looking down on it in full sunlight it seemed so small, the burn on the rug, with the dense design of the still growing valley around it. They must have run away, off the burned patch on to the green. But where? The valley, wherever he looked, was still, as if men had worked it to perfection and then abandoned it.

There was that wailing again. The lamb. It began low and shaky, then it rose, gathering strength from a growing consciousness of pain. There came a moaning cry to meet it. And in a little while a third joined them, a whimpering sound. The Lieutenant listened to these sounds as if they were a part of a movie. They were making a movie of the war to show the people at home what it was like. He had often seen them, the Signal Corps cameramen. They were always turning up in strange places. But how had he gotten into it? Why was he here?

He focused the glasses and moved them deliberately over the torn earth, until he came to the blasted and blackened carcass of the ox. The snakes that crawled to attack it . . . were its entrails. The low hills in the valley moved like waves. He doubled over and threw up; and could not stop it; and then did not want to stop it.

When it was over, when he was emptied out, he lay down on his back and shivered with the cold, staring straight up into the sky. The great blue emptiness of sky was too much for him. It made him dizzy, sick; it was turning over so that he might fall into it. But he went on staring up into it, unable to turn or to close his eyes. He wanted to get up and go away, but he was waiting for something, what it was he did not know, and he could not move. He thought he was waiting to find out what had happened, and what it had to do with him. He did not know where he was, or where he might go. He thought that he might have been killed, that he was dead like the others. Which others? All the others, all those who had died and would make the earth of this place fertile with their bodies. What more could any man do? He was very tired. He lost interest.

The sky took him in. Daydreaming on a hilltop in

the sun. Detached, he rose into the high blue. To meet Anne, who was not ashamed of her nakedness. Was she his wife? Was the war so long over? He did not know. She soothed him. She was not Anne any more, she was the dark girl of the moon in the piazza, the girl with the beautiful strong legs. A voice in him said, It would be nice if she were here now, we could lie here together and I would—. Then there was nobody. There was not even himself. Only this infinity, this eternity of blue.

The moaning came up to him through the stillness. It did not sound like either animals or men.

He heard the crackling of a mechanical voice. It was the voice in the phone. But he did not know it.

The sun broke into the cold sea where he floated like a corpse with its eyes open. He felt the grass under his hands. He began to think again that none of it had anything to do with him. It was the war. It was the guns. It was nothing personal. It was like living on the slopes of a volcano. Anything might happen. How could he help what happened? Or any man. He laughed at himself. Soon it will be over and we can go home and lie on the beach. And forget it. There had been some kind of terrible accident. Someone had been killed. But it was over.

He got up with his back to the valley and was surprised by the towers of the town, and the toy castle. His eyes drifted to the path that went back through the brush to where . . . there was someone else. He wanted to see some other living thing.

But he stopped and turned himself around to go back to the edge and look down again. If there were the bodies of dead men there he wanted to see them. With his naked eye he looked and saw a horse on its back with two legs sticking into the air and two legs missing. But no men. He picked up the glasses from the ground and looked again. There was nothing. The glasses moved automatically and framed the stripped branches of an olive tree that bore as its fruit half of a man's body, naked except for the shoes.

Chiarello came through the trees in time to see the Lieutenant plunging and stumbling down the steep slope into the valley. He fell and rolled and got up to keep going down. He was shouting something but the radioman could not make out what it was.

By the time Chiarello got to him the Lieutenant had seen everything he wanted to see. He had looked at what he could find of the men, and touched them. He had begun to dig a grave with his hands.

20

And then the crying again—the child, the lamb, the men who had not yet died—always louder than the distant guns. But there were no guns. It was the sea. He wanted the sea to come up and take him, to lose himself in its darkness. He did not want to see the sun rise again—see it rise and strike the earth, see the earth erupt at its touch.

On the sand at his side the woman sighed and stirred. A stranger, anonymous in her nakedness. A woman who spoke his own language, to whom he could not speak.

It was a journey in a strange country, moving, stopping, moving up. They were on their way to some reward, some final haven. Up and up and up. But the rest were gone, they had left him. He was moving backwards now, down from the high clear places; he was alone and he had no destination.

Each night on this beach he listened for the sound of guns; but there was nothing. Finally he gave up listening and gave himself up to the sand, the sea, the soft nights of summer. And to the hunger of his body, that would not die. In this place that he had come to there were women of his own country; they came to look for him at night on the beach and gave themselves to him. He did not know how or why this was. They came, night after night, first one and then another. It seemed to belong to this carnival of fire and flesh from which there was no escape.

Night after night—this beach, a woman; it did not matter which one; one was like the others. He was cold, and there was heat in their bodies; beyond that he knew nothing of them. They wanted to talk, but he could not talk; he lived with a cry of anguish locked in his throat, his whole body an unexploded shell.

One night was like another: the mild darkness and the lapping of the sea and the hungry women; so that there was no counting the days or the nights or the women. Outside of time he seemed to crawl upward on the slopes of a volcano, to reach the mouth, to escape the burned valley that lay below him. The tormented bodies of olive trees seemed always to surround him, awaiting the eruption.

His time was inverted: the future was behind him; and ahead the past awaited him, a volcano, its mouth choked with the bodies of the dead. The present was a narrow ledge: he was afraid to go backwards or forwards. It was only for a moment each night, in the bodies of the women, that he could come to rest.

2

This woman—he did not know who she was, he could not tell her from the others. After dark he had come to the beach and she was there waiting. She wanted him, as the others did. They were nurses and they had seen too much (but never enough) and they were hungry with a desperate hunger. A moment ago he had felt the struggle of her body under him, writhing to free itself, to explode. But the excitement generated in her by the mutilated bodies of young men was too deep to find release in her body; she could never get enough. These men fresh from the mysteries of killing . . . initiated . . . endowed with some secret knowledge . . . But they would not be serious. Or they mocked you with their silence. Something was held back.

For weeks he had hidden himself from the sun; he came out only at night. It was as if in that final moment of his life he had looked too long into the rising sun; he had not been able to turn away; he had seen the inside of the sun, and of the earth: the inner exploding core. The core was fire, it was blood. And then his eyes had filled with blood and gone dark; and now could look only into darkness. In the darkness he had come upon the stars, their mysterious design, their sudden burning and falling. They were cold as he was cold, they became his element.

Among the stars, far outside himself and his time, he could look down and see himself. Somewhere, in some now distant time, he saw himself sitting on the ground, talking, waiting for the light. Somewhere else he saw all the men and the guns and the trucks of the carnival rushing ahead in bright sunlight to that unknown haven that awaited them. They did not know where it was, this haven. It was somewhere beyond the mountains. Which mountains? No one knew. They kept going toward it, wherever it was, blind and bleeding. When the sun came up he shouted to warn them, but they did not hide. They kept going.

And he himself, the Lieutenant, the good soldier, was nowhere. It was as if he had jumped clear of a runaway train, and fallen backwards, off-balance, downhill, through a long dark night; until he arrived here, by this quiet sea. Here was a hospital; it seemed to be surrounded by sand and sea; he had seen orange trees and caught the scent of pine; that was all he knew of it. The women did not speak of it, what happened in it was their secret. After they had had all he could give them of his body (it was young and strong and whole and therefore rare) they begged him for his secret. But they could not break through his silence.

3

It was the same night; for him it was always that same night, before the coming of the light; he prayed that the sun would never rise. *The pillar of fire had faded and the circle of darkness was complete again.* It was quiet, there was no sound of guns. Was it an island, then, encircled by this calm sea? Circles within circles: a circle of water, and a circle of the warm flesh of women, and of darkness . . . He told himself that it was an island, that nothing could reach him here. The sun could not reach him, he lived—if he lived—in the night. In the long hot days he slept.

He lay on his back, the sand cool against his body, forgetful of the woman, watching the stars to see if they would fall. Out there, there is no direction. No haven. No destination. Millions of millions of suns, beginning and ending nowhere, exploding to make new suns and earths and suns, without end. He lay in the cooling sand as in a shallow grave, waiting for the moment when the shells would begin to fall again, the earth to explode, the men to die again, praying that this time he might die with them and that it might then be over. But his body was young, it had not yet begun to die. It mocked him with its heat. It went on expecting, making promises. It clung to the earth. He listened. He heard the words, *Like a sun hath risen.*

It was McGovern, the dark-haired pink-cheeked Irishman who had cornered him in the latrine one early morning, laughing, giddy. How could he turn away from a blind man, one who laughed? "Last night," McGovern said, "someone stole our clothes. On the beach. She almost died. I told her we were Adam and Eve. Without so much as a pair of socks. She took me by the hand and led me in. We get halfway back and she starts to run for it. I grab her, and you know what I say, I say, Listen baby, you know what you are? You're a priestess in the temple of love. That stopped her. I hang on and while she's thinking it over she's guiding me in. Listen, I tell her, copulation is a prayer in the sight of God. That really got her. She stuck with me, Florence Nightingale to the end, and in we go through a window. More, she says, tonight I want you to tell me more. It ain't what you do, buddy, it's what you say that gets 'em."

He laughed and shook his eyeless head. "The temple of love. The entrance into heaven. The more you give them, the more they want. What is it, friend, what's happened to the American girl?"

The Lieutenant could not take his eyes from the hollows where the collapsed eyelids stared back at him. The face changed, the crooked smile was gone, twisting, settling to the dreamy earnestness of a choir boy. The voice was soft, almost sweet: "Are you still there?" Waiting, then abruptly: "Tell me sonny, what are you going to be when you grow up? A soldier? How nice. You know what I'm going to be? A priest. The blind shepherd. Ahhh, smell those flowers, son, 'tis the spring of souls today" (the voice changing again, swinging in erratic curves from banter to solemnity to a sound like angry weeping). "Christ hath burst his prison, and from three days' sleep in Death, like a sun hath risen. And you, who are you? Can't you speak? Did they tear out your tongue then? Are you deaf?"

He came toward him, his hands outstretched, groping. The Lieutenant backed away, afraid of the tense searching hands. "Can't you speak? Who are you? Are you a man? Are you one of the sacred whores of this temple? I'm blind. They took my eyes. Can't you see that I'm blind? Don't go away. Wait. I have something to tell you. These women are ghouls. They'll suck your blood. Do you hear me? Do you?"

       . . . *like a sun hath risen.* He listened. It was the sea. Was the blind man trying to find him? Was he crying, was the lamb crying? A voice in him moaned, Wake up, wake up, it's a dream. The guns are gigantic toy animals in a parade. A carnival. Or was it that he had died with the others and that this was his death?

4

    The war had gone on across the Arno and through the hills heavy with the end of summer, and into another range of mountains. But the Lieutenant knew nothing of this; he did not know how far he had come, or how he had come; he did not know what part of the night this was. It was a journey, he moved in circles, in smaller and smaller circles, in and out of the valley where the men had died; and each time he came back they died again, on their knees, praying to him. They were as large as life, and so close he could almost touch them. He could see the contortions of their eyes and mouths, he could hear the crying of the lamb.

    A star fell blazing across a million miles of sky. For a moment he went with it and was gone, released. But his body was on the ground; it brought him back.

    "Oh! Look!" she cried. "Did you see it? A star. A falling star. Ohhh." He did not hear her. Silence. She could not understand it. He was a hero. He was unwounded. Why was he here?

    What does she want, he thought. What do any of them want? Her starving mouth. Her tongue. Hard. Prying. Hunger. For what?

She had tasted the death in his mouth. She wanted more.

The sand was cold now; and the sea was cold. He watched for a sign of the sunrise, to guard against it. He was cold but he withheld himself from her body. Sleeping. Let her sleep. She did not talk in her sleep, and her face was less hard. Why did she want to talk, a woman who has slept with a hundred men, or a thousand, who has said it all and heard it all? Why did she come here? She was a stranger to him, like the others. Every living thing was strange. Only the men who had died before his eyes were known to him. No one knows me now, he thought. No one will ever know me.

She stirred and sighed, turning to face him. "I'm cold," she said. "Gil, it's cold. We must have fallen asleep. Gee but I'm cold." She waited. "Gil? Honey?"

He watched the stars, waiting for a sign. The huge suns that shine and give no light. And fall, burning, to strike nowhere.

The great black emptiness of sky was turning over and he was falling backwards into it. They were there. The target. They are men. They are running. Into the field glasses they come up very close, running straight at him. No. In reverse: The pieces of flesh reform themselves into the shapes of men, they run backwards in circles, they come up from their knees, they stop praying, they put the fruit back on the trees, they put the animals back in the farmyard; they fall back into place under the olive trees, under their blankets, and sleep. The white snakes that are his entrails run back into the belly of the ox, he stands up whole, yoked to the plowshare in his great patience.

The sun falls back down in the east, it is night, the circle of darkness is complete again, there is peace. The tall bony man stands up before his superiors in the baronial hall

(the food is back on the table, the lamb around his neck still
bleeds) and announces that Christ will establish paradise on
earth. Here. Now. A falling star will be his sign.

"What are you thinking about?" she asked. She
moved toward him in a spasm of pity and self-pity. "You
don't care about me, I know you don't. I'm cold. Please. Talk
to me. Won't you warm me? Honey? I want to help you.
Can't I help you, huh?—I'm all alone and I'm sad and you
never talk to me. Why don't you ever talk to me?"

He heard her, but he did not hear what she said. His
fingers dug into the sand; he hung on against the backwards
spinning of his mind. His eyes reached for stars that would
hold him in place.

"Honey, honey, I'm so cold. Warm me. Be a good
boy and make me warm, won't you? Huh? Don't leave me
alone."

She pressed herself to him; with her mouth and her
hands she clutched at his body. This was her life; the war
was her chance to live. She was not young any more, her
hands were chafed and rough. The body of a boy, aged into
hardness; starving, and the more she ate the more she was
emptied out. Live, her hands said, I want to live. In groans
that were almost words she said, *Tell me. Tell me what to do.*
"I'm crazy about you, I'd do anything for you. Do you
hear?"

The sea washed it all away for a moment and then it
came back.

She let go and fell away from him. "Men are all
alike, all they want is—" The quiet voice startled her. He said,
"All they want is to live before they die."

"What did you say, honey?"

He turned away.

"Why aren't you nice to me? You never say anything, you never—." He lay so still. She shivered, her hand

came up, stopped, afraid to touch him. Cold. "We've got to get back soon," she said. "I'm on duty in the morning. She's been watching me. Dear Dorothea. Captain Hawley. The old bitch, she knows. She knows everything. She's jealous. It kills her. What a laugh." She laughed alone; she threw the words after each other into the dark. "Even one of the blind ones wouldn't touch her." She threw them like pebbles to break the silence. Against the lapping of the sea her voice rose, and the sound of it excited her. "I hate her. I hate the whole thing. I wish the war would be over. I hate this country. Don't you hate it? I can't stand it any more. Do you hear me? I never know if you hear what I say. I can't stand it." She paused to listen. "Why can't you settle for one girl, why do you have to screw around like that? Why? What's the matter with you?" She babbled until a gasping sob choked the words off in her throat. The crust broke, she fell through; an animal moaning.

Without knowing what he did he put out a hand and touched her. "Don't. Don't. You'll be all right."

Trembling, she came up on her knees, close to him, and laid a hand on his belly. "Do you want me?" she whispered. "Darling. Do you? We could do it again now, we were sleeping—couldn't we? Couldn't we try? Come on, please. Make me warm. I can't stand it. I'll do anything you want."

Her hand moved in a small circle. It was rough and hard and insistent. But it was dark, he did not know who she was, or care—she was only this hand, a woman's hand, a living thing, holding him to the earth, among the living. The pleading voice had stopped; it had not reached him. But her hand reached him; it knew that it reached him; it became sure and slow. His body refused the death he offered it; it followed her hand.

"I love you, I'm crazy about you," she said, and clung to him. "You're so good, you're not like the others." She came up over him and pressed her small breasts to his chest. "What happened to you? Tell me. Tell me what happened." She played with his hair. "Tell me, come on, please, you've never told me. Was it exciting?" Close to his mouth she whispered, as if to pry it open. "Why do you play around with all the girls, why can't I be enough for you . . . You're a devil. But I like it, I like you because you're a man. You're the strong silent kind, aren't you?" She laughed. "But you're mean to me. Don't you know that I'm proud of you—?" Her hands moved, touching, caressing. He stirred, unaware of her, but she held on. His hands came up to find her shoulders, and gripped them suddenly, the delicate small bones; he knew her, she came from his own country, he was sorry for her, starving, her dry body feeding among the wounds, among the erotic dreams of helpless men . . . From his own country . . . anything to escape . . . their hair was cut short, their bodies were thin and hard, they hungered for sensation . . . He tried to remember . . . all his life moving up, up, up . . . a journey . . .

"I'm your girl, I'm all yours. The other girls don't care, all they care about is screwing. Why don't you tell me—?"

He turned his head to look up at her and felt her quick hot breath on his face; he heard her tongue come out of her mouth to wet her lips. He could not remember her name. Her mouth came down and she drove her tongue between his teeth, searching; and wrapped her arms around him. "You're brave. You're a man. You killed a lot of Germans, didn't you? They say you killed hundreds of them. Isn't it true? Tell me how it was. Please. You're wonderful, I'm proud of you, tell me—"

His fingers tightened on her shoulders. His voice

came flat. "You stick your thumbs into their eyes and push and the eyes fall out . . . You chop pieces of them off with an axe until they are dead." A sharp fragment of a laugh broke from his mouth. "Would you like to see a man being killed, would you like me to kill one for you? You like it, don't you—?"

"Oh but you're laughing at me, that's not—." She screamed. "Don't, you're hurting me. Don't." The fingers dug into her shoulders. His eyes were wide open, his teeth clenched behind the lips stretched back as if in pain.

With a cry she tore herself free of his hands. She backed away, clutching at the sand for her clothes. She could not find them. Turning, she ran heavily in the sand.

5

The Lieutenant was a hero. It was in all the newspapers. A human interest story, something to bring the war close to the people at home. Something they could get their hands on. Sink their teeth into. *In the last resort it is the individual fighting man who* . . . And so on. (What can you say about a corporation—that it is fighting hand-to-hand, and will emerge victorious?) It said in the paper that the Lieutenant, a college man, tall and soft-spoken, had wiped out, single-handed, one Panzer Regiment—more or less—with all its armor. Written with enthusiasm by a man who prided himself that he knew the smell of death, the story was syndicated in three hundred papers. The army newspaper picked it up and played it big. Yes, they said, it's about time somebody gave the artillery a break.

The nurses read it. It gave their war a meaning. They watched him. A hero. But he had cracked up. A mystery. Yet he was a real hero. It said so. And he was a tall, good-looking kid, very straight. And his eyes, something there—he had seen something. They watched him and whispered. All they knew was what they read in the paper. They made a mystery around him; it broke the routine. They had a dream: At the edge of the world there was a fire where men were burned alive and purified. He had been there. He was the hero of the dream.

On that bright June day three weeks before, they had brought the hero back to Brigade Headquarters, where a ceremony was arranged. It was time for some medals. Flags were flying. The visiting generals arrived smiling in their cars. One of them made a speech. *This crusade . . . a great team . . . a job well done . . .* They pinned the Silver Star on him. A French general kissed him and hung the Croix de Guerre on him. They looked solemn and then they smiled. In a cool stone house on the edge of the sun-dazzled piazza they broke out a bottle and drank to the wines of Tuscany. For the brass, it was all in a day's work.

Around the piazza, in the shade of the projecting roofs, the officers who had been decorated stood chatting in groups: the fraternity of victorious athletes. The Lieutenant, with Chiarello at his side, moved like a man walking in his sleep. Near the church he stood apart, mute. In these three days he had spoken to no one. His face, thin, stretched tight, showed nothing. His eyes were wide open and dead.

They were of the underworld, his eyes, alight with the yellow-green-black iridescence of flesh rotting in the sun. With his own hands he had changed the valley of his dreams into a blackened crater, and there he lived in a new world, the world of the unburied dead. The unready dead, whose new blood has run into the ground, who lie in the fields or sit by the roadside unwilling to go into the ground. They are young, they have the force of numbers, they are swollen too big for their uniforms, they are hard to handle. Having died like animals, they are now not quite men. Yet they are a real presence, they insist on their place in the scheme of things. Rob them, turn out their pockets to see what they might be worth —but do not molest them; they are dead but they are young, and there are so many of them. If you touch them they will overpower you. Their strength is from the sun; the sun ripens them, to the bursting point. They have the secret of life.— So he thought of them; so he lived with them. So he watched them die, and died with them.

The stones of the piazza were ablaze with sun. The Lieutenant moved past the young men talking, toward the dark opening in a wall that had been part of a church. Chiarello followed him. A hurrying voice cut in on them: the war correspondent, sweating, was saying, "Lieutenant. Congratulations." Chiarello tried to wave him away. The man pressed in, he saw nothing. "Congratulations. I hear you really cleaned up on the bastards. Listen, how about a story, Lieutenant, tell me something about yourself. Tell me—." The Lieutenant kept on moving. Chiarello stopped, to explain. The puzzled face of the hurrying man came closer. It was the face of the outsider, a hungry uncertain face. The soldier shrugged and turned away.

The correspondent breathed hard in the heat, watching them disappear into the church, out of the sun. He knew the type. OK. He would get the story somewhere else. It was a hell of a good story.— In the end he got it, though he had to take what he could get. What he couldn't get he supplied out of his head. He needed a story. He always needed a new story. It was always the same story, but people were hungry for it, they could never get enough.

A hero. On the basis of the Headquarters maps of the previous day he and his driver had gone six miles inside the German lines, had destroyed a key point of enemy resistance,

had saved no one knew how many lives for the French infantry.

Given the confusion, all this might be true. Or it
might not. At Headquarters they knew this. But who was to
say it was not true? The man had been through hell. Something had happened. He had killed a great many of the enemy.
Who was to deny the possibility of heroism? What man
among them did not relish the drama of a one-man show? Out
of the dumb mechanical mass one man comes up and shows
them how it ought to be done. The story has spread through
all the battalions of the brigade, it has given the men at the
guns a lift. The Fifth Army historians have been looking into
it; if they handle it right it might go into the history books. A
legend, even; the kind of thing people expect from a war.

6

They did not forget Chiarello; they gave him the
Bronze Star.

Chiarello had brought the Lieutenant back. He had
put an arm around his shoulder and led him back through the
heat of the morning as one leads a blind man, a man who has
just had his eyes put out. Without words he had taken the
impact of the other man's shock; had somehow gotten him
into the jeep, in no man's land, to confront the labyrinth of
small deep valleys. It was for him to do, to search, alone.
Once, on the brow of a hill, in sight of the layered blue-
hilled distances, hopelessly lost, he turned to the other and
caught the full emptiness of the wide-open eyes. And went
on, through the hanging gardens of the terraces, winding,
gambling, to find a way back. The sun beat down, the valleys
were close and hot and very still in their green; everything
had changed in the light. A country of peaches and figs,
almond, apricot, pear, cherry. Wheat, in shining steps. Back

through the silent winding roads crowded with convoys of the dead in postures of flight, where the planes had caught them. High-banked rivers of stench where the sun ripened the flesh from white to yellow to blue-yellow to black.

Where the bodies of men and horses choked the narrow road the jeep weaved, churning the white dust, barely moving. Chiarello forced the wheels in among them, over them—slipping, sinking, grinding in four-wheel drive. Caught in the silence of the dead the machine roared as it squirmed.

At his side the Lieutenant rode silent, erect, stiff. Bareheaded, his face masked with dirt, his eyes drifting. Like a man caught under water, pulled down, surrendering to it; a man who even if he comes up again will have left some part of himself on the bottom. In his eyes there was no life in the world—only this, what he could see, the new world of the unburied dead. The other world. The deathless dead, watching him, following him, staying with him. From a ditch one raised a skinny hand and waved. Grinned. He was known to them. He was moving away from them—up and around the side of a hill—and they were moving toward him; they were everywhere. They were there one moment, torn and twisted and reaching out toward him, and then they were not there. (If the jeep moved, if Chiarello spoke, he did not know it.) They looked up from the roadbed and down from the shattered wagons. In the hot sun they had ripened quickly; in the life after death they were growing larger than life. Some had reached the edge of the vineyards. In the ditches they seemed to climb over each other, as if to rise.

He could not shut his eyes against them.

This was where it began, the journey, in circles, in among the dead and out and in: the tight spiralling descent into hell, down, away from the sun. The engine roared. Then it was silent, stalled where the dead lay sprawling in the rubbish of plunder and weapons. A roaring of flies: the sun breeding flies whose roar of pleasure in the broken flesh was the same as the roaring of the sun in his head. They were going down.

Down through a blaze of sun into pools of green: peach, apricot, pear, cherry. In the eyes of the Lieutenant it was yellow-green and it was rotting.

7

When they reached the battalion it was as if they had come among strangers. Here nothing had changed. They cleaned the guns and cared for them; they spoke of moving up. Chiarello stayed close to the Lieutenant; they moved in the detached way of a blind man and his guide among the questioning faces around the guns.

The guns were clean; their black muzzles shone in the sun, thrust upward through the olive branches. In the wash of sunset light the gun crews were at ease, sitting under the trees, like farm workers at the end of a harvest.

In the olive grove far back from the guns Chiarello laid the Lieutenant's sleeping bag on the grass and helped him into it; his hands were cold, he was shivering.

Chiarello went in search of the Executive Officer and was glad when they told him that he had gone with the Battery Commander to Battalion Headquarters. Only then could he give himself up to sleep, not knowing what to tell them, what answer to make to the questioning eyes that followed him through the battery position. He had not slept in twenty-four hours. But he could not sleep until he had gone back among the olive trees to assure himself that the other man slept.

Until the early morning the Lieutenant slept. It was quiet, the war had run away again, the guns were silent. He dreamed that he was lying in snow, freezing to death, and awoke to see ice on the olive leaves in the moonlight. In the clear cold light he got up and wandered away from the battery in search of the valley. He went in circles, his legs soaked with the dew, until Chiarello found him in the ruin of a house on a hillside, hiding from the rising sun. (When the sun came up and caught him in the open he went down on his knees and prayed for darkness; when the guns began to speak and the shells roared over his head like subway trains he crawled to the shelter of the house.) When Chiarello brought him back he was cold, his face a stone; he lay under a tree, on the earth that trembled, drowning in the storm of gunfire.

Chiarello stayed with him. The others were afraid of him; they left him alone.

When they came to take him to the ceremony at Brigade Headquarters, he had gone without a word, passive, as if still in sleep.

Not until the moment when the general came up close and raised his hands to pin the ribbon on his chest did he awaken.

He saw the hands coming up with the ribbon in them. His mouth opened and shut, soundlessly, and then a low sound broke from his throat. Their eyes met, the hands stayed raised; the general flinched, recoiling from what he saw there. He looked down and saw his hands and dropped them, and moved on down the row of chests waiting to be decorated. The Lieutenant stood motionless in the bright morning sun, a tall man in battle dress, a perfect figure of the soldier, the helmet casting a deep shadow on the rigid face. The rest were moving, they seemed to be very far away. He was alone.

He was in the broken church and he was alone. It was small and dark after the sun in the piazza. The glass coffin was empty, the altar stripped bare. On the tile floor were the arms and legs and heads of saints. There was blood and bandages and the smell of human excrement. He heard echoes of many voices. Bowen and the lamb. He tried to pray; the words echoed in the hollows of the church, mocking him. He ran back and forth in time, looking for the beginning and the end of the journey, the steps leading up. The half-remembered voice said, *We are one body. We are one body. We are—.* The sun is not yet up. There is time, he thought. But he did not think: it was a rush of sounds from the blood, the bone, the nerves. Running, looking for a way out, he threw himself against the walls of his mind. He was not alone.

The sound of a rat running turned him around. Through the holes in the roof long columns of sunlight burst and burned on the floor.

When Chiarello came to tell him that they were ready to go, he said, "You go. I want to stay."

"Stay?"

"Where should I go? I have no place to go." He turned away.

He did not see the battalion again. That same afternoon he was taken to a field hospital, where he waited in silence. Later they sent him to the other hospital by the sea, with the new-made amputees, and those whose faces were to be restored, and the blind. There the psychiatrists talked to him; but they could not reach him. He spoke of a journey. They did not understand. He asked if he was still in Italy. Then he was silent. And slept. Let him sleep, they said, maybe he'll come out of it.

Day and night for a week he slept. Or lay sleepless, listening, waiting for the guns to begin again. Then he was forgotten. There were so many others. He had his bed in an officers' ward, among those who were thought not to be violent. What was he after all? Another psycho, another case, another second lieutenant. There were so many—subdued men looking for a way out.

The war rolled away, like a summer storm, beyond the mountains. The hospital was isolated, in the new dimension of stillness. The faces of strangers (yet not quite strangers) came and went. Through most of each day he slept, and in the night was gone. No one noticed. The nurses knew—but that was their secret.

8

The brass of the hospital bureaucracy had forgotten him. But after a while someone noticed that he seemed pretty normal ("Look at the way he takes on those nurses"); so they called him into the office of the Commanding Officer one day and asked him if he would like to go home. He hesitated, and did not reply. They urged him. Here was a well-publicized hero, it would be a shame to waste all that publicity.

"How about it, Lieutenant," the Adjutant said with a smile, "how'd you like to go home, take your convalescent leave, and then maybe help out the war effort by traveling around to boost morale in the factories. Someone's got to tell those people it's not all steak and gravy. Maybe talk at a few war bond rallies. On per diem—a regular expense account. A pretty nice life. How does that sound to you?"

He didn't say anything, only looked at them. They looked away from his cold eyes, at each other. The Colonel drummed with his fingers on the desk.

"Well, Lieutenant, what do you say? We don't get an assignment like this every day." The Colonel cleared his throat. "Why not tell those people at home what you've seen. Give 'em a shot in the ass. Eh?"

He said nothing, looking at them. He could almost have laughed. They shifted in their chairs, uneasy now.

He said, "I don't want to go home. I want to stay."

The old Colonel smiled. "Can't tear yourself away from all the good food, eh?" He winked.

Out of a tense mouth the Lieutenant laughed in his face. "I like it here." Then his voice was very quiet, and flat. "I like this country. I've got to stay here."

The Colonel flushed pink and red, and turned away. The Adjutant took the Lieutenant's arm and led him out. "You just threw away a good thing, buddy," he said. "A damn good thing."

When the psychiatrists heard about it they were puzzled. But not the Colonel. He was a hard-headed failure from West Point and he knew a dodge when he saw one. This man, though it had to be said he had a good record, was playing for the whole hog—he wanted out, pure and simple. But the hospital reports said he was fit for rear-area duty, and the Colonel knew of just the job for him. It was a regular Siberia, a lousy little wop town without so much as a coke machine or a movie, and with hardly another American in miles. Since the invasion of southern France the Colonel had been hard put to supply men for this kind of operation. For a wop-lover this one was made to order. Down the coast a way in this lousy little fishing town they were setting up a laundry; they needed an officer who understood Italian to run it. They'd make this boy the boss and he'd learn to know a good soft war-bond junket the next time he saw one.

21

Again the journey. South. A high road above the sea. Rocky coves, distant headlands, screened by slopes of pine and cypress. Jade-green sea gleam, in flashes. Where am I going, he wondered, and where will I go? Am I going home, he thought. Is there such a place? What do they do there? Do they give their lives for each other? *Home.* He said it aloud. *My country.* The driver looked at him and looked quickly away. The driver was a man who liked to drive. The machine responded to him. It held on the curves, it climbed, it picked its way relentlessly through the starving gazing children of the towns. The power of the machine made him what he was.

The Lieutenant watched the driver's hands and feet, their pleasure in action, in movement, in power. My countryman, he thought, thinking *Where does the machine end and the man begin?* For a moment everything was clear. *My country. No man's land. No man—.* But the sun came around the side of a hill and hit him in the eyes, to blind him. *What do they make of themselves? Money?* Out of chaos words came to his mouth. *No man's land.* And he spoke them.

"Huh?" The driver heard the words as a question.

"Hell no. This is ours, we took it weeks ago. Where you been, Lieutenant?"

Shapeless fragments of understanding shifted in his mind; were related, and broke apart again. Dimly he heard the answer to all questions resounding in the unexplored caves of his being. *No man's land. We come from* . . . He heard the words, but it did not seem to be his own voice. From far down in the underground passages of memory he heard: *It is war. Your country is always at war.* And another voice, that said: We call ourselves a Christian nation. But we are alone, we are the loneliest people on earth, brothers, and the children of Christ are never alone. We kneel, brothers, Sunday after Sunday we kneel to be at one with Him. We come together, we kneel—but we are not together, we are alone: for we do not know and we do not care who kneels beside us.

He looked down and saw his hands come together, palm to palm, finger to finger. In anger he broke them apart and drove them down his thighs to clutch at the knees. Glancing, the driver saw it, saw the wide staring eyes, snapped his head straight ahead, let his foot go down hard on the gas.

Leaping, freed by the movement of the machine, words broke upward in him, as from a fountain in spring that breaks through the detritus of winter,—and carried with them the decomposed matter of nightmare and memory, the decayed flesh of old hopes, old beliefs. Uphill: for a long moment as they climbed he was in the open, unburdened; he saw himself clearly, simply: a man like other men.

From the top he saw the sea, blue and still and empty, and the white cubes of a village on the distant headland. He took them in, he accepted them not as visions of paradise but as parts of a world, parts of himself; himself a being in the natural world—driven by storm and fire and hunger—who came out of the earth and would return to it.

High on this hill above the sea he laughed and cried to himself in the pain and joy of release; the deep layers of rot broke and rose in him, a fountain. From underneath, a man who had been buried, stirred, saw light, saw a way to emerge. He made no sound. The jeep went down in a hot wind into the heat of a valley that opened to the sea. His eyes were open and seeing: he saw the green of the hills and a river that broke green from them to meet the sea; and he was grateful for them.

But as they came down he lost himself in the fire of the sun above and of the sun that burned in the motionless sea below. He closed his eyes against them; the fountain in him erupted to become a volcano. He saw red, he saw through the film of blood the earth rising as if it were itself explosive. The earth spurting into the air, hanging for a moment, falling back. And in this rain, falling, fell pieces of men and trees and animals. The sea, coming closer, roared to echo the roar of the machine and its wind. The sun-struck earth lifted itself toward him in convulsions, the machine was pulled down into its heat. And out of the falling black spray the torn half of a man rose higher than anything else.

2

They were on the flat now, close to the sea, and the broken bones of the next town came at them, alive with the black crawling of children who had become animals in their hunger, who watched them pass out of black animal eyes.

It was noon, the sun was high, it burned. It burned without shadows. On their left the hills rolled down in green fires to the road; on their right the sand burned down to ash even to the edge of the water, and the water burned.

The journey south. Down. Out. And to the north the guns moved, up, in, chewing and spitting: earth and mortar and the unripe bodies of men. Men as fertilizer. And other men, their servants, moved with the guns, still obedient to them, in awe. Fighting for the final freedom—from death. And then home. Home. Home and a job. To make money, make it, make it new. The same old money. To pay for the car, to go to the job, to get away on Sundays, to go like hell. Mom and Dad and the kids and the car and the house and the next payment and the power of the car, to keep going. Not to die. Not to die young and in a strange country far away and your mouth full of dirt that has nothing to do with you. No. Go home to get lost in a white houseboat on the prairie seas, payments in time will make it yours before you die. Home and a job. Will there be a job? What kind? Do you like your work? Making money? It's your life. If you live. Digging ditches, hiding, running, moving up, burying the dead. It's always safer to work for a big corporation. Back and forth to the job, the pendulum swinging, pursuing time and pursued by it, in circles. But never mind that, home is home, it is purple mountain's majesty above the fruited plain. It is better to die at home. It is better not to die under the axe-blows of a machine. It is better to lie in your own soil that you have bought with your own money. (Return passage will be paid, dead or alive.)

Go back. Go back. That first day in the army, the Reception Center, the new men marching bewildered through the streets of barracks, the ironic veterans of a week mocking them with shouted advice: Go back. Go back.

Now the driver was in a hurry. This Lieutenant, the funny look on his face—he didn't like it. Slowed in the street of a town, where the road narrowed, surrounded by the sores and clutching hands of begging, thieving kids, he forced the jeep in among them, to give way or lose a leg. They opened the circle, and before they could close it again he was through, flinging them back into the rubble.

With his whole body the Lieutenant ached for the release of rage. But the confused anger piled up in him, again and again, and wore itself away to dazed indifference.

Down the coast road in the heat of July they moved against the stream, against the new units and the truckloads of replacements streaming north, moving up. But they were not the only ones going down. Behind and ahead of them the trucks moved south along the old Roman road. They were not empty. Some carried the walking wounded. Some carried the earth-eaten dead from their shallow graves to the new military cemeteries. New blood and waste products in the bloodstream of the corporation.

Shit. Shit, man, it's hot. It's goddamn hot. Held in the hot steel bodies of the trucks, they griped as they moved north with the stream. These were new men, virgins, to be offered up on the mountains north of Florence.

Outside the next town traffic was held up, the two streams waiting side by side. The driver turned and looked into the back of one of the troop-carrying trucks. "Hey, whattsa matter you guys, too hot for you?" He grinned, looking them over; for the man of experience there is always something funny about a virgin, and funnier still when they come in bunches, all neat and tidy and dying to know. "Soak up some sun, boys, looks like there's gonna be some more winter sports on them mountains." He smiled and shook his head. "Huh, Lieutenant?—what they don't know won't hurt 'em. Right?" Embarrassed by the silence on both sides of him, the driver chuckled to himself. "Live and learn, huh?"

Then the roaring of motors again and they were moving, in both directions. Trucks on a road, men passing and moving on, casual labor on the way to a job—strangers, countrymen. Like home. "Them kids," the driver said, "it's like taking a kid into a dirty movie. Kids. What the hell do *they* know?" All that space of promised land, all the traffic booming back and forth, all looking for that which was promised. And the armies of the unemployed—now they found work. Another day, another dollar. But more than a job: war offers such promise; anything can happen.

It's like home. They keep moving, they keep going home and away from home, a people on the move. They strain uphill and go down fast, encased in steel bodies; the steel against wind goes *whoom, whoom, whoom* as they go by. They meet and die at the cross-roads, mangled. There are corpses under the wheels. They are killing one another, but they keep moving; they are running toward their deaths, to escape time, which is right behind them. Young men on the way up. Go west, young man. Go north. Go. Keep going. Up. There is a way up and there is a way down. There is no standing still. Go up and kill to live. On the slope of the hill the infantry sergeant stands up and yells *Follow me. Come on! Do you want to live forever?*

Drum-Taps! Comrades, listen! Listen before you go. The good gray poet is calling to you. Listen to his song of manly love, the love of comrades, conceived in a war of brothers and dedicated to the proposition that all men are made mad by the fear of death, are made hungry for love. So he says. *The last sunbeam* (nostalgically he says it) *is looking down a new-made double grave* (for a father and son, brothers in arms and in death). *No danger*, he says, *shall balk Columbia's lovers. If need be a thousand shall sternly immolate themselves for one.* Sternly, sternly, do you hear? *Those who love each other shall become invincible. They shall yet make Columbia* (Mother of All, he calls her) *victorious. I hear*, he sings, *the great drums pounding. And ever the sounds of the cannon far or near (rousing even in dreams a devilish exultation and all the old mad joy in the depths of my soul)* . . . *And bombs bursting in air, and at night the vari-colored rockets.*

Listen. The rapture! *Now* where is the rapture? Who is this mother, this corpse-loving Columbia? Are these her sons, then, who ride silently in the trucks, looking into the face of death, seeing nothing else, knowing nothing, hoping that this is the right road home? These virgins who are no longer sure that they want to lie down with a woman who calls herself Experience and smells of death? Listen to him sing of war. *The strong terrific game,* he calls it. He sings like a virgin.

Up and down the coast road. The Roman road. "Look, Lieutenant—see them kids? In all that rubble. They're digging in there to get out a body that maybe they can get something off. Something new every day, huh? Live an' learn." He laughed a little. Christ, he thought, whattya say to a guy like this, you gotta say somethin'.

"Ya know what I saw in Rome once? There was one of our guys got throwed outta the whore house with a colored guy an' they were both on the street on their backs, only he wasn't as drunk as the colored guy, who looked like he was drowned. So the colored guy was layin' there on a pile of junk and this other guy was sittin' up holdin' a bottle like it was a baby, and along comes these guinea kids who are in the business, an' he says to the kids, 'Hey, ya wanna buy a black man?' These kids get it right away, they're really in business. So finally they settle for a thousand lire an' the kids haul this stiff in a hallway an' take every damn thing off him including his underwear, an' they must of really cleaned up on him. Funny, huh? Well, a buck's a buck. Only that dope could of got two thousand easy if he'd of stuck. That's what gets me—these guys grab a fast dollar, no argument, an' they never even think what that does to the market. Last time I was down there ya couldn't get no more than four dollars for a pack of cigarettes if you stood on your head on top of the goddamn Colosseum."

3

The road was full of holes. The Lieutenant's eyes jumped from hole to hole. (Was this the road home?) Watching the road unwind. (Home, he thought, to the virgin cities? Where nothing has been touched.)

Ahead of them the road filled again; the southbound trucks moving slowly in a long line. It was too slow. The dead lay baking in the steel bodies of the trucks. In the heat of the afternoon the road was hung with the smell of death. They kept moving, in the slow traffic. The driver gave up his talk.

Here and there on the hills above the sea one of the old farmhouses still lived, grown deep into the earth. But the earth, trees, walls, roofs crumbled before him and were sucked down into the whirlpool where he went down, where he saw again the men he had killed, his blood brothers. (Brothers? No. Strangers. To kill a man with your hands, in anger, is one thing. To wrestle, to embrace, in heat, in the purity of rage. Face to face. But to sneak in on him, to trap him, to inflict death by machine . . .)

The smell of death and the smell of the machine seemed to come out of himself. A thing (not a man) to be loathed. As if dead, and unburied. Alone.

Maddened by the fear of death, the soldiers kill with whatever weapons are put into their hands; they kill so that the face of death shall become familiar, no longer the unknown. But there is no relief. Those who kill are driven mad. It becomes a dance of madmen. To the music of the machines, the music of a Black Mass in which men eat of each other's flesh and drink of each other's blood, and die of it. It begins as a mission: to save the world. It ends as another victory for the machine. The perversion of nature: the guns, the hermaphrodite killers, the castrating machines. The big gun: a blind eunuch, finally; like all machines a neuter, emasculating all whom it touches.

In its passage along the road the machine had left disorder. The towns and villages that had been an order were now a disorder. But the people, searching in the stones for a way to begin again, had not become a formless crowd. They held together.

Yet what was it to this man who was going down in the wake of the dead?—he did not see the living among the broken stones. He could smell the dead. He could see them. *They* were his people.

The words shouted themselves, *What have I done?*, into the spaces of the catacombs where he now wandered alone, where the men he had killed stood in rows and grinned. A shout, drowned in the roar of the motor as they went down.

Up and down the hills of the coast road, the earth— as he saw it—burned black by the sun.

A man buried alive, who struggles to free himself, to rise. Caught between the living and the dead he gives himself up, unable to move; he is not one man but two, the man who wants to live and the man who wants to die. He goes with the machine. It moves.

The machine takes over and he goes with it. Lulled by the machine, he passes through a tunnel (a deep narrow valley) that becomes, to his eye, a telescope. Through it he sees their faces (those of the men he has killed), and the faces are all the same, all familiar. And then he sees that each face is his own, and that they are closing in a circle around him— and in the center there is someone who is himself and not himself. They are holding axes and they are going to kill him.

So he lives and dies as the machine carries him through the shifting scenes of disorder.

It is a journey, he moves in circles, in smaller and smaller circles, in and out of the valley where the men have died; and each time he comes back they die again, on their knees, praying to him, who belongs to the machine. They are as large as life, and so close he can almost touch them.

He saw the sun suspended over the sea. He could not tell if it was coming up or going down.

Walls came up to enclose him, orange and gold in the sunset light. A piazza. And faces, coming closer as the machine stopped moving, full of quickly burning life, full of eyes that pulled him up out of his darkness.

He was among the living.

There was no escape from these eyes. They lived. But he shifted quickly from face to face, afraid—afraid that if they looked into his eyes they would see the catacombs where he kept his dead, who were also their dead. (By way of these dead, these who lived became his people.)

At the center of the piazza the jeep was stopped by the crush of bodies. The terrible eyes closed in a circle around him, lit by hunger. The motor was cut, there was a moment of silence before he heard their voices. The words, almost whispered, came like stones to his fear. *Pane. Lavoro.* The faces, the hands, the eyes, coming at him. Reaching for him. To kill him? He saw anger, hatred of him who had killed them.

Bread, they said. *Work*. But he did not hear what they said. The machine had passed over them, crushing them down. Now they sprang up.

Out of the machine he came; he was among them. The machine man. Their blood on his hands. The machine

that killed would now give them work. He had come out of
the machine: a rebirth, the still-born god out of the machine,
who came to them at the point of starvation.

A strange god, a killer; and now they would kill
him for what he had done. Or loathe him, because he was a
machine-part and could not be killed.—Or so his fear told him.

They pressed toward him, shouting now. They cele-
brated him as a god out of the machine; the machine, for them,
was miraculous, it could do anything. It was America, wasn't
it, the great fruitful engine of their dreams?

He heard them. Suddenly his heart was roused; his
blood beat hot through his fear. Many were dead. But these
were not dead.

They had heard of his coming. They had waited in
the piazza for three days. Some had prayed. Others had been
confident of the miracle. They were starving.

They touched him. They grasped his hand. Unbelieving he drew back. They smiled and touched him. He
could not speak; he tried to meet their eyes, grateful for their
mercy. A woman came forward to embrace him.

They were starving. Yet those who were closest to
him saw what was in his face and knew that he was not one of
those who spat and made money.

Something passed between them, between him and
them; a spark that hung for a moment and then burned in him.
In that moment he took life from them into himself, and did
not vomit it up. The tears stood large in his eyes, and fell.

They saw it in his face, the first signs of life, the
pain of it, and paused; then the voices began again. Nothing
was clear.

"What the hell do they want, Lieutenant? Why
don't you tell them to break it up?" Through the flat frightened voice of the driver he heard the words now. *Pane.*

Lavoro. Bread and work. Lightheaded with hunger, they saw him as young and strong, with all the promise of the new world in his hands.

Pane. Lavoro. The sounds of the Italian pierced him and filled him—an old music, an order.

He was out of the machine and in among them, moving with them as they showed him the way, their speaking hands raised to him, as they showed him that it was good to be alive.

He was out of the machine, blinded by the quick surge of his blood; moving with them across the piazza, not knowing what he would do, unsure of everything but that they had touched him and given him their hands. The living, speaking hands.

They feared him as one of the profligate gods out of the machine. Yet they had touched him, and he was of flesh. And they had seen in his face the convulsion that brought it back to life; they had seen their own yearning for life mirrored in his eyes, the eyes flaring up out of ash to burn again.

His feet on the worn cobbles, moving with them across the square of honey-colored stone, he knew himself as one separate man, no longer captive. The machine was behind him.

It was as he walked with them across the piazza that he heard a voice in him say, I am not dead. Many are dead, but I am not dead.

Across the square they moved in a circle around him, a dance, their hands, their voices celebrating the end of starvation. He did not know what they were celebrating; he had never starved.

They were alive, they belonged to this place and to each other; even in hunger they were more than a formless crowd. Across the square, smiling with hope, they led him to the house where the two sergeants of the Quartermaster Corps, the laundrymen, were waiting for him, waiting for the job to begin.

4

At the sound of the crowd the two sergeants came to the door of the house. They saw him, the tall young officer among the small dark ragged figures of the Italians.

One moved, and then the other, to greet him. Then stopped dead, their mouths still open, as he came close and his eyes swung to find them. His eyes were alight and yet remote. On his face was an expression of a kind they had never seen. He seemed to smile with his eyes, yet his mouth was tensed to cry out. They stood frozen, waiting for the cry. It was the face of a condemned man who stands reprieved on the scaffold, on the edge of life, unable to believe, unable to take the first step back. It was a face that said, *Look, these are the living. Look. These live. They are not willing to die. I am still with them. I am not dead.*

Frozen, in awe of the unknown, the two sergeants watched him, unable to take their eyes from his face. It was torn open. It was the bared soul. They were stricken by what was revealed there. They saw the gold bars on the shoulders of the familiar green combat uniform—yet they could not accept this face as one of their own. It was, now, the alien face of the blind man, who does not see, yet sees other things than we see. How were they to know what the blind man feels at the moment when he regains his sight?

In that moment both men were thinking, Does he see us? He sees something. What does he see?

They stood face to face, ten yards apart, the two and the one. For a moment he saw them: they were waiting, they were ready. It was a job.

Then he no longer saw them. In the midst of these people who had received him his elation surged and fell and in a sudden calm he saw himself, known and yet a stranger. It was himself, and it was someone else. There was strength in his hands; the blood beat fast in his body; he was warm. Warm and cold, as if he were a corpse being warmed into life by the sun.

He turned away. Along the uneven cobbles of the streets that led down to the sea, in the shadow of the high crumbling houses, he walked as if he had lived here all his life, as if these were his people. But there was something more: it was as if there moved in him, submerged, some unknown man who was also himself, but more himself; and as if it were this self who had always lived here in the sun, who had no relation to the machine, who had not killed, who would not kill; who was alive and knew what it was to be alive.

He walked away from what he had been.

It was a journey, in search of a place that was dimly known to him, and in this place he would meet and know this other man who was also himself, who would emerge to meet him.

Many were dead, but he was not dead.